# THE
# CHASE

# Also By Pamela Humphrey

## Hill Country Secrets

*Finding Claire*

*Finding Kate*

*Finding Treasure*

## Other Books

*The Blue Rebozo: A Novella*

*Researching Ramirez: On the Trail of the Jesus Ramirez Family*

# THE CHASE

PAMELA HUMPHREY

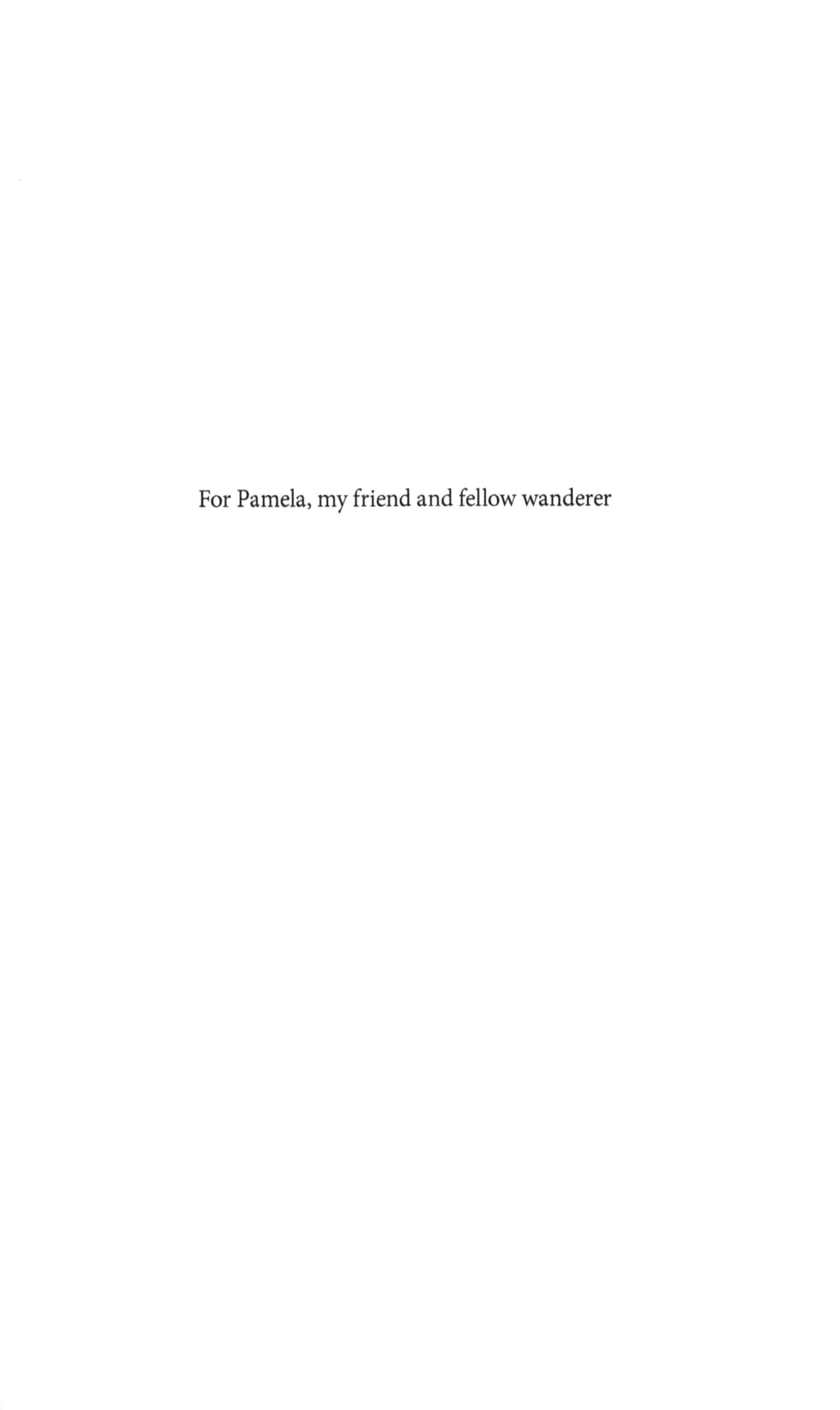

For Pamela, my friend and fellow wanderer

# CHAPTER 1

## *Friday, April 8*

Detective Ben Torres turned and moved the phone to his other ear, leaving his partner shaking his head. Taking a personal call at work wasn't typical for Ben, but when his friend, Alex, called a second time without leaving a message, Ben guessed there was trouble.

He rubbed the top of his head "Slow down. She what?"

Alex took a deep breath before repeating the news. "Some guy ran Kate off the road. She's okay, but her ankle is messed up. She's in a cast up to her knee. Car is totaled, I think. It definitely wasn't an accident and has to be connected to the break-in."

Ben dropped into his chair. In the time he'd known Kate and Alex—three short months—she'd been in trouble more than once.

Miller grew impatient with the phone call and waved a case folder before dropping it on the desk and tapping a name.

Ben pointed to a picture on the computer screen to appease his partner's frustration, then continued his conversation with Alex. "This just happened in the middle of the day? Where? Any leads?"

"About an hour ago here in Kendall County on one of the country roads. Maddox is investigating. The guy dropped a note in her car."

Ben tensed. "What did it say?"

"Says to give it back or people get hurt—or something like that." Alex's unease tremored in his voice.

Ben wanted to support his friend, but the case that had just landed on his desk, the one that had Miller so ready to jump, would keep them busy late into the night. Besides, Kendall County wasn't Torres's jurisdiction, and Captain Maddox, who would be working the case, was good at his job.

"What can I do?"

"Nothing right now. I'll keep you posted." Voices echoed over the hospital PA system as Alex ended the call.

"What's going on?" Miller rattled his keys.

Ben flipped through the open file on his desk. "You remember that case from January—the woman found at the mall and her sister, Kate, who'd been kidnapped?"

"Yeah. She's the one that remembered who she was, then found out it was all a lie? And had the guy with her, the one that lived in a cabin."

"We've become friends. Anyway, someone broke into her place a couple days ago. She hid in a closet the whole time. But Alex just called to say that someone ran her off the road. He was on edge before. This is about to push him over."

"Hope they figure it all out." Miller tapped the file, ready to move on with the case in front of them. "The picture you pointed to. Is that the one the witness mentioned?"

Ben shoved thoughts of the accident aside and focused on the case in front of him. "Yeah, that's the guy. But we don't have an address for him."

The situation at the hospital faded into the background as he and Miller worked their leads.

Marisa rehearsed what she wanted to say as she walked up to Paul, but when she noticed him standing near the damaged front bumper of his car, she stopped. "What happened?"

"Fender bender. Guy stopped in front of me, slammed on his brakes for no reason." He didn't look at her, which meant he didn't see her roll her eyes. In every situation, someone else was always to blame.

"That's terrible." She said what was expected, though she had little pity for him.

"I'll be home later." He didn't wait for her to respond before getting in the car and backing out.

His taillights disappeared down the street.

For the last two days, she'd planned to break it off with him and move out. After introducing him to her brother and his friends, the attentive older man she thought adored her seemed slimy and overbearing. Mari had paid close attention when they all gathered at Kate's. Watching Becca interact with her husband, DJ, and seeing the way Alex looked at Kate revealed Marisa's relationship with Paul as a cheap counterfeit. The fact that she suspected of theft—a suspicion prompted by a recent discovery and something she hadn't shared with anyone—unraveled any last threads of affection for him.

Her brother, Kate, and their friends had all been polite, but Marisa hadn't missed the looks. No one understood why she was dating Paul. When she thought about it, she wasn't sure either. Months ago, convinced that he loved her, she'd moved from Austin to San Antonio to live with him.

His friend had even found her a job with the local realty company where he worked. A new town, a new job, and a doting boyfriend made life fun and adventurous until Paul morphed into someone different.

Checking her phone when he thought she wasn't looking, asking her not to go out with friends, demeaning her in little ways whenever he found an opportunity—these things flashed like neon after she'd introduced him to Kate and Becca.

Marisa needed out of the relationship.

She couldn't wait until he returned to give her rehearsed reasons, her explanation of why the relationship wasn't working. The need to be away from him consumed her. Loathing the thought of him, she raced up the stairs to pack her bags.

As she walked inside, she called Kate. "Hi, it's Marisa. You busy? Can I come over?"

Maybe she would let Marisa use the guest room until she found a place to stay.

Paul's off-color humor and wandering hands—behaviors he'd put on display while at lunch with Kate and Becca—embarrassed Marisa, and she wanted to apologize. His behavior that day gave enough reason for Marisa to leave him. She didn't need to mention her suspicions about him being a thief. Alex loved Kate, and giving her a bad impression of the family was the last thing Marisa wanted to do.

Kate answered in a groggy voice, sounding half-drunk. "Whoa, slow down. I'm in the hospital. Can I call you when I go home?"

Panic grabbed Marisa. "What happened?"

"A car ran right into me. Shoved me into a tree. On purpose."

Marisa stared out the window at the parking space vacated minutes before. Paul had acted weird whenever Marisa mentioned the break-in at Kate's, but she'd dismissed it. The coincidence of his damaged bumper was too much to ignore. Suspecting him of stealing made it easier to believe he could engage in other illegal behavior. But breaking into Kate's house? Running her off the road?

"Marisa?"

Marisa snapped back to the conversation. "The hospital? Are you okay?"

"Yep. Mostly. My ankle is hurt pretty bad, so they have my leg in a cast, and I'm really sore. Otherwise I'm wonderful. Your brother is taking good care of me. Oh, I forgot to call you. I wanted to know Paul's last name." Kate's words disappeared in a fog.

Worry pounding in her head, Marisa hung up without responding. She needed to report her suspicions, but how? And where? If Paul was capable of intentionally running Kate off the road, he was more dangerous than Marisa thought.

If she left now, he'd assume she knew something. Nothing good would come from that. He'd likely go after Kate again, and Marisa wouldn't risk that. She grabbed her purse and ran out to her car, forming an exit plan that didn't tip off Paul but eliminated him from the picture.

When she pulled into the lot at work, it was empty except for one other car. Marisa hoped that Ted—the owner of the black Corvette—was immersed in his own work and would leave her alone.

She held her keys in her fist as she tiptoed into her office. After swinging her office door closed, she flipped through folders until she found what she needed. Before stepping into the hall with the files, she opened the door and listened. Ted jabbered on the phone in his office down the hall.

Marisa slipped into the workroom. At the large machine that did almost every office function conceivable, she made copies, one file at a time. When she finished, she rushed back to her desk, glad to have completed her task without Ted's prying eyes watching her. She stuffed the copies in her large purse and glanced toward the door before returning the folders to the filing cabinet. His voice echoed down the hall. After sliding the files back where they belonged, she pushed the drawer closed, relieved.

"Well, hello. What brings you back to the office?" Ted stood in the doorway, looking ready to pounce, his brown eyes boring into her.

"Just following up on something. Checking files." She didn't dare share her real reason for copying files with anyone, especially a friend of Paul's.

"Have time to go for a drink?" He stepped closer to her. Tall and fit, he acted as if every woman wanted to be with him.

"No, thank you. I should get home. Don't want Paul to worry about me." Marisa hoped that by mentioning her boyfriend, Ted would back off and not persist in asking her out.

"Okay, then." He turned but stopped a couple steps out the door. "I hope you used the right code for the copies you made."

Marisa picked up her purse and slung it over her shoulder. "I'm careful with details like that, Mr. Jenner." She hurried out the door before he could ask any more questions.

The sun had disappeared from the sky by the time Ben got to his car. He texted Alex as he slid behind the wheel. *Kate okay? Any suspects?*

The response appeared almost immediately, meaning Alex wasn't getting much sleep, as Ben expected. *In pain, but okay. No leads yet.*

He called Alex and put it on speaker before backing out and driving toward home. "Alex, are *you* okay?"

Worrying about Kate was something Alex did often but didn't do well. Very much in love, he didn't deal well when she was in danger. Tortured would be an accurate description.

"She could've died. You should see her car. The guy slammed her into a tree."

"Maddox is good at what he does, and he's her uncle. He won't let this drop. They'll get whoever did this."

"We don't even know what he wants."

"You just take care of Kate and let Maddox worry about the rest. And if you need anything, please call me."

"Thanks, Ben."

Ben turned up the radio, letting the classic rock help him unwind from the busy day. Nothing about the accident made sense. He ran through the details Alex had shared, shaking his head. *It's not your case.*

When he walked into his apartment, he tossed his keys on the coffee table. Even though it was late, after changing out of his work clothes, he did his routine of pullups and pushups, then warmed leftovers.

Feet kicked up, he turned on the Xbox and spent the next couple hours as artillery blowing up tanks.

～*～

Marisa woke up when the front door opened. Disappointment weighed heavily on her. Set on leaving Paul, she hated the idea of sharing a bed with him even one more night. Her stomach soured, and she swallowed back the bad taste that accompanied thoughts of him. Disgust tasted rancid.

She laid still as Paul banged around the apartment. When he slipped into bed and wrapped his arms around her, she pretended to be asleep. His hands wandered as he whispered her name and dotted kisses on the back of her shoulder. She resigned herself to suffering the choices she'd made and rolled onto her back.

# CHAPTER 2

*Saturday, April 9*

Ben headed for the elevators. He'd managed to get away from work early, which meant he'd make it to his nephew's birthday shindig.

He answered his phone before stepping onto the elevator. "Hello."

"Are you coming?"

"Yes, Mom. I'm going to the birthday party. Carlos is how old?"

"Ay, Ben, you don't know? He's turning three. Will you be bringing a date?" His mom sounded eager for a yes to the last question.

*Who brings a date to a kid's party?* He hadn't yet met the woman he'd subject, or rather introduce, to his family. "You're right. I should know how old my nephew is. And, no, I'm not bringing anyone with me."

"*Mijo*, you're thirty-three. Will you ever settle down?"

He listened patiently as his mother repeated her encouragement for finding a nice girl, the same speech he'd heard many times before. When she wrapped up her mini lecture, he rolled his eyes. "Love you, Mom. I'll see you over there." He hurried onto the empty elevator as he checked the time. He didn't have high hopes for arriving at the party before it started.

Ben slipped on his sunglasses as he stepped off the elevator. If he hurried, he could grab a gift, change clothes, and make it to his brother's house before the piñata broke open. He'd hoped to take off all of Saturday, but criminals didn't take the weekend off. Absorbed in his thoughts, ticking through the five million items on his to-do list, he nearly plowed into a woman who stepped in front of him.

A long-legged brunette, with stunning green eyes, flashed a nervous smile. Her deep red dress hugged every curve. He hoped his reflective sunglasses hid his stare.

*Eyes up.*

In her heels, she stood nearly his height. "Excuse me. I need some information."

He glanced over his shoulder at the front desk, ready to send her that way. Only paces away, it buzzed with uniformed officers ready to answer questions, but something in her expression halted him.

"How can I help you, ma'am?" He nodded toward the far wall, out of the way of foot traffic, and pushed his sunglasses to the top of his head.

She scanned the room, inching closer to him before she explained. "If I wanted to report a possible crime that happened in a different county, can I do that here?"

Marisa had never seen a look like that before, at least, not directed at her. His soft brown eyes held her focus. The wish that they'd met somewhere else, under different circumstances popped in her head and surprised her. In slacks, dress shirt, and tie, he looked the part of a detective. She glanced at the badge on his belt.

He gave information but not without asking questions. "You'd need to report it in that county. What type of crime?"

"A burglary and an—I guess it would be called an assault." She glanced back over her shoulder, hoping Paul didn't walk into the station. She worried that he might have followed her. If he discovered what she was up to, no telling what he'd do, but he needed to pay for his crimes. Everything she'd observed pointed to Paul being guilty. She wouldn't let him hurt her friends without consequence.

Concern registered on the detective's face. "Assault? Are you okay?"

"I'm fine."

"Were you the victim? Did it happen in a nearby county?" The detective kept his voice low; his gaze stayed focused on her.

Marisa didn't want to drag anyone else into her tangled mess. "Oh no. Not me. I'll run out to Kendall County to file a report. Thank you so much for your help, Officer …?" She couldn't leave without, at least, knowing the man's name, not that they'd ever meet again.

"Torres. Detective Ben Torres." He made sure to include his first name.

"Thank you again." She clicked away on two-inch, red heels, perfectly matched to her dress.

Distracted, he failed to put together all the facts while she was still in front of him. Burglary? Assault? Both incidents in Kendall County? It seemed coincidentally similar to what happened to Kate.

He ran after the woman. "Ma'am."

She turned, surprised. "Yes?"

"The assault—was that with an automobile?" He phrased his question deliberately, trying to determine if he'd jumped to a wrong conclusion.

Her eyes went wide, and she touched his arm. Long, slender fingers with red manicured nails pressed against his bicep. "Yes. He hit her, slamming her into a tree. She's in the hospital."

He didn't need to hear anymore. "When you get to Kendall County, talk to Captain Pat Maddox. He'll want to hear what you have to say." Ben gave a quick nod and started to put on his sunglasses. With each minute he spent next to her, the weaker his grip on rational thought became. Women reporting crimes and looking over their shoulder weren't the best candidates for dating. She had trouble written all over her, but asking her out had occurred to him multiple times during their short exchange.

Her fingers still resting on his upper arm, she shook her head. "Please, Detective, don't say anything. I'm going to report it, but I want to tell them myself, please. I'm not even completely sure he did it."

*Them?* Did she mean Kate and Alex? How was she connected? By the look on her face, she wondered the same about Ben.

"I can't promise not to say anything, but I don't even know your name."

"Then I guess I have nothing to worry about, Detective Torres." She cocked an eyebrow and forced a smile. Fear hovered in the barely-noticeable lines of her face.

*She's young. And afraid of someone.*

As she slipped her hand off his arm, he took notice of the empty ring finger. *Leave it alone. Whatever it is, you don't want mixed up in it even if she is beautiful.* He slipped on his glasses. "Have a good one." He rushed out the door before rational thought disappeared completely.

Marisa watched the detective hurry away. She clutched her purse close to her, almost as a shield, as she walked out of the building. Her phone beeped, and the distinctive tone she'd set for Paul's messages stopped her. She read the text notification on the screen: *Where are you?*

She threw the phone in her purse and glanced around. Ducking back inside the building, she entertained the idea of going home and keeping quiet, but her conscience wouldn't let her. How had she let herself get entangled in such a mess? On her own since her high school graduation, she didn't need anyone keeping tabs on her, yet she'd put up with it from Paul. And for what? He treated her more like a plaything than a person.

The phone beeped a second time reminding her of the unread message. Deciding the consequences of ignoring his text were better than slipping up and letting him know where she was headed, she ignored the phone. After stepping back outside, she lingered on the top step, gathering her courage, determined to follow through with reporting her suspicions.

Ben made it as far as the bottom step. The fear in her eyes wouldn't loosen its grip. Rushing back up the stairs, two at a time, he almost ran into her.

"Detective?" She put her hand up to stop him and left it resting on his chest.

He couldn't walk away without protecting her, but unwilling to let her know she'd made such an impression or how much he liked the feel of her hand on him, he tried to make a valid sounding argument for staying near her. "It'd be irresponsible of me to let you go and not ensure you actually reported the possible crimes. Need a ride?" He glanced down at where her hand rested just above the pocket of his dress shirt and wondered if she could feel his heart thudding. *This isn't exactly leaving it alone.*

She hesitated before letting her fingers slip off his chest. "Okay." She clicked along next to him as he made his way to the parking garage.

When they neared his car, he gestured toward it. "The Jetta is mine."

"The beige one?"

The color he'd chosen because it was unobtrusive and worked well in the Texas heat suddenly sounded plain and boring.

"Moonrock Silver." Why was he defending against a beige car?

"Looks beige, not silver." She pointed at him. "Even though you're giving me a ride, I'm still not telling you my name."

He put up his hands. "I'm only here to make sure you arrive safely to file a report."

"You'll give me a ride back?" Her question reminded him of where he was supposed to be.

"Of course." He tapped out a quick text, letting his brother know to expect one less for the party. Ben would let his brother pass along the info to their mom.

The woman stared at Ben, her eyes betraying the distress that lay underneath the beautiful exterior. "You said safely. Why?"

He hadn't expected such a direct question. "Are you in danger? Afraid of someone?"

"Is my fear that obvious?"

"Only to my keen detective eye." His attempt at humor was rewarded with a small smile, but his quip sounded way too much like flirting. *Just get her to Maddox and walk away.*

Marisa studied the detective while he drove. Although extremely fit—his shoulders framed nicely by his dress shirt—his best feature was his eyes, light brown and expressive. If he'd noticed her fear, she had to be better about not letting it show. Paul would pounce on that with fangs bared.

She tried not to check the side mirror too often, thinking her chauffeur might notice. The fact that he knew about the incidents made her curious. Alex and Kate didn't have a wide circle of friends. Did he know them personally? "You have friends in Kendall County?"

"Yes." He gave answers like siblings shared candy.

"How did you know to ask about a vehicular assault?" Marisa wanted to know the detective's connection to her brother and his girl-friend.

"It happened to a friend of mine."

Marisa stared at Detective Torres, tempted to stay silent until she got back to her car. He knew Kate, which meant he had to know Alex. If anything about the exchange in the station was mentioned, Alex and Kate would know who the detective was talking about.

But in the precarious place Marisa had wedged herself, she needed to trust someone. "I know you said you can't make the promise not to say anything, but you can see that I'm reporting it."

"I'm more worried about you than your friends." He didn't drop any names, as if maintaining the vague references offered her the anonymity she craved.

Responding risked saying too much, so she stayed quiet.

Forty-five minutes later, after they'd left the city behind and entered the more rural Hill Country to the west, he parked outside the Kendall County Sheriff's Office. "If you're concerned that someone might harm you, you can file a restraining order. And don't stay in a bad situation." He gripped the steering wheel so tight his knuckles turned white. "Please."

*If only it were that easy.* If she left, Paul might suspect something and leave or do something worse. Either way, he'd never get justice for what he'd done. Besides, it had only happened to Kate because she knew Marisa.

She had to make it right. "I'll be fine."

Inside the lobby, the detective followed Marisa to the front desk.

She smiled at the receptionist. "Hello, I need to speak with Captain Maddox."

"Sure, can I get your name?" The woman's pen hovered over a notepad.

The detective leaned over the counter, keeping his voice low. "Ma'am, can you tell him that Detective Torres would like to speak with him. She's with me."

"Of course." The receptionist picked up the phone.

Waiting, Marisa clutched her purse while the detective tapped out a drum solo. A middle-aged gentleman appeared in a doorway at the other end of the front desk. Detective Torres stepped up and shook hands.

Wearing boots and a Stetson, the man looked like a wiry cowboy.

After a brief exchange, the captain waved Marisa over. "I'm Captain Pat Maddox. Thanks for coming in. We can talk back here." After escorting her into an interview room, the captain stepped back out, leaving the door ajar.

He stood in the hall talking with Detective Torres, but, much to Marisa's frustration, their conversation was drowned out by the buzz of the air conditioner and office chatter.

Ben prepared himself for Maddox's questions. Giving facts without tipping his hand about his attraction wouldn't be easy.

Maddox glanced back toward the woman in the red dress. "Who is she?"

"I don't know her name, and I don't want to. She asked me about reporting a crime. She wanted to report a burglary and vehicular assault in Kendall County. Said a woman was slammed into a tree." He lied about the not wanting to know part, but for now, her safety was his priority.

"A bit of a coincidence."

"It has to be related to what happened to Kate, so I sent her to you. Whoever she is, she's afraid—looks over her shoulder, checks her mirrors. I drove her here to make sure she made it safely."

"Help yourself to coffee in the break room. I think someone made a fresh pot sometime today." Captain Maddox stepped away, then turned back. "I find it surprising that you don't even want her name. I mean, you're single, and she's…" Maddox raised an eyebrow and shrugged.

Ben skipped the coffee and settled in a chair in the lobby. He'd met Pat Maddox through Alex and Kate. Maddox's good-natured ribbing didn't surprise Ben. Even in the short time they'd known each other, they'd become friends.

Maybe the mystery woman would give Maddox the break he needed to solve Kate's case and ease Alex's worry. But, that didn't help Ben protect the mystery woman.

Marisa spent almost an hour recounting to Captain Maddox every detail she remembered. She included all her suspicions about Paul breaking into Kate's house and running Kate's car off the road. Maddox scrawled notes as she told him about lunch with Kate and Becca, the surprise visit to Kate's house that same night, and the damaged bumper.

"Was Paul with you all night after you returned from Kate's?" Maddox gazed at Marisa over the top of his reading glasses.

"If you'd asked me the next day, I'd have said 'Absolutely.' But now, I'm not sure. He made me a cup of tea; we went to bed; and I don't remember anything until morning."

"So, you can't vouch that he was home all night?"

"I can't."

"Tell me about the damaged back bumper."

"It was the front bumper. The passenger side took the brunt of the damage."

Maddox asked details about the lunch, then moved on to the night at Kate's. He asked question after question and scribbled down Marisa's every answer.

Afterward, he reviewed his notes, flipping through pages in his notebook. "What time did you see Paul near the damaged bumper?"

"It must've been about five thirty or so."

"Anything else you need to tell me?"

"I think Paul has been breaking into houses, but I don't have real proof." She pulled the files out of her purse. "These are the houses that have been broken into."

"Why do you think he did it?"

"I'm a realtor. Most of the houses I've listed have been broken into. I saw a piece of jewelry in his drawer that looked like one that was stolen. He doesn't know I saw it, but it wasn't there when I looked later."

"Where did these robberies happen?"

"One here in Kendall County, the others in San Antonio."

He shuffled through the papers, selected the house in his county, and handed the others back to her. "Tell me about the one that happened here. The others you need to report to SAPD."

She told him all she knew about the theft from the house in Kendall County. When they wrapped up the interview, Maddox encouraged her not to delay in reporting the other thefts.

"I'll do it today." She tapped her purse. "Captain Maddox, please, can you keep my name out of this when discussing it with Kate and Alex, or *anyone*?" She glanced out to the hall, hoping the meaning was clear.

"They won't blame you."

"Please. I need to tell them myself. Give me time to do that."

He reluctantly agreed to keep her name under wraps. "Are you safe?"

Ben must have told Captain Maddox that she was afraid of someone.

With her most convincing smile painted on her face, she lied. "I'll be fine, but let me know as soon as ..." She left the statement dangling, not sure how to finish it.

"I'll let you know if we arrest a suspect related to your complaint."

"Thank you." She stood up, ready to leave the small room.

"Thanks for coming in." He pushed open the door to the lobby.

She scanned the room.

The detective stood to greet her. "Ready to head back?"

He and Captain Maddox exchanged a look and a nod. How much info would be shared between them? She kept stride next to the detective as they walked to his car. He opened the passenger door, and she slid into the seat.

"Do you two know each other well?" She gazed up at him, trying not to let concern show in her eyes.

He smiled and closed her door.

～✳～

Ben climbed into the driver's seat. "He won't tell me anything. Whatever you told him isn't any of my business." He swallowed back all the questions that popped in his head. The hardest to dispel was the question about her safety.

"I appreciate your discretion." She stared out the window.

Ben hated to see her tense. "Have you lived in San Antonio long?"

"Are you investigating me, Detective?"

"Just making conversation." He wanted her to feel safe while he was around to protect her.

"I've lived here most of my life. You?"

"Born and raised."

Casual but guarded conversation continued as they drove into the outskirts of San Antonio. He worried she was in real trouble, but forcing her to accept help wasn't an option. Encouraging her to seek it was the only thing he could do.

"Maddox is a good guy. If you need help, give him a call."

"I said I'll be fine." She chewed on the end of a strand of hair. "Do you know where I file a theft or burglary report?"

"You'd want to report that at the substation near where it happened." He checked his mirror. "What part of town?"

"Northwest."

"We can stop by that station if you'd like." Expecting a yes, he changed lanes, preparing to exit.

She touched his arm. "You don't have to give up any more of your Saturday."

"It's not far from here." He kept his eyes on the road as he navigated the surface streets to the station.

As they pulled into the lot, she asked, "Why are you helping me?"

"It's more obvious you're nervous when you chew your hair." He jumped out without giving more of an answer. He didn't have one, not one that made any sense.

He cringed as she scanned her surroundings when they walked toward the building. Inside the lobby, he stopped. "I'll be right here when you're ready."

She walked up and spoke with the woman behind the desk.

Ben dropped into a chair in the corner, sorting through the information he'd gathered. If the mystery woman had spent most of her life in San Antonio, she probably knew Alex. But how?

A few moments later, she sat down next to Ben. "She said they'd find someone for me to talk to."

"You okay?"

She nodded, staring at her hands.

He wanted to erase the tension from her shoulders, to see the fear wash out of her green eyes. "I won't tell Alex about bumping into you."

A soft gasp let Ben know the name struck a nerve, but he didn't look up.

She grabbed his hand. "Please, Ben, you can't."

When she squeezed it tighter, he glanced up and met her pleading gaze. "I said I wouldn't." Promising not to say anything was a bad idea. He knew it in his gut, but if it opened a door for her to trust him, he had to risk it.

He made a point not to look at her hand wrapped around his fingers, hoping she'd leave it that way.

She might have if she hadn't been waved over to the desk. "I'll be back."

"I'll be here." He'd gotten way too invested to walk away.

He waited almost an hour, sitting and answering texts from his mom. Eventually she'd forgive him for missing the party. He was careful not to mention that he was helping a beautiful woman, which was easier because he didn't know her name. Instead, he texted his mom: *A friend needed help.*

It was true that the woman needed help. Whether she'd become a friend remained to be seen.

When she joined him back in the lobby, he didn't ask any questions. He followed her to the car and opened her door. "Let me buy you a late lunch before we head back."

"I can't risk that but thank you." She squeezed his arm before sliding into her seat. "Even riding with you concerns me."

"Let me help you." He'd given up not getting involved. If she trusted him enough to let him help, he would.

She wouldn't even look at him as she shook her head, and for the first time all day, she wiped at tears. On the way back to the station, more than once, she pulled a strand of hair into the side of her mouth, then immediately tucked it behind her ear.

"Parked in the garage?" Ben dreaded watching her get out of his car.

"Yes, black Passat, second level."

In the half-empty garage, it was easy to spot. He pulled to a stop behind it.

"Detective." She stared at him and chewed her bottom lip. "I hope we meet again sometime, but under different circumstances."

Ben nodded. "Me too. Take care of yourself and remember what I said." He bit his tongue, wanting to say so much more. Every added minute he spent around her, the more the world felt tilted, just a slight bit to the left. After hours together, the lean had become unnerving. He jumped out and opened her car door. "I hope everything gets resolved."

"Thank you, Detective." She slid into her driver's seat.

Ben climbed back in his car. Before he pulled away, he stole one last glance. The green-eyed mystery woman gazed into her rearview mirror. He forced himself to drive away. *She doesn't want your help.*

Marisa drove to a diner and tucked into a corner booth. She ordered food and answered emails on her phone. After she ate, she stayed burrowed in the corner of the restaurant Paul didn't frequent. For hours, the waitress, whose nametag read *Livvy*, refilled her coffee cup, casting curious glances but never implying that Marisa had overstayed her welcome. She appreciated the kindness of that waitress.

Long after the sun had set, Marisa paid her tab, added a hefty tip, and headed home. She hoped Paul might be asleep by the time she returned. She'd ignored his texts the entire day. The less time she spent around Paul, the safer she was. At least she hoped that was true.

She slipped into the apartment, steeling against the barrage of questions he would throw at her if he was awake. After a deep breath, she ventured down the hall.

"You're late. I hope that means you sold another house or two." He stood in the bedroom doorway.

"No. It didn't work out." She kicked off her heels and hurried past him into the bedroom.

He caught her by the arm. "That's all you have to say? I texted you several times."

"I'm sorry I didn't answer. I didn't mean to make you worry." She couldn't let him see her fear. "I'm pretty beat. I think I'll tuck in."

He pulled her up against him. "Sleep can wait. You've been gone all day. I want your attention." His leering look made her want to cry.

"Not tonight, Paul. I have a terrible headache." She wriggled out of his hold and locked herself in the bathroom. How long would it take to investigate her report? How long would she have to stay so that Paul wouldn't be tipped off? Whether he'd done what she suspected or not, the relationship was over. She wanted nothing to do with him. As she washed off her makeup and changed into flannel pajamas, she thought of the detective with the schoolboy stare. Why couldn't she have found someone like that?

Ben laid in bed, staring at the ceiling, concern for the woman keeping him awake. *Is she in danger?* He should have done more, maybe given her his number, but he found her so captivating it unnerved him. She was too young and, as they say, out of his league—far more stunning than any woman he'd ever dated—not exactly the kind of girl he pictured taking home to meet the parents. Her repeated assertions that she was fine left him with a gnawing worry that she was anything but.

He tossed back the covers and dressed for a run. After locking his apartment, he took off downhill. He lived near campus, in an area dominated by college students, and almost never encountered an empty street.

Chasing away the frustration and concern, he doubled back at the bottom of the hill and started the uphill trek back to his complex. As he crested the hill, he turned around again. Over and over, up and down, he ran. An hour later, after multiple passes up and down the street, he headed home. Physically exhausted, he'd sleep regardless of what needled his brain.

# Chapter 3

*Monday, April 11*

Marisa parked outside her office. She'd been so excited to hear from Kate and meet her for lunch, but it hadn't gone as anticipated. Startled by the news that whoever ran Kate off the road left a note, Marisa had acted the coward and left without admitting she thought Paul was the culprit. She couldn't even imagine how mad Alex would be when he found out. It wasn't the idea of his anger that bothered Marisa. He'd be hurt. He was so in love and happy. How could she admit to introducing Kate to someone that inflicted harm?

Besides, Maddox was working the case. Before walking into the office, she called him to check in, to get reassurance that the case was progressing.

He answered after three rings. "Maddox."

"This is Marisa Ramirez. I wondered if you'd had any, um, success with what I told you."

Rustling preceded his answer, but just before he spoke, Marisa heard her brother's voice in the background. "I haven't. Listen, can I call you later? Are you safe?"

"I'll be fine. Please don't tell my brother I called." She hung up and hurried into the office. She needed work to distract her from the awful mess.

Ben fumbled with his phone, trying to answer as he unlocked his front door. "Hello."

"Torres! What's up? Got a date?" Married for at least two decades, Miller ribbed Ben about his relationship status weekly, just for good measure.

"Wouldn't tell ya if I did." He dropped his grocery bags on the table. "Need something?"

"Calling about Thursday. You're coming, right?" Miller didn't sound like he'd take no for an answer.

Ben had no idea what he was supposed to attend. "Thursday?"

"Dinner. I told you last week. You said this month you wouldn't miss it."

"Oh, yeah. I'll be there. Send me the info again, will you?" Ben shoved the perishables in the refrigerator.

"Will do. See ya Wednesday."

"Bye." He ended the call and tossed his phone on the table.

It wasn't that he didn't enjoy dinner with Miller and other friends from the office, but being the only single guy in the group sometimes made it awkward. The ribbing he could handle. The offers to help him find the perfect someone—usually from the wives—he didn't like near as much.

# CHAPTER 4

*Tuesday, April 12*

Marisa held her breath. Pinned to the wall, she waited, praying Paul's mood would change. "I'm going to be late for work."

He slid his hands up her skirt. "What's more important?"

"If I don't do a good job, it will reflect badly on your friend. He got me the position. I don't want to cause trouble for you." Framing her escape as a benefit to Paul was her only hope of avoiding having his sweaty body on top of her without risking him uncovering what she was up to.

He unbuttoned her blouse, unmoved by her argument. His moods darker, his urges stronger, he'd been a different person after Kate's accident. Daily, Marisa questioned her decision to stay. So far, allowing him the illusion of control helped her navigate the uncomfortable predicaments.

"Paul, please. Not this morning." She closed her eyes, bracing for his anger.

He squeezed her thigh. She'd learned to cry out, giving him the reaction he wanted, though what she wanted most was to shove a knee into his groin and leave, never to have him touch her again. He left bruises, but they were always where others wouldn't see.

"Do you want me?" He continued to tighten his hand around her leg as he whispered in her ear.

"Yes." *Not at all.* She said her lines, playing her part until she could safely get away.

Her phone squawked.

Paul released her and pulled it out of her purse. "Your brother." He threw the phone at her and stomped away.

Clutching her blouse closed, she ran out of the apartment as she answered.

Early in the afternoon, Ben parked outside Kate's house and waved to the security guard before walking onto the porch.

Alex opened the door. "Thanks so much for doing this."

"What else am I going to do with my day off? I ran errands this morning, got stuff done. I'm happy to do it. Big plans today?" Ben silenced the questions he wanted to ask about a tall brunette.

"I appreciate it all the same. Becca's here with Kate."

"And I saw the guard." Ben pointed back over his shoulder.

Alex wrinkled his nose. "Yeah, after what happened in January, I can't get myself to trust them as the last line of defense."

"I get it." Ben waved at Kate as he made his way into the kitchen, making mental note of Alex's dodge of the question about plans. "Hey, how's the ankle?"

"Don't ask." She hobbled toward Ben, her cast clunking with each step, and wrapped him in a hug. "Thanks for babysitting."

"Anytime."

Kate handed him a small cooler and a bag. "I packed you some snacks."

"Thanks." Ben nosed through the bag. "You know where I'll be if you need anything. Just text me."

"I will." Kate pulled a Coke out of the fridge and handed it to Ben. "But it's not like I'm helpless and alone."

Her friend, Becca, poked her head out of the den. "Yeah, she's not alone. I'm here."

"And we all feel safer because of it." Ben chuckled as he walked to the door.

Alex followed Ben out. "I'll be gone a few hours. DJ may beat me here."

Becca's husband, DJ, worked as deputy in the next county over. He covered some of the watch shifts when Alex was away.

Kate closed the door, and Ben listened for the flip of the bolt.

"She locked it." Alex stepped off the porch.

"I'll hang out as long as you need." Ben slid into the driver's seat and settled in for a long watch.

"I appreciate it." Alex strode away to his truck.

Ben passed the time listening to the radio and watching the people of the little town of Schatzenburg.

After a couple hours, he dug snacks out of the mini cooler. As he munched carrots, the security guard nodded, the signal that a vehicle was approaching.

A Tahoe pulled into the grass, and two minutes later, DJ slid into the passenger seat. "Hey, quiet afternoon?"

"Very."

"Well, you can take off. I'm going to head on inside." DJ yawned.

"I'm going to stay. You go see Becca and relax."

"You sure?"

"Yeah, yeah. I want to chat with Alex a bit before I leave anyway." Ben had nearly convinced himself to ask about the mystery woman. He needed to be sure she was safe, and more than that, he wanted to see her again. Asking without mentioning that he'd bumped into her at the station would be tricky.

After DJ wandered inside, Ben swapped out the veggies for chips. The uneventful little town made for a boring watch, but he wouldn't complain. Boring was a good thing.

Snacking, he waited and watched.

An hour and a half later, Alex climbed into the passenger seat after parking the truck. "I can't thank you enough for doing this."

Ben caught sight of a small box shape in his pocket. *So that's where he's been.* "She just stumbled to your door?"

Alex's eyes went wide, and he laughed nervously. "You know how Kate and I met."

"It just seems crazy. She wandered around in the dark after escaping a kidnapping and landed at your door, and that chance meeting led to … what y'all have." Ben wouldn't rob Alex of the surprise.

"I'm just glad our paths crossed." He gazed at the house. "I can't imagine life without her."

Ben shifted, stifling questions about the mystery woman who had crossed his path. "Listen, DJ's already inside. I just stayed as a precaution."

Alex focused on Ben and rubbed the cleft in his chin. "Can I ask you a question? In confidence?"

"Sure." Ben anticipated a question about Kate. If Alex wanted assurance that she would say yes to his proposal, Ben could give it without hesitation.

"If you thought someone was being abused by a boyfriend, what would you do?"

Ben chewed his lower lip, trying to hide the fact that the question rattled him. "Have you talked to her about it?" He blinked, the image of the woman's fear-filled green eyes imposed on the back of his eyelids.

"You don't know this girl." Alex gave a humorless chuckle. "She's strong-willed and independent. Admitting she needs help isn't in her playbook."

"What makes you think she's in trouble?" Ben had his own list of reasons for assuming that was the case.

"Her boyfriend rubs me the wrong way. I know that's not a reason." Alex raked his fingers through his hair. "But I talked to her earlier today, and I swear she was crying. When I asked, she denied it. And she's not a crier."

Ben rubbed his buzz cut, which was in desperate need of a trim. "Have you seen any signs of abuse? Bruises?" He wracked his brain, trying to recall every visible inch of her. He hadn't noticed anything, and he'd been concerned. But he'd also been reminding himself over and over to be a gentleman and not let his eyes wander. Had he missed something?

"No black eyes or bruises that I've seen."

"Have you shown up unannounced at her house?" Ben was close to doing just that, if only he knew where it was.

"She hasn't given me the address. I don't even know for sure there is a problem." Alex slid out of the car, tapping his pocket. "Forget I mentioned it. You coming in for a bit?"

"I'm gonna get going. I'll see ya later." Ben waited until he was alone before he squeezed his eyes closed, choking back nausea. The woman Alex was worried about had to be the same one Ben met at the station. He felt it in his gut. She'd asked him not to say anything, and he'd kept her secret. Would she suffer because of it? He glanced back at the house. Should he run after Alex, describe the leggy brunette, and confirm what he thought? That still didn't help Ben get to her. Instead, he shot Maddox a text: *What's her name?*

He answered within seconds: *Stay out of it.*

# CHAPTER 5

*Wednesday, April 13*

Staying out of it hadn't gotten the green-eyed bombshell out of Ben's head. After what Alex told him, Ben worried about her almost constantly. Back in his days in uniform, he'd been called to domestic abuse cases—those were never easy. In homicide, he saw the devastating aftermath of abuse.

After forcing himself to focus on cases, as soon as his partner left for lunch, Ben made the call he'd been pondering all morning.

"Maddox." The captain's soft drawl sounded hurried but polite.

"Hey, it's Torres. Any news?"

Papers shuffled in the background. "I can't talk about it, but you know that. What do you really want to know?"

"Is she safe?"

"I wish I could say." Maddox sighed. "As soon as I have enough to make an arrest, I will. But until then, I don't know. I'm sorry."

"You won't give me her name?"

"I think it's better, safer if you stay away from her right now. Besides, what happened to 'I don't want to know.'?"

Ben rubbed the back of his head. "I'm worried about her, but I'll let you do your job."

"We can't force people to accept help." Maddox sounded as weary as Ben felt. "I gotta go."

Ben stuck his phone in his pocket to keep from tossing it against the wall.

❦

Darkness cloaked the street. Marisa had stayed out late, limiting her time at the apartment. As she walked toward the door, she chatted with her brother, hoping to reassure him that she was okay. She ended the call as she walked into the apartment. As soon as she stepped inside, the door slammed behind her, and Paul threw her against the wall. She cried out as his fingers dug into her arm. He was getting less discreet about where he hurt her. She'd have to wear long-sleeve blouses until the bruises healed.

"Who were you talking to?" His paranoia had ramped up the last few days, and he jumped every time a phone rang.

"Alex. I called Alex to check on Kate."

He let go of her, his demeanor changed. "Are they home from the hospital?"

She nodded, feeling awful for telling the fox where the chickens were.

He ran a finger down her arm. "You should've just told me who was on the phone and not made me ask you."

"Okay." She'd learned to acquiesce, and it kept him from getting angry, most of the time.

"You're late. Again."

"Trying to get caught up at the office." Marisa backed away from him. "I should've called. I'm sorry."

"You coming to bed?" He pulled her close and kissed her cheek.

She tensed, knowing that eventually Paul would balk at her excuses to avoid being intimate. "Not now. Is that okay?" Begging his permission garnered a yes more often than opposing him.

"Sure, baby." He unfastened her top button, slipped the blouse off her shoulder, and planted kisses along her collarbone. "There's no one else, is there?"

Images of the detective flashed in her head. "Of course not. Must be allergies. My head's been killing me most of the week."

"Anything I can do to ease your pain?" He pressed her against the wall and undid the next button of her blouse.

*Leave.*

"No. I'm going to sip on a Coke and watch some television."

"Too many of those will make you fat. That would be a horrid shame." He raked his eyes over her.

She joined in the laugh and bit back curses when he slapped her butt. "I'll probably be up for a while." She couldn't bear the thought of sleeping next to him. The couch was much more inviting.

Ben breathed in the night air as he stepped out his front door. He trudged down the stairs, weary and wound up. Between working open cases and worrying about the mystery woman, his mind never shut off. Physical exhaustion earned him at least a few hours of sleep, so he set off on a run.

An hour and a half later, when he crawled into bed, he replayed the conversation with Alex, then the conversation with Maddox. Hopefully an arrest would be made soon. Once he knew the woman was safe, he could resume his normal life, and hopefully sleeping, without her camped in his thoughts. Maybe. He still wanted to see her again.

# CHAPTER 6

## *Thursday, April 14*

Marisa limped into her office. That morning, she'd managed to fall through a weakened floor board at the dilapidated old house when showing Kate a property in Schatzenburg. Even though it was only a scrape and a bruise, it hurt to move. Marisa rubbed her hip, hoping it would heal quickly.

As she leaned over her filing cabinet reaching for a folder, a hand brushed against her backside.

"May I help you?" She didn't have to turn around to know who it was.

"Hey, Paul mentioned he was working late tonight. You want to grab some dinner with me? Just two friends out for a good time." Paul's friend, Ted, had gotten her the job, but had she known that he assumed strings were attached, she would never have said yes.

"No thank you, Mr. Jenner."

He closed the distance when she stepped back. "Please, doll, call me Ted." He let his gaze drop from her face, and a greedy smile spread over his face. "Do you have the file on the Wheeler place?"

"Yes. It's right there behind the desk. Let me grab it for you." She moved away before reaching over to grab it.

Once again, he invaded her personal space.

"Could you please move back?"

"I'm sure Paul wouldn't mind. We've been friends a long time." Ted's creepy vibe had doubled as Paul had gotten more aggressive.

"I mind. Do you need anything else?"

Always standing too close and calling her doll, Ted irritated Marisa. "Need or want?" He laughed.

"If that's all then, I'm late to meet a friend. She'll wonder where I am." Marisa snatched up her purse and raced out to her car. She'd fibbed. No one was expecting her, but she could change that. As she drove home, she called her friend, Lexi. "Hey, Paul's working late. Want to grab dinner?"

"Yes. I just got home. Where do you want to meet?" Lexi lived moment to moment. Spontaneity was her middle name.

Marisa had met Lexi at the realty office. She worked the front desk and had befriended Marisa on day one.

"Food trucks?" She never had trouble finding something good to eat at the food truck park not far from campus.

"Sounds great. See ya in a half hour."

Marisa changed clothes, yanking on a long-sleeve t-shirt despite the warm weather. With Paul working late, she got a rare night out of the apartment without enduring questions, but spilling her secrets to Lexi was not part of her plan.

Ben scanned the crowd, then made his way to where Miller sat with his wife. "Hey, Dana."

"It's so good to see you." She jumped up and hugged him. "How are things? It's been a few months. I almost didn't believe it when Jack said you were coming tonight." Always warm and caring, Dana was on a quiet campaign to marry Ben off, at least that's how it seemed to him.

"Jack pointed out that I'd missed too many monthly dinners, so here I am. Other guys coming?" He sat down at the table.

"Nah, Daniels and his wife are at a school play. Robbins and the misses are celebrating their anniversary. You know Andrews? Dana knows her from church. She might join us." Miller chuckled as Dana glared at him.

Ben shook his head. "You set me up?"

"Bethany! You made it." Dana beamed as her blonde friend took a seat next to Ben. "Have you two met?"

Officer Andrews focused big brown eyes on Ben but didn't say anything. Her long hair out of its usual ponytail, she looked attractive. He hadn't paid much attention before.

"Yes, hi. We've met a few times." Ben shot Miller a sideways glance.

"I've seen Detective Torres, I mean Ben, around the office." Bethany scanned the food trucks.

Dana waved toward the lines. "Go grab food. We'll talk when you get back."

Ben walked along next to Andrews, deciding what he wanted to eat.

She smiled up at him. "You eat here often? What's good?"

"Trucks change from night to night, but I'm a fan of the Korean tacos."

"Sounds interesting. I'll try those then." She followed him as he wove through the tables to his favorite taco truck.

He stopped in line behind two women. From the back, one reminded him of the woman in the red dress. *Quit thinking about her.*

Andrews commented on the nice weather. Ben agreed. After a minute of quiet, he asked her about how she'd met Dana. Intentionally giving his back to the woman who drew his thoughts away from the present, he listened as Andrews explained.

"We worked the nursery at church together several times and became friends." She smoothed the wisps of hair blowing in the breeze. "I hope this isn't too strange."

"Strange?"

"You know how married people are, always trying to set up single friends." She shrugged apologetically, giggles dancing in her eyes.

Before he answered, a group of guys in a heated discussion bumped into Ben knocking him into the brunette behind him. When she whipped around, familiar green eyes widened.

"I'm so sorry. They crashed into me. I didn't mean to bump you." Ben waited on her cue about whether to act as if they'd met.

Marisa grabbed his arm for balance. Her hip still throbbed from the earlier fall, and she winced in pain but tried to cover it with a smile. She glanced from Ben to the short blonde next to him. "No problem, *sir*. Don't worry about it. I'm fine."

The sting of seeing him with a date surprised her. He owed her nothing, and she'd flat out refused his help.

He glanced at the ground, kicking at a small rock. "Fine? Are you sure?"

She understood his question but couldn't risk being honest. She nodded when he looked up again.

Lexi leaned in close, but not close enough. "Who is *that*? Yum! Maybe you should invite him to eat with us." She had no filter.

Marisa spun Lexi forward so that they both faced the front of the line. "Stop. He can hear you."

"Truly, I don't care. And he isn't looking at me. Dump Paul. This guy is way better looking."

"Lexi, please." Marisa imagined the twinkle in those brown eyes and almost glanced back. Then she remembered his date.

Lexi gave up all pretense of whispering. "Look at him. I hardly ever see guys that fit at the gym. And he's not bad looking either."

Ben chuckled.

Lexi glanced back and winked before stepping up to the window to order.

With Lexi busy at the window, Marisa took advantage of the moment and dropped her purse. As she expected, he bent down to retrieve it.

Leaning down, she whispered, "Thank you, Detective."

Their gazes locked, she was tempted to give him a clue about how he could contact her, a thread he could follow if interested, but the hand that touched his arm stopped her.

~*~

Ben didn't notice Bethany speaking to him until the woman in front of him glanced at Bethany's hand on his arm. "Sorry, what was that?"

"Someone you know?" Officer Andrews wrapped her hand around his arm and stepped closer. The giggles disappeared from her eyes.

"No. Not really. I bumped into her on accident, then she dropped her purse." He noticed the woman's pained expression, and that concerned him.

"I saw all that. Just seems like you know her."

"Uh, no. Don't know her name or anything."

"I find that hard to believe, *Detective*." Andrews had a future as an investigator. She hadn't missed the whispered exchange, but Ben couldn't set it right without explaining more than he wanted people to know.

He forced himself not to watch the mystery woman walk away. Turning to Bethany, he stepped up to order. "Order whatever you want. My treat."

"No, thank you, Ben." She ordered and paid for her own food. "I'll meet you back at the table."

And the blind date ended before he'd even started eating. His thoughts circled back to the mystery woman. Concern mingled with interest in the thought campground dedicated to her.

# CHAPTER 7

## *Friday, April 15*

Ben stood at the stove, making dinner. The week had been stressful and long, and work was only part of the reason. When a familiar number lit up his phone, Ben lunged for it, knocking the salt shaker crashing to the floor. He had quite a mess to clean up and hoped the superstition didn't hold true.

"Alex? Everything okay?"

"My sister hasn't answered her phone all day. I've called three times. It isn't like her to ignore my calls."

*His sister?* Ben remembered those vivid green eyes. *Of course.* He'd spent hours wondering about the connection between Alex and the mystery woman, and it should've been obvious. "Is this the one you were asking about the other night?"

"Uh-huh, but I really don't know if there is anything like that happening."

"She's not answering or she's ignoring?"

"After one ring, it goes to voicemail."

She was in trouble, but Ben didn't know enough to get her out of it. His interference might even worsen her situation.

"And you don't know where she lives?"

"With that boyfriend, but I don't know where that is." Alex's voice cracked. "That makes me a horrible big brother. I let her down after Ellie died, and now—she doesn't even ask for my help. I don't know what to do. I don't want to talk to Kate about it. She'll worry."

Ben's mind raced, trying to think of a solution. "Have you tried asking Maddox? He talked to her after the break-in, didn't he?" He hoped that tidbit had come from Alex.

"Good idea. I'll do that." He hung up before Ben could ask to be kept in the loop.

*Maybe it's better if I don't know.* He didn't believe that. Sleep was over-rated anyway.

Marisa wiped her eyes and slid into the tub, trying to ignore the bruises on her arms and legs. She wasn't sure how much longer she could tolerate the charade. Locking herself in the bathroom under the guise of soaking in the tub provided her a respite from Paul. Her hip still ached, but she'd managed to hide the injury from him. She didn't want to draw any more attention to Kate.

If Maddox called today, hopefully he'd been careful. Marisa had been very clear about not leaving messages on her phone or sending texts. Paul allowed her very little privacy.

He'd hung around with her all day, in possession of her phone, answering some calls and sending others to voicemail. For the short spans she was away from him, he kept her phone.

Alex was probably sick with worry. He'd called at least twice, and both times, Paul sent it to voicemail. Biting her tongue, she opted not to speak up and anger him more.

Paul's paranoia ratcheted up after Maddox interviewed them both the day before about the night of break-in, routine questions since they'd been at Kate's just before it happened.

Paul knocked at the bathroom door. "Marisa. Are you ever coming out?"

"Soon."

"No need for clothes when you do, baby." Words, coated in slime, slid off his tongue.

She submerged under the water and held her breath. How long did she have before he broke down the door? Would she drown before he made his way into the bathroom?

When stars danced on her eyelids, panic grabbed her. *No.* She'd walk away before harming herself. She sat up, tears mixing with the bath water. *Justice. He needs to pay.*

She wiped her face and breathed in deep. She could handle it a few more days. After stepping out of the tub, she opened the drain and grabbed a towel. Burying her face in the blue terrycloth, she gathered her nerve.

"Hurry out." Paul's clipped demand scared her. Would she be able to put him off another night? Or would he take what she wasn't willing to give? The last week, using feigned headaches and whatever other creative excuses came to mind, she'd managed to put him off. Her list of excuses had been used up. The thought of him touching her twisted her insides, flooding her with a wave of nausea.

She dropped to her knees by the toilet and expelled the contents of her stomach.

"Yuck." Paul's reaction made her smile. "Forget it."

She heaved a few more times, thankful for the unexpected reprieve. After toweling off, she put on her flannel pajamas. When she got to bed, her phone lay on her pillow. She sent a quick text to Alex: *Can't talk now, but I'm okay. I'll call soon.*

Paul flopped onto his side, giving her his back. "You better not be pregnant."

That thought kept her awake half the night.

Ben collapsed on the floor of his apartment after a longer than normal run. He glanced at the screen when his phone beeped. Stress loosened its iron grip on his chest as he read Alex's message: *My sister texted. Says she's okay.*

Trusting Maddox to do his job wasn't easy, but given the intense feelings Ben harbored for the woman, his way of taking care of the problem might land in him serious trouble or land her in the hospital. He couldn't risk the latter.

# Chapter 8

*Sunday, April 17*

Marisa spent her Sunday morning at the office, wrapping up paperwork before she went to meet clients. Early in the afternoon, she returned to the apartment, hoping to find her phone before she left for her appointment. She searched the couch cushions and the floor. Paul hadn't said anything about taking it, and he flaunted his power by telling her he'd rescinded her phone privileges, which he'd done a couple times in the last two days.

The phone linked her to clients. She needed it.

She searched each room over and over until she risked being late. She couldn't miss the appointment. It would cost her a large commission. She grabbed her bag and left without the phone.

Just as she pulled up to the curb in front of a house in a Hill Country suburb, a ringing emanated from her center console. She yanked it open. Her phone lay half hidden under a receipt. Before the ringing stopped, she answered. The woman Marisa was supposed to meet apologized for the late notice and canceled, only five minutes before their scheduled appointment.

Marisa hung up, shaking her head. In all the time she'd had the car, she'd never put her phone in the center console. She scanned her emails, then her texts. The world started to spin as she read the text exchange with Kate on her phone, a series of messages Marisa hadn't sent. Paul had impersonated her. He'd acted as if she wanted to visit Becca's house. Kate had texted the address.

*Why does Paul want Becca's address?*

While trying to figure out what it all meant, Marisa dialed Maddox and drove toward the highway. When he didn't answer, she left a message. "Paul wanted Becca's address. She was with us at lunch that day. I don't know why he wants it, but maybe he plans to break into *her* house."

Speeding down the interstate, she called her brother, trying to decide if she should head to Schatzenburg or Kerrville.

"Hey, Marisa. Everything okay?" He sounded worried in every one of their recent conversations.

"I need to talk to you. Are you at Kate's?" She couldn't bear to tell him over the phone.

"No. I'm in Kerrville. What's wrong?"

"Where can we meet? I'm on my way."

"Burger place at the first exit. See you in a few."

Marisa took full advantage of the seventy-five miles per hour speed limit. Miles disappeared behind her as minutes ticked by. She made it to the restaurant before Alex even arrived.

She parked near the back of the lot and waited. Rehearsing how to explain the secret she'd been keeping, she gave in to tears. When his blue GMC truck pulled into the lot, she climbed into the passenger seat as soon as he parked.

"Marisa, what's wrong?" Tears always rattled Alex.

"Please don't hate me. I'm worried that Paul might hurt Kate or Becca." She told her brother about her suspicions and about the text exchange. She couldn't let Paul hurt anyone else.

Personal details like bruises and confiscated phones, she left out. Alex didn't need anything else to worry about.

Marisa wrung her hands while he raced back to Becca's. He called

DJ while they were on the way, warning him to get there as quickly as he could. Marisa regretted keeping the secret so long.

As they drove up the street toward the house, a patrol car stopped, and deputies ran into the house.

Alex skidded to a stop. "Wait here."

Marisa sat, worrying and bracing herself for the worst.

Minutes ticked by. Knowing it was her fault Becca and Kate were involved, Marisa stayed in the truck like her brother had ordered. Usually she wasn't good at following orders.

A few minutes later, the front door opened. She leaned forward in her seat. A familiar figure, hands cuffed behind him, trudged along next to an officer. Paul was being arrested.

She clenched her jaw and squared her shoulders. He wouldn't see her upset, but he'd see who turned him in. Sitting in the truck as police loaded him into the backseat of the patrol car, Marisa met his stare. *Finally. Behind bars is where you belong.*

Ben had been on edge all weekend. He'd pestered Maddox a couple more times, only to be told "Let me do my job" and "Stay out of it." But there was no staying out of it anymore. Tomorrow, in the office, Ben would do whatever he could to find an address for the mystery woman. Whether she wanted it or not, she needed his help.

"Look at me, Uncle Ben." His nephew whooshed down the slide.

"Wow. That was fast." It took effort for Ben not to let his family see his stress. Hanging out in the backyard, watching his nieces and nephew play, offered a distraction.

When his phone vibrated in his pocket, he yanked it out. Alex's number showed on the screen.

Ben answered on the first ring. "Any news?"

"They made an arrest. I'll finally sleep tonight."

"Is everyone okay? Who'd they arrest?"

"Everyone is fine. Kate is okay. Please keep this under wraps, I don't want the whole world thinking badly of her."

"Kate?" Ben hoped Alex would mention his sister.

"My sister. Her boyfriend—ex-boyfriend now—had some sort of

a scheme stealing from houses she'd listed. Don't know the whole story. They think it was about getting back something he stole."

"What did he steal?"

"That's the kicker. No one knows. He won't say." The lingering loose end irritated Alex. That was clear from his tone.

"Is your sister okay?"

"For now. But when I'm done with her ..."

"Alex, she turned him in, right?" Ben added the last word, not wanting to sound too informed.

"She did. And if he'd found out, he'd have hurt her. Just thinking about it makes me want to vomit."

"Will you swing me, Uncle Ben?" His niece swayed back and forth, dragging her white sandals through the dirt.

Ben let his body relax after days of worry. "I'm glad everyone is safe. I'm being paged. Can I call you later?"

"Yeah." Alex hesitated. "Please don't say anything about our discussions."

"I won't." Ben hung up the phone and pinched the bridge of his nose.

Whatever her name, Alex's sister was unharmed. And with her boyfriend behind bars, she'd be safe. At least until he was out on bail.

Ben wondered how he could arrange to see her again, then he remembered Kate's surprise party. Surely Alex's sister would be there. He smiled.

~*~

Marisa sobbed on her brother's shoulder, something she hadn't done since they'd buried their parents. "Can you ever forgive me?"

"Just promise me that you won't date guys like that anymore. He could've hurt you."

"I have to get my stuff out of his apartment."

Maddox nodded. "You have a key."

Alex laid a hand on her shoulder. "Let me check on Kate, and then we'll get you moved out."

"Thank you." She hugged Alex as he turned to go. "I'll meet you at the apartment."

"Text me the address."

She messaged him the information before getting in her car. Driving back, she blared the radio, attempting to drown out her thoughts. Guilt hounded Marisa after watching her brother worry about Kate. After three years of cutting himself off from most of the world after losing his wife, he was finally happy. Kate was the reason. Introducing them to Paul had put that at risk.

And Marisa had put herself at risk. Her brother hadn't even had her address. If she'd needed him, he wouldn't even have known where to find her. Her stupid decisions taunted her. Mistakes had taught her more in a week than a lifetime of lectures. Things would be different. She would be different.

She stopped for boxes before going to the apartment. Tense, she let herself in, wishing she hadn't come alone. She changed clothes, then started packing her things. She carried clothes, still on hangers, out to her car. Back and forth, trip after trip, she separated her life from the man who'd hurt and degraded her. That he never loved her was easy to see in hindsight.

While she was gathering her toiletries, Alex called. "I'm on my way. Sorry it took me so long."

"See you in a bit." She tossed all her makeup in a bag. As she emptied the bathroom cabinet of what belonged to her, she shuddered. She needed to buy a pregnancy test, but she didn't want her brother to know. That would only lead to a whole new level of worry.

She ran out of the apartment and drove to the nearby pharmacy. Tucked between the feminine napkins and prophylactics, several brands of pregnancy tests lined the shelves. She picked up a box without reading it. Spotlighted by fluorescent lights, she couldn't escape the store fast enough.

Ben ran into the pharmacy to grab chips, a Dr Pepper, and another bottle of pain killers. Headaches and worry the last week had wiped out his supply. As he made his way to the snacks, he glanced down an aisle. There she stood.

He hurried toward her. Seeing her raised his blood pressure and calmed his fears all at the same time, until the package in her hand hit the floor. *A pregnancy test?*

Her eyes misted with tears, and she shook her head. Her earlier plea etched on her face and played in his head. *Please, Detective, don't say anything.* She chewed her bottom lip as she rushed past him.

He stood in the empty aisle, staring after her. *More secrets.* And he still didn't know her name.

Marisa crossed her arms. "You can't do all this by yourself."

"Head on out to the cabin. Here's the key." Alex tossed her a purple key.

"Since when do you buy purple keys?"

"It's Kate's. She'll need it back."

She tucked it in her pocket. "Alex, please. Let me find someone to help you. Let *me* help you."

Alex didn't even look up as he shuffled boxes. "Don't worry about me. I'll get help."

"Alex, *please,* let me help." Marisa carried a suitcase toward the truck.

He set a load in the bed and focused his big brother stare on her. "Marisa, *go.*" He used his don't-argue-with-me tone. "If you don't want to be alone, go to Kate's, and we'll unload your car later."

She hated when he told her what to do, but she wasn't in the mood to argue.

~*~

Ben paced in his apartment, picturing teary green eyes. If she was pregnant, her life would only get more complicated. She still needed help.

Concern needled at him. He called Alex. "Any more news?"

"You free? I've got a load of boxes to move to the cabin." Exhaustion weighed heavy in Alex's voice.

"Tell me where, and I'll be on my way."

Alex rattled off the address.

"I can be there in five minutes."

The last ten days, the mystery woman had been living less than ten miles from him. Packing up and moving showed that she was breaking ties. That was good but much more tangled if kids were in the mix.

When Ben arrived at the apartment complex, Alex had already loaded half the pile.

"Hey." Alex hoisted a box onto the tailgate. "I think it'll all fit."

"Only boxes?"

"She's leaving everything else."

"Whatever doesn't fit in the truck, we can squeeze in my car."

They loaded the rest boxes into the bed of the truck and stashed suitcases in Ben's car. Once they finished loading, Alex tied down the load.

"I'll follow you."

"Thanks." Alex's shoulders sagged.

The strain etched in Alex's face weighed on Ben. His friend had been put through the wringer the last few weeks, and he didn't even know the whole story. If Alex knew what Ben knew, anger and rage would stomp out the strain.

"We'll get it all unloaded and then you can get back to Kate. I bet after what happened, she'll be happy to have you home."

"Home. That's funny. The cabin was home until recently." Alex pulled his keys out of his pocket. "You're coming Thursday, right?"

"I wouldn't miss it."

Alex stepped up into the truck but left the door open. "I'm planning to propose, but don't say anything."

Ben had suspected that was part of the big surprise, but having Alex confirm it shocked Ben.

*Another secret.* He added it to his list. "Kate will make a beautiful bride."

Alex smiled for the first time all evening. "Yeah. She will."

Following the truck out to the cabin, Ben hoped the green-eyed brunette was not at the cabin. Seeing her again with Alex around would be awkward, and Ben couldn't shake the image of her dropping that box.

When he pulled up to the cabin, he breathed a sigh of relief. The black Passat wasn't there.

# Chapter 9

*Monday, April 18*

Marisa parked outside the title company and checked her makeup in the rearview mirror. Last night's sobs had left her eyes puffy. She freshened her lipstick and gathered her paperwork—the documents she always had on hand at a closing, just in case.

She glanced at her full schedule. Busy was what she needed. Putting the past behind her, she could move on. She contemplated moving back to Austin but didn't want to run away. Besides, the detective lived here, and seeing him again wouldn't be horrible. Maybe she'd run into him since he knew Kate and Alex.

Then she remembered dropping the pregnancy test in the pharmacy aisle. Ben wouldn't be interested. He knew too much. The thought stung, but it was true. If he was what he seemed, he wouldn't be interested in a girl like her.

Before climbing out of the car, she sucked in a cleansing breath. Kate was quick to forgive, but Alex hadn't been real talkative last night. His truck pulled into the lot as Marisa stepped out of the car.

Kate's smile reassured Marisa, but apologizing again wouldn't hurt.

She met Kate at the passenger side door. "I am *so* sorry. I never meant for any of it to happen." Marisa backed up as Alex stepped in to help Kate out of the truck. Getting in the way of their little ritual seemed a bad idea.

Kate closed the gap and pulled Marisa in for a hug. "Like I told you last night, it wasn't your fault. I'm not mad."

"And I don't want you to think I was just keeping his secret. I reported him right after your accident."

"Everything turned out okay." Kate clutched Alex's arm and smiled up at him. "I'm ready for us to sign some papers."

"About that." Marisa strolled alongside them. "The owners aren't signing until tomorrow, and I can't give you the keys until both parties have signed."

"Well that's a bummer." Alex pulled open the door. "You'll bring Kate the keys once they've signed?"

"Absolutely." She followed Kate through the door. "I'll let you know as soon as I get word."

Marisa smiled. Including Alex's name on the papers was significant, but she'd chosen not to spotlight the fact. She guessed it wouldn't be long before her brother proposed.

# Chapter 10

*Tuesday, April 19*

Ben slid out of bed later than normal and put on his running gear. He detoured from his usual run and made his way into the hills nearby. Subdivisions filled with lavish homes lined the road. Pounding down the sidewalk, he tried to clear his head. Maybe he'd pick up lunch and surprise his parents or go get the groceries he desperately needed. One thought overshadowed the others. He wanted to see her again. As he ran, he tried to figure out how to make that happen.

After a long run, exhausted, Ben trudged into his apartment. Visiting Alex and Kate provided the best chance of seeing his sister, but Ben couldn't show up sweaty and nasty. He stripped off his clothes as he ran to the shower, planning how he'd invite himself over.

Still wet and only half-dressed, he called Alex. The ringing stopped abruptly, and a text popped on the screen: *What's up?*

Ben replied: *You free?*

As expected, Alex extended an invitation when Ben mentioned

pizza rolls. Declining the call and responding via text was a bit concerning.

Ben texted: *Everything okay?*

Alex's response didn't offer much info: *Mostly. At Kate's. Come whenever.*

Marisa grinned as she texted Kate: *I've got the keys! Place is all yours. You home now?*

Kate's reply made her laugh: *Yes! COME RIGHT NOW please.*

Already in the car, Marisa tossed her phone in the cup holder and drove toward Schatzenburg. After yesterday's closing, Kate left mildly disappointed that the sellers wouldn't close until sometime on Tuesday. The key couldn't be released until the entire process was complete. As soon as Marisa had received notice all the paperwork was signed, she'd grabbed the keys.

When she arrived at Kate's, she parked behind Alex's truck and ran to the door. Kate yanked it open before Marisa even knocked and wrapped her in a hug.

"I'm so excited. Thank you for driving all the way out here."

"Of course! Besides, I wanted to see your happy face. And my commission on your purchase wasn't shabby. Thank you for choosing to work with me." Marisa handed over the keys. "Hey, Alex."

The worn expression on Alex's face pricked her. He wore a smile, but Marisa could see through it. He hadn't quite recovered from Kate's brush with danger.

Her brother bear-hugged her, not his typical hello. "Where'd you park?"

"Behind the truck."

"Mind if I move your car into the garage, and we'll take mine over. My vehicle has better clearance."

"I can just park mine on the street."

"Nah." He reached out, snagging the keys dangling from her hand. "I'll move it."

Kate's eyes were red and puffy; Alex wore tension like a sweatshirt. The combination bothered Marisa. She was likely to blame.

While he moved cars, Kate put on her shoe. "You coming with us?"

Alex and Kate needed to share the moment alone. Even though there'd been no talk of a wedding, Kate adding Alex to the ownership papers spoke volumes. If they weren't already talking about marriage, the conversation was just around the corner.

Marisa shook her head. "If you don't mind, I'm just going to hide out here and relax."

"You sure?"

"I am. The house on the property is still full of stuff, but I can arrange to have it cleaned out. The owners didn't want any of it."

"Ready?" Alex dropped the keys in front of Marisa but focused on Kate. "We can figure out where to build my new cabin."

His stress seemed to fall away, and his eyes glimmered as she limped toward him, a broad smile on her face. Marisa caught a sigh before letting it escape. She couldn't be happier for her brother.

"Have fun!" Marisa laughed as Alex scooped Kate into his arms and carried her to the truck.

~*~

Ben texted Alex as he left the restaurant with two dozen pizza rolls: *On my way. Just picked up food.*

Alex replied quickly: *Let yourself in. Back door is unlocked. We're looking at Kate's new spread.*

Driving toward the little town, Ben wondered if there'd be any mention of Alex's little sister. He was interested in learning all he could about the brunette.

When he got to the house, he parked on the street and ran around to the back door, pizza boxes in hand. The truck wasn't in the driveway. Since they weren't back, he'd keep the food warm and wait.

~*~

Marisa watched the knob on the backdoor twist. Kate and Alex hadn't been gone very long. She stood as the door swung open and gasped. "Detective."

Pizza boxes bobbled. His eyes wide, he stopped in the doorway.

She took one step forward. "I didn't expect..." Delighted to see him, she smiled, her excitement tempered by the fear that her secrets wouldn't remain as such and that her excitement was misplaced.

"Alex told me to let myself in. Sorry, I didn't know you … I mean, anyone else was here." He stepped inside and kicked the door closed.

"Marisa. My name is Marisa."

"Hello, *Marisa*. I'm glad to finally know your name."

She motioned toward the den. "You want to sit down?"

"I worried about you for days." He turned away and adjusted the temp on the oven before sliding the boxes inside. "Kate usually has a stocked refrigerator. Want a Coke?"

"Dr Pepper if she has it."

He opened the refrigerator and grabbed two cans. His fingers brushed along her hand as he handed her the drink.

*Was that intentional?*

Staring at her hands, he opened his mouth, then snapped it closed and sauntered into the den. He stood next to the couch and didn't sit until after she did.

She laid a hand on his arm. "You can say what you started to say."

He focused soft brown eyes on her. "Did he hurt you?"

"Please don't tell anyone." She tugged her sleeve down. "You going to tell Alex I talked to you at the station?"

"And let him know I knew about it more than a week before you told him?"

"Then I guess I have nothing to worry about, Detec—Ben." Pangs of regret pounded in her chest. She should never have put him in that tight spot. "But I'm sorry. I shouldn't have—"

"I made my own choices. No need to apologize."

Silently, they sipped their drinks. He stared at his Dr Pepper can, giving her ample time to study him. She guessed he was in his thirties, worked out often, and had a woman somewhere waiting on him to come home. He might be single, but unattached didn't seem possible. He hadn't been alone at the food trucks. She envied the woman that got to curl up next to him. Good-looking, but not staggeringly so, he had a manner and presence—and if she was honest, his physique— that made him more than desirable.

"Marisa." He said her name as if testing the feel of it on his lips. "Pretty name."

Alex's truck rumbled into the driveway, and they both jumped up and hurried into the kitchen. Ben, standing behind her, leaned in close as the truck doors slammed. "Your secrets are safe, Marisa."

She whipped around and faced him, but before words formed in her head, the backdoor swung open.

"Kate solved the case! Maddox is on his way over." Alex's voice pitched with excitement.

"I know what Paul stole." Kate hobbled to a chair and laid a photo on the table. "Marisa, you mentioned having the stuff cleaned out of that house. Please don't." She dropped into a chair. "Can you believe that place is connected to my client's family? Anyway, I found this picture." Pointing at a photo, she told them about a brooch.

Marisa tried to pay attention, but with Ben standing right behind her and leaning around to view the picture, her heart raced. Her thoughts occupied with him, the brooch and photo paled in interest.

The day they'd met, he'd taken up residence in her head. Going out of his way to help her and keeping her secrets carved him a permanent place in her heart. What she felt for him was different than gratitude. He'd become what other boyfriends never were—what she wanted. In her heart, the truth stabbed at her. She didn't deserve him.

~*~

Anticipating Kate would give the long version of events, Ben pulled out a chair and motioned for Marisa to sit.

Alex dropped paper plates and napkins onto the table while Ben grabbed the food.

They ate, and Kate continued her story.

Ben listened as Paul's actions were rehashed, a reminder of the danger Marisa had faced.

Kate pointed at Ben. "You remember that night. You were here. DJ and Becca came. We sat around the table eating pizza."

"The neighbor showed up with wine." Alex rolled his eyes.

Ben stifled a laugh, remembering how put out Alex was about the neighbor hitting on Kate.

"Marisa, that was the day we met you for lunch, then Paul acted so weird and dragged you out here that night. All of this started then."

"He must have dropped something in one of the bags at lunch."

Marisa rubbed her temples. "I'm so sorry. He insisted on coming out here because he wanted to know where you lived."

She hadn't been there when Ben was there. He'd missed meeting her, probably by only a few minutes. The thought unsettled him. How would events have been different?

He spoke—focused on her—without giving his words much thought. "I left before you showed up, I guess."

His impulse to highlight the missed connection surprised him but not as much as Marisa's reaction did. She popped out of her chair and darted down the hall.

When Alex jumped up to chase after his sister, Ben stopped him. "Let me."

Down the hall, he slipped through the half-open door and closed it, making his presence known. Marisa stood at the window, looking out, dabbing a tissue to her eyes.

Watching her cry unnerved him. He stepped closer, trying to decide how to comfort her. He wasn't even sure why his observation had upset her.

She sighed before turning around. "Alex, I'll be fi—"

"I didn't mean to make you cry." Ben offered an apologetic smile.

Her eyes widened, vivid with anger. Tears lingered on her lashes. Jaw set, she crossed the room and poked a finger at his chest. "I don't need you running after me."

Ben bit back the retorts that bounced around in his head and moved out of the way, so she could leave the room. He hadn't seen that landmine, and he had no idea what he'd done to trigger it. The logical response would be to walk away, but the pain that flickered in her eyes, masked by anger, tugged at him. He wasn't any less interested, maybe even more so.

When he joined the others, he avoided her gaze as he shook hands with Alex. "I gotta run." It wasn't a lie. Ben planned to go home and run several miles, far enough to shed his frustrations.

# Chapter 11

*Thursday, April 21*

Ben tossed the GPS enabled keychain in a gift bag and shoved red tissue on top. Hopefully, Kate found the humor in his gift, but he also hoped she'd use it. After hunting for her twice—make that three times—he thought the GPS keychain an appropriate gift.

Alex was lucky. Not because of all the trouble that had hounded him and Kate in the last few months, but because he'd met her. They were happy together. There was no question how she would respond to his proposal.

Ben wanted that, not Kate, obviously. Was it too much to hope that serendipity would land at his door? He locked up his apartment and headed out, wanting to make it to the cabin before Alex arrived with Kate.

Marisa would be at the party. Ben was eager to see her, but he'd have to be more watchful of landmines.

Marisa helped Becca set up the table and draped it with the new red tablecloth. Alex had given Marisa a list, and she'd spent her non-working hours the last two days shopping for Kate's surprise birthday party.

"Who's coming?" She didn't want to ask about the detective by name, but she hoped he'd be attending.

She'd been less than kind in their last exchange. His coming after her had caught her off balance, and if she was honest, it scared her. She'd wanted his attention, but when he gave her that attention, she lashed out, guarding herself. He either wasn't a nice guy—she didn't need another loser—or he was having fun at her expense because no way would a nice guy be interested in a girl like her.

Men like him didn't want girls like her, did they?

"I wish I knew. Alex didn't give me a list. The only ones I know about are Gram—have you met DJ's Gram? She lives down the street from Kate."

"I haven't met her, but Alex and Kate have mentioned her."

"Everyone loves Gram. Anyway, friends from Colorado are coming. I could probably guess who else. There are supposed to be…" She tapped her forehead. "Twelve, plus the two of them. So, it's probably— let's see—the three of us, Gram, Beth and Pat—"

"Beth and Pat? I don't think I know them."

"Maddox. Kate's aunt and uncle."

A cold tremor rushed down Marisa's spine. How would she make it through the evening without everyone in attendance knowing everything that had happened?

"Where was I? Five and the two from Colorado. Kate's sister—I don't like that woman—and her husband might be coming, maybe Phillip, the new neighbor, and hmmm. Who else? I'm missing someone obvious." She shrugged. "It'll come to me. But, oh, I'll introduce you to the neighbor. He's like a magazine cover and loaded."

"I'm not really wanting to meet anyone new right now, not like that."

"I guess that makes sense. Sorry. Can you drape this cloth on that small table? We'll put gifts over there."

Unless the detective was someone obvious, Marisa was out of luck. If he did show up, she needed to apologize.

~*~

Ben eased his Jetta down the caliche driveway. Cars lined both sides. How would Alex pull off a surprise with so many vehicles parked in front, not that there was anywhere else to park? Someone had set up cones, marking off a spot, presumably for Alex's truck.

When Ben got to the front door, it swung open before he even knocked. He froze, but there were no reflective glasses to hide his stare.

Serendipity stood in the doorway looking for all the world like trouble.

Marisa smiled and stepped aside to let him enter. "I wondered if you were coming."

Looking more stunning than the day they'd first met, she made him want to sweep her into his arms, drive out to the middle of nowhere, and talk for hours under a blanket of stars—any more than that would have to wait. She'd had a rough go of late. But he wouldn't leave, not knowing what Alex had planned.

They stood, gazes locked until she broke the silence. "You going to stand in the doorway all night?"

"Hello, Marisa." *Of course she has the same name as Grandma.* Ben grazed his fingers along her shoulder as he stepped in the door, then leaned in close and made sure no one else was around before asking his question. "He hasn't come after you has he? Since making bail?"

His worry had only eased some. She still dominated his thoughts.

Tears rimmed her eyes, and a nearly imperceptible shake of her head shut down any more questions on the topic.

She pointed to the table decorated with a colorful tablecloth where other presents lay. "Gifts go over there."

"Is that you, Ben?" Becca bounced out of the kitchen, carrying a vase of flowers. "Have you met Marisa?"

"I have." He tossed his gift with the others. "How can I help?" Reining in his runaway emotions, he regained a measure of control.

"In here." Becca motioned him toward the kitchen.

"Be right there." He turned to Marisa. "I'm glad our paths crossed again. Maybe we can talk more later?" He hoped they'd have lots of time to talk during the evening.

"I'd like that."

Marisa stood near the office door, watching the other guests and waiting for Kate and Alex's arrival. Ben peeked out the window over the desk, ready to pass the word as soon as the truck turned down the drive.

Becca dragged Phillip across the room. She clearly hadn't taken Marisa's earlier comment to heart. "Have y'all met? Phillip, this is Alex's sister."

He tugged at his collar. "Hi."

"We met at Kate's." Marisa wondered if the detective was listening from inside the office.

Phillip flashed a wide grin. "We did. As I recall, you and your boyfriend were there. He talked about his trip overseas. Nice guy."

"We aren't dating anymore." Embarrassment set her on edge, and Marisa hoped no one had mentioned the ordeal.

"Well, that's good news." Phillip stepped closer as Becca retreated. "What do you say you and I go out one night?"

Papers toppled in the office, and Marisa hid her smile. Did someone not like Phillip's invitation?

She'd dealt with unwanted advances before, not always in the best way. "You're the one playing This Old House down the street from Kate?"

"I'm restoring the blue Victorian."

She crossed her arms. "It sounds like you have your hands full already."

Reacting to her body language and tone, Phillip put his hands up in front of him. "Didn't mean to step on any toes." He leaned in closer. "I suppose there is someone else."

*As if that's the only reason I won't go out with you.*

Repulsed by his complete arrogance, she glared at him, swallowing back the not-nice words she wanted to spew at him. "Let me make it clear and simple. You're not my type."

She'd dated enough self-absorbed men to recognize one, and

she wasn't interested. Phillip smirked, shaking his head, and strolled away without another word.

Marisa leaned back against the wall. She didn't like Phillip. He was hiding something, and his playboy personality seemed like a façade. In fact, it surprised her that he'd been invited to the party. *What was Alex thinking?*

Ben spied headlights and waited an extra minute to ensure it was Alex's truck coming up the drive. As the blue GMC truck passed the window, Ben grabbed his beer and hurried out of the office. "They're here!"

Excited, he scanned the room, taking in everyone's position as Becca ran for the light switch.

*Where's Marisa?*

The flip of a switch cloaked the room in darkness before he could spot her. Knowing Alex's surprise made it hard to wait. When the truck door slammed, he clenched his fists in anticipation and stepped back toward the wall. A hand stopped him.

"Marisa?" he whispered over his shoulder.

Her breath tickled his ear, her hand still on his back. "Your muscles are tight." She shifted, pulling him to the wall next to her. "You have a secret."

Her fingers slipped into his hand, and he squeezed, a natural response, as if holding her hand was a regular occurrence. Before he had a chance to respond, the door opened, and light filled the room.

"Surprise." Everyone in the room shouted and cheered.

Marisa let go of his hand to clap and shot him a sideways glance. "Is he going to…?"

Ben nodded, impressed with her perceptiveness.

When Alex dropped to one knee, a collective gasp went up from the room. Kate answered "yes" as Ben expected she would. While the party guests sighed and wiped their eyes, Alex and Kate ignored the rest of the room, whispering and kissing near the door.

Ben glanced at Marisa. Stunning green eyes focused on him. The woman skewed his perception of reality and tangled all logical thought. Pressing her to the wall and tasting her lips was the loudest thought in his head.

She touched his elbow. "The other day—"

He caught her hand. "You don't have to explain."

"Why are you even talking to me?"

"How else will I get to know you better?"

The warmth evaporated from her green eyes. Her fingers chilled, and she shot him an icy glance. "Don't you know too much already?" She shook free of his hand and walked away.

He leaned his head back against the wall. She switched from hot to cold faster than Texas weather during an autumn cold front. It would definitely make getting to know her a more interesting process. For the rest of the evening, he'd keep his distance, following her cues.

Marisa watched him during the rest of the party as he interacted with her brother, Kate, and others. When Ben blushed during a conversation with Gram, Marisa wanted more than anything to know what had been said.

Every interaction painted him as a good guy, and he'd been clear about his interest. Marisa had to find his flaw and soon. Pushing him away proved successful. He walked wide circles around her. In the cabin, that wasn't an easy feat. In stories shared throughout the evening, his frequent help was recounted, highlighting his character.

Marisa guessed that she'd seen the last of Ben. He would leave after the party and forget her. She, on the other hand, wouldn't be able to do the same. He'd kept her secrets and still tried to protect her, qualities she couldn't forget.

As the party wrapped up and guests started to leave, Captain Maddox pulled her aside. "What you did was brave, but next time, if there ever is one, leave. Some things aren't worth the risk. Your tip helped us put together a strong case. I'm confident he'll spend a while in jail after it goes to trial."

She hugged him. "Thank you. And I promise. There won't be a next time, not like that."

Trying to collect herself, Marisa tucked into the office and discovered the detective on the phone.

He stood up. "I'll call you back. I gotta go." He shoved the cell-phone in his pocket. "Sorry. I was talking to my mom."

"Is everything okay?" She stepped closer to him.

"My brother's wife had her baby." He brushed past her. "I'll get out of your way."

Marisa reached for him. "Ben, stop. Please."

He stopped, back to her, hand on the doorknob.

Her hand still resting on his back, she swallowed the lump in her throat. "I'm not. Two tests, same result." The compulsion to tell him she wasn't pregnant overrode her discretion. He didn't want to know that. Likely, he didn't care.

"I'm glad, for your sake, but"—he turned around and opened his arms—"either way, it doesn't change who you are or my interest. I would like to know you better."

She stepped into his embrace, satisfied that the low-light of the office hid the war of emotions on her face. "Thank you. But—"

"After you get to know me a little better, if you don't like me, tell me to go away. Until then, how about we take it slow?"

She nodded against his chest, fighting the urge to bolt from the room. "Really slow."

He slipped his phone out of his pocket. "May I have your number?"

She typed her number into the contact he created. Nervous, she avoided his gaze.

"Thank you." He pulled her close for a moment and whispered, "Goodnight" before slipping out of the room.

Ben congratulated Alex and Kate, prepared for her to hug him as usual. "I'm really happy for both of you. Can't say that it was much of a surprise."

Kate threw her arms around Ben. "Thank you for coming. And for being such a good friend."

"Y'all make it easy."

"Thank you ... for everything." Alex embraced Ben but focused on Marisa a moment before meeting his gaze. "Glad you were here tonight."

"Wouldn't have missed it." Ben waved as he walked out the door.

Walking past the black Passat, he glanced through the window into the cabin, hoping for a glimpse of its driver. He hadn't expected to see her standing just inside, staring out at him.

All forward motion ceased. He wasn't sure how long he stood there, transfixed. When light spilled out of the cabin as the front door opened, he jumped and hurried to his car. *Waiting until tomorrow to call is taking it slow, right?*

On the way back to his apartment, he wondered about the flicker of pain. She pushed him away for reasons he didn't understand, but she was clearly interested.

~*~

Marisa bagged trash and wiped down tables. In the empty cabin, alone with her thoughts, she had time to entertain regrets. She'd intended to apologize, but instead, she'd overreacted like before. But even with the way she'd treated him, he'd proclaimed his interest. Didn't he know too much? He'd likely never call, but she'd get over it. At least she had a better idea of what she wanted. She wanted him to call her.

Alex pushed open the door, all smiles. "Thanks for cleaning up."

"I didn't think you were coming back tonight." She tied off the bag and dropped it near the door. "Aren't you staying at Kate's?"

"Danger's past, so not until after the wedding."

She shook her head. "You and your outdated ideas."

"Something you know nothing about." He shot her his big brother look. "Did you have fun tonight? I know you didn't know many people here."

"It was fun. Y'all have great friends, except that Phillip guy. He's different."

Alex chuckled. "I asked him to come just so he could see Kate say yes to my proposal. I think he's a nice guy, just odd." He broke down the tables and leaned them against the wall. "You saw Ben again."

"Uh huh." She faced away from her brother, unwilling to risk letting him notice a change in her expression. "Seems like a nice guy."

"Marisa Ramirez!" His laughed echoed as he disappeared into the office and closed the door.

# Chapter 12

*Friday, April 22*

At 6 pm, Ben started his engine, but didn't back out of his parking space. Nearly twenty hours had passed since she'd typed her number in his phone, and he felt an award was warranted since he'd taken it slow and waited so long to call.

Since he'd pulled away from the cabin after the party, he'd thought about what he wanted to invite her to do. Movies were no good because it didn't allow enough time to talk. Dinner was typical. He wanted something memorable.

He'd searched back roads and wildflowers and decided a drive in the Hill Country would create lots of time to talk. A picnic was romantic, right?

He touched her name in his favorites and waited.

"Hello."

"Hi, Marisa. It's Ben."

A door closed before she answered. "Ben, hi. It's good to hear from you."

"What's your weekend look like? I work Saturdays, and I know realtors are often busy Saturdays and Sundays, but if you have some time on Sunday, I thought we could drive through the Hill Country, oooh and ahhh over the wildflowers." He tried to keep a casual tone.

"I'm free most of Sunday."

"Great. Want me to pick you up at the cabin?"

"No."

She answered so abruptly, he thought maybe she'd changed her mind. "Is there somewhere else you'd like to meet?"

"I'll be in San Antonio that morning. What about meeting at the park and ride under 1604 & I10?"

That location would be convenient for him. "Perfect. Ten?"

"I'll be there."

He connected the dots and realized why she'd suggested someplace so far from the cabin to meet. "Marisa."

"Yes?"

"Would it be okay if, maybe, we just see how this goes before saying anything about us to our mutual friends?"

"Sure. Of course." The tension washed out of her voice. "Bye, Detective. See you Sunday."

"Bye." Grinning, he backed out of the space. He had forty hours to plan the perfect day.

Marisa ended the call, her hands shaking. He hadn't waited long to call. She couldn't wait to see him, but he would inevitably realize she wasn't his type.

She picked up the phone, intending to cancel when someone knocked at her office door.

"Marisa? You still here?" Lexi was almost never in the office after five.

"Come in." Marisa tucked her phone away. "I was just getting stuff done while traffic dies down. What's up?"

"How'd that party go last night? It was for your brother's girlfriend?"

"It went great. Kate was surprised. Then he surprised everyone by proposing."

"Wow! So sweet." Lexi dropped into the extra chair. "My roommate gave notice. I have to find a new one or a cheaper apartment."

Marisa had no interest in having a roommate after all that happened. "Sorry. Hope you find someone."

"I'm sure I will. But if you hear of anyone looking…" Lexi stretched, then jumped up. "I'll get out of your hair."

"Lexi, you aren't in my hair. I'd say let's have dinner, but I promised Kate I'd go over after work."

"No problem. See ya later."

Marisa gathered her bag and purse and followed Lexi out. "Have a good evening."

By the time she arrived at her car, canceling on the detective sounded like a bad idea.

# Chapter 13

## *Sunday, April 24*

Ben loaded the cooler and blanket into the trunk and laid the bouquet of sunflowers on the passenger seat. He ran through the list on his phone, making sure he hadn't forgotten even the smallest detail.

Excited, he ended up at the park and ride ten minutes early. So, he waited … impatiently.

At two minutes to ten, her black Passat pulled into a space. He jumped out and headed toward her. Like a scene out of a movie, she put a white tennis shoe on the ground, and above that, all Ben could see was leg, gloriously tanned and well-toned. Another joined it.

*Slow.*

"Right on time." He held out a hand to help her up. "You look great."

Her white blouse was pulled off her shoulders and hung loose. Her jean shorts hugged all the right places. Counting the frays on the bottom edge of her shorts would've been in poor taste, so he focused on her green eyes.

"Really great."

"Thanks." She punched a button on her keys and looped her arms through his. "Lead the way."

Ben walked her to the passenger side and watched her face as he opened the door.

～*～

Sunflowers bundled in pretty paper and tied with twine lay on the seat. Marisa whipped around. "Ben, they're beautiful."

"So are you. Seemed fitting." His smile made his eyes come alive. "I had the lady put those little water things on the ends, so they wouldn't wilt on our drive."

"Thank you." She scooped them up before sliding into the seat.

She eyed him as he pulled out of the lot and made his way to the interstate. Flowers were usually an apology or a signal that men wanted something. What did Ben want? What plans did he have for an afternoon alone in the middle of nowhere?

She tried to corral her thoughts, reminding herself that Ben wasn't like the others.

*Then why is he on a date with me?*

He moved his hand and rested it on hers. "Figured we'd drive out toward Fredericksburg, take some of the back roads. Then stop at the wildflower place, maybe."

"Okay." Too quiet, she tried to shake the fear that he wouldn't like her once he got to know her better. She needed to be the woman he asked out, the woman he met at the station. Tossing her hair over her shoulder, she raised an eyebrow. "Sounds like you have our day all planned, Detective."

He shot her a sideways look. "Would you rather do something else?"

*Here it comes—the change of plans. He'll probably suggest going to his apartment.*

"Whatever you want to do is great with me."

He laughed, so robust and full it should've been sipped out of a glass.

"What's so funny?"

"You have an opinion. I want to hear it."

Marisa hadn't expected that answer. "I like what you've planned, but I hope food is on the schedule somewhere."

"I packed a picnic." He winked.

"You went all out."

Focusing on the swaths of flowers on the side of the road, she relaxed. The date had potential. He let go of her hand a few times to shift gears, but always returned it to on top of hers. She liked it there.

Once they were out of town, into the next county, she asked, "Why did you become a policeman?"

"The uniform. Girls like uniforms, *and* I get to carry a gun."

"I'm being serious."

"Sounds cheesy, but I wanted to make a difference, help people." He glanced over at her. "Now you see why I gave the other answer first."

"Why did you help me?"

He squeezed her hand before letting go to shift. "The fear in your eyes. You were afraid, but you were there anyway, determined to report him."

Why had she brought that up?

"The wildflowers are spectacular this year. Look at all the fire-wheels. They are my favorite."

"The red and yellow ones? We used to call them blankets or something. Firewheel suits it though. I like that name." Ben exited the highway and turned off on a two-lane side road. "I read that this road has several spots to stop and take pictures."

"You going to model for me?"

"The goal is to make you want to spend more time with me, not have you run away screaming."

"Whatever. I know you heard what Lexi said about you."

"Oh, yeah. I still need to pay her for those comments. Did they help?" He'd been so much more reserved and intense when they'd met before.

"You're different today, not as serious."

"I can be funny."

"You try." She grinned when he let loose that laugh again. "It's nice."

They poked along the road, admiring fields full of reds, yellows, and blues. Small patches of pink lined the edge of the road. At one of the pull-out spots, Ben eased off to the side and shifted into park.

"Want to snap a few pictures?"

"Yes, but I do want you in at least one."

He ran around and opened her door, offering his hand. "Walk up near the fence. I'll join you after I grab my camera."

She slipped her phone in her back pocket and picked her way through the flowers, not wanting to crush any.

Ben unzipped his camera bag and swapped out lenses. In her denim and white, it was as if she dressed for a photo shoot. He couldn't wait to snap pictures. The camera around his neck, he walked toward the fence line. She leaned against a post, gazing at a field of bluebonnets.

He raised the camera. Just before he mashed the button, she looked back over her shoulder. Click.

"Hey. Give a girl some warning."

"Sorry. It was the perfect shot. I couldn't resist." He captured a few shots of the flowers, without Marisa as the focal point. "So, what made you want to be a realtor?"

"I stumbled into it, but…" She paused, moving stray hairs away from her face. "It suits me."

The conversation continued as he took pictures of her and she snapped pictures of him. They even took a few together with her phone.

"Will you text those to me?"

"If you're nice to me." The smile on her face was tempered by a shadow in her eyes.

He didn't understand the disconnect. Her words were flirtatious, but her eyes showed hesitation.

"Let's keep going. We can picnic at the next stop."

She caught his hand. "Can't wait to see what you brought."

Ben kept reminding himself to take it slow. He wanted to pull her into his arms, much the same way he'd thought of doing when he met her at the door of the cabin, but she needed him to exercise restraint.

He started the engine. "Favorite movie?"

"Princess Bride. Yours?"

"Goonies. Love that movie."

She laughed. "'I'm setting booty traps.'"

He hoped beyond anything that he'd see more of her. She was his kind of girl, younger and better-looking than he'd imagined he'd meet, but definitely his kind of girl. "Exactly."

"Did you ever see Cloak and Dagger?" She brushed a finger along his hand.

"Are you kidding? It was filmed here, you know."

"Yeah. Every time I'm at that one section of the Riverwalk, I think of that movie." She chuckled. "My brothers thought the video game stuff in it was so cool."

"I'll have to remember that tidbit." Ben spent more time looking over at Marisa than he did at the colorful fields on either side. They couldn't arrive at their picnic spot fast enough.

Marisa gazed at the acres and acres of flowers, conscious of the fact that he watched her almost as much as he watched the road. They tossed questions back and forth as if they were speed dating, but without the switching tables part.

Her courage increased the more time she spent with him. "Ben, earlier, when I changed the subject—I just want you to know that it's hard for me to talk about. I don't want people to know, especially not my brother."

"I'll keep your secrets, Marisa. And you can make any topic off-limits." He rested his hand on hers. "Slow, remember? You can set the pace on that."

"You are the only one that straight up asked me if he'd hurt me. Not sure why I didn't just lie to you." She was glad for the warmth on her hand. "I probably should have let you help me that day. Things hadn't been too bad up to that point. I thought I could handle it. He wasn't the first guy who…" She couldn't make herself finish the sentence.

Determined to keep her emotions in check, she stared out the window, silent.

Ben eased off the road and stopped at the picnic spot. The quiet gnawed at him. "I still want to help, if I can."

What he really wanted to do was line up every guy she'd dated who treated her like that and beat them to a bloody pulp—not the healthiest of attitudes.

"I'm ready to eat." She clutched the sunflowers as she stepped out of the car.

He wouldn't push, but letting her set the pace for that conversation was difficult. The wait gave the buried anger time to ferment.

"Let me grab the cooler and blanket. Wasn't sure if there would be a table, but we can use the quilt as a table cloth."

She took the quilt from him, touching his hand more than once in the process. "Let me help."

"Thanks." He slammed the truck closed and followed her to the table. "True confession time. I didn't cook this food. I bought it already prepared."

Grinning, she poked through the cooler. "You bought stuff I like. How did you know?"

"I paid attention on Thursday. Catching details is part of my job."

She served herself a plate while he popped the tops on two glass-bottled Cokes.

"Was helping me part of the job?" Her focus stayed on the table.

Ben leaned down to catch her eye. "I'm not here because of the job. I'm not here because of your brother or because of Kate." He reached for her hand. "You are the only reason I'm here."

"The guys started out nice. Always. Things would usually change slowly. With Paul, it was almost as if someone flipped a switch. He didn't hurt me until after the break-in at Kate's."

Ben listened, trying to choke back his rage.

"I was really scared by the time they caught him. It didn't help that—never mind."

"I'm here. You can talk to me." While he'd been eager to get to know her, hearing her recount what had happened with barely any emotion registering in her voice made a few truths clearer: she had good reason to take it slow and he was more invested than he thought possible for the short time he'd known her.

"I still have bruises." She pulled up her sleeve, revealing faded greenish circles up her arm. "That's why I wore long sleeves. My others are where people can't see."

Forcing himself to stay in his seat, his heart rate double its normal pace, he squeezed her hand. "I'm glad I wasn't there the day they arrested him."

Visions of slamming Paul against a car did nothing to ease Ben's fury.

"I was." She looked up at Ben. "He saw me. He knows I turned him in."

A volcano went off in his head. Still holding her hand, he pinched the bridge of his nose. *Breathe.* Silent, he revisited multiple crimes scenes where an ex had exacted revenge. He couldn't look at her, wouldn't let her see his fear.

"Ben?" She slipped her hand out of his.

"If he comes after you…" He threw his arms open, knocking the glass bottle to the ground.

Marisa jumped up and backed away from the table. "I knew it. You are just like the others."

"Wait. No. That was an accident."

She crossed her arms. "Take me back to my car."

"Marisa, please. Finish eating at least."

"No." Tears brimmed in her eyes. "I don't want to be here anymore, not with your temper." She spun around and stomped to the car.

He rubbed his buzzed head, frustrated. After returning the food to the cooler, he cleaned up the shards of glass. The entire time, she sat in the passenger seat, staring out the front window.

He had to figure out how to make it right. Complicated and deeply hurt, she reacted unpredictably.

Her sunflowers lay on the quilt, right next to where she'd been sitting. He cradled them while yanking the quilt off the table. The trunk repacked, he slid into the driver's seat and handed her the flowers. "You forgot these."

"Don't want them."

"I never meant to scare you." He crossed his arms over the steering wheel and rested his head on them. "But I won't apologize for caring or for being mad. At him. Not you. You know that, right?"

"Can we go now?" She'd walled herself off.

Ben wanted to punch something. Instead, he started the engine and began the long drive back toward the park and ride.

# Chapter 14

*Tuesday, April 26*

Ben dialed Marisa's number for the third time since dropping her off at the park and ride on Sunday. She hadn't spoken a word all the way home, and she left without even a goodbye.

Every time he called, it didn't just roll to voicemail. The calls were cast off to voicemail halfway through the first ring. He'd left rambling messages, apologizing.

He sighed as the recorded message played, Marisa's voice chipper and friendly encouraging callers to leave a message after the beep. "It's Ben again. I'll stop bothering you, but I would like to see you again. You have my number."

She didn't answer his calls, and he couldn't talk to her brother without violating her trust. Ben wouldn't do that, but walking away was not an option. He worried about what might happen. At least she was staying at the cabin. She'd be safe there.

How much he cared rattled him. He stared at the sunflowers in a vase on his table and hoped that before they lost all their petals, things with Marisa would be on better footing.

"Night, Alex." Marisa closed herself off in the bedroom at 9 pm. She hoped he'd assume she was tired.

He knocked. "Everything okay?"

"I'm fine." If she said it enough, maybe she'd believe it. She held her breath waiting for his footsteps.

He padded away.

She curled up under the covers and opened a book. Staring at words that made no sense, she never even turned a page. Over and over the glass bottle shattered on the ground. *Ben.*

She'd ignored all his calls, but he was friends with Alex and Kate. She'd see Ben again sooner or later. How would she handle it? Moving back to Austin felt like running away, so she vowed to stay—not for her brother, not for Kate, but for herself—even if it meant seeing Ben again. And part of her hoped she would.

# CHAPTER 15

## *Wednesday, April 27*

Marisa snapped a photo of the kitchen, trying to capture the layout and natural light. "This is a beautiful kitchen. It will be a big selling point."

"Thank you. I will miss it when we move." The homeowner glanced at her phone. "Excuse me. I need to take this call. Take all the pictures you need." She disappeared into the office, and Marisa winced.

When clients were around, Ted kept his hands mostly to himself, but alone with him, Marisa had to remain aware to avoid being tapped or pinched. Behavior she should have reported, she put up with it because her job rested in Ted's hands, or so it felt. She focused her camera for a wide shot of the eating area when he stepped up next to her.

"Beautiful, doll. Here, maybe if you take it from this angle." He wrapped his arms around hers, moving the camera to match his suggestion. "It's all about the right position."

"Of course." Marisa snapped a few other shots, then moved into the living room, Ted never more than a few steps behind her.

After months on the job, he still insisted on accompanying her when his schedule allowed. She thought little of it at first, but as months dragged on and he continued, touchier than when she started the job, she recognized it for what it was. How to handle it wasn't as straightforward.

"Paul came over last night, with his new squeeze." Ted leaned over her shoulder to give his opinion on the photo.

Marisa swallowed back surprise. She hadn't expected to hear Paul's name mentioned. Knowing he was out on bail, awaiting trial, unnerved her, but she tried not to let it show. "I'll take a few of the back yard." Marisa stepped lightly on the balls of her feet as she moved through the thick, plush grass.

Like a puppy, Ted stayed on her heels. Stepping backward for a better angle, her heel sank in soft dirt. She teetered, and Ted caught her around the middle, a bit higher than her waist.

"Careful, doll." He didn't show any urgency to remove his hands.

She took another step backward, trying to catch her balance. Her heel landed on something much firmer than grass.

Ted yanked his hands away and grabbed his foot.

Marisa hid her grin. "I'm sorry. Standing close to me can be dangerous, I guess."

Ted sneered. "I can't imagine why he misses you."

"Mr. Jenner, please. I don't care to talk about my personal life with you at work." She hurried inside, hoping the homeowner was off the phone.

When she made it back to the realty office, she made a quick list of items that needed to get done in the morning before she packed up for the day. Thankfully, Ted said he had something to take care of and didn't hang around her office, leaning over her, touching her, wanting to peruse all the pictures.

Marisa slung her purse over her shoulder and walked out to her car. Texting her friend who had gone home early, she dropped into the driver's seat.

Lexi responded: *I hate cooking. Let's go out. You choose.*

Marisa chose a place and sent Lexi the name of the restaurant.

She tossed her phone aside and started the engine. When she glanced up, she put the car back in park. A single red rose lay tucked under the wiper blade.

Her heart skipped a beat. Had Ben left it? She picked up the rose, uncovering a small note.

*I'm never far away.*

He would never have left a note that creepy. Marisa scanned the lot, a wariness giving eyes to the shadows. She tossed the flower on the ground and left.

Maybe she'd mention it to Lexi or maybe even Ben, but that would require speaking to him, which meant not avoiding his calls. Marisa didn't want people worried about her, especially since it was probably just Paul trying to frighten her.

Ben counted pullups, staring at Marisa's image superimposed by his thoughts on the white textured wall. Awake, asleep, she was there.

He dropped to the floor finishing his workout regimen with push-ups. Miller's casual comment during lunch about Officer Andrews hadn't been lost on Ben, but calling Bethany when another woman dominated his thoughts wouldn't be right. He couldn't explain any of that to his partner.

Sweaty, he shed his workout clothes and made for the shower.

# CHAPTER 16

## *Friday, April 29*

Ben slammed his apartment door, locked it, and rushed down the stairs. Staying home was a recipe for madness. He opted to meet friends at a local dance hall. Almost every weekend a group met to go dancing. He'd likely sit and listen to the live band, watching others dance, but it beat sitting at home alone, stewing.

On the drive, he wondered what Marisa was doing with her evening. Was she hanging out with Kate and Alex? Ben had purposefully avoided calling his friend. Seeing Marisa with others around would not be ideal given the way things ended.

He parked and opened his door. Marisa's voice carried from not far away. One foot on the ground, he sat and listened, trying to decide what to say to her. Leaving wasn't an option. Petals had already started falling off the sunflowers.

"I really like the place, and I can move in on Wednesday.... No, I have enough." Marisa walked past the back of his car. "I'll be late.... I don't know what time.... Okay, bye."

*Moving?*

Ben slipped out of his car. He pulled his license out of his wallet as he walked toward the dance hall. Every time he came, he got carded by the bouncers.

Glancing up from his wallet, Ben grinned. Marisa held out her license for one of the bouncers, the big guy.

Ben hung back, watching. He didn't want to catch her off guard.

The big guy looked at her, then the card. He took his time before handing back her ID. When he motioned for her to go on in, his gaze followed her.

Ben cleared his throat when she was out of earshot and showed his ID.

"Sorry. Got a bit distracted." The bouncer chuckled. "Have a good night."

Ben hurried in, so he could find the source of distraction. She stood with a group of ladies at a table right beside the group he was meeting.

As he made his way through the crowd, he formulated yet one more apology in his head. He had an opportunity to make it right, but he needed to tread carefully. He waved as he skirted past the table from work and was almost behind her when someone shouted, "Torres!"

Marisa whipped around. A smile lit up her eyes but didn't touch her lips.

He took a few steps toward her and raised his eyebrows. When she moved his direction, he closed the distance. "I'd ask if you were following me, but you got here first."

"Are you following me, Detective?" Dark hair danced on bare shoulders. A tease played on her lips. The disconnect reappeared.

"I wouldn't. I swear this is just…"

"Serendipity?"

"I'd like to think so. Please, forgive me." Ben held his breath, waiting for her answer.

Some overgrown thirteen-year-old slapped him on the back. "Torres, introduce me to your friend." A detective from White Collar Crimes gawked at Marisa, apparently expecting her to fawn over his blond hair and bedazzled jeans. Was that sleazy grin considered charming by anyone with a pulse?

Ben didn't even look back. He stepped closer to her and offered his hand. "Would you like to dance?" Taking the time to put the frat boy in his place wasn't on Ben's schedule.

"With you? Or with that kid?" In true Marisa form, she made her point. Winking, she slipped her hand in Ben's. "Did you put a GPS tracker on my car?"

"I'd never—" He halted before they stepped into the throng.

"It was a joke, Detective." She stepped onto the dance floor. "I forgive you."

He put his hand on her back, conscious of keeping a polite distance between them. "You come here often?"

She closed the gap on the first step. "You use that line on all the girls?"

Ben enjoyed the closeness, but aware that her flirtatious behavior was almost a shield, he reminded himself to take it slow.

~*~

Marisa tried to relax. She hadn't expected to be so excited to see him again. "I've come once before. I wasn't allowed out much in my previous situation." She tried to make light of her past.

Ben steered her around another couple. "You've been dancing more than once. Surely."

"I have. Just not here."

A good dancer, he bumped her toes whenever she leaned in close. Controlled in almost every way, he didn't seem the type to be easily distracted. To see him misstep made her wonder what was running through his head.

"People from work come here a lot. I had no desire to spend the evening alone. Hearing your voice, seeing you was a pleasant surprise." His soft brown eyes expressed the sentiment as much as his words.

"I wasn't sure I'd have anyone to dance with."

He laughed. "Like that would be a problem. Anyway, if I'd known you were going to be here, I'd have dressed up a bit more."

There was absolutely nothing wrong with the way he looked.

"Next time then." She kept her hand on his chest even after the music stopped.

He didn't seem to mind. "So we're okay?"

Marisa nodded. "I spook easily. I'm sorry."

The music started again, and he raised his eyebrows in invitation. "Another?"

"Yes." She'd dance every song with him if he wanted. "You live near here?"

"Not really. I'm closer to the university. Just outside the loop. Kinda close to … you know what area I mean."

She knew exactly what he meant. He lived near where she worked, near where she would be moving. Maybe once she moved, she'd bump into him more often.

*There's a happy thought.*

She had little doubt that the detective wanted to see more of her, or at least see her more often. Maybe taking it slow was a bad idea. She shifted her hand up until her fingertips brushed his neck.

A smile cut across his face.

～✳～

"I forgot to bring it up the other day. At the food trucks, it seemed like you were hurt. I'm sorry. I felt horrible about that." Ben tried to focus on not bumping her feet.

She distracted him, no matter what he was doing.

"That wasn't because of you. When I was showing Kate the land behind her house, I fell. The house on the property isn't in good shape."

"You're okay, though?"

"Yes. I'm fine. Bruise is healing."

His gaze dropped to her hip, then he caught himself and focused on her face. "It's pretty cool that she bought that place. I wonder what's she'll do with it."

"Not sure. I doubt Alex is going to build there now."

Ben chuckled. "They'd be married before he had time to finish anything."

"How long had you known?"

He hesitated. "I had my suspicions. But the night we moved your stuff to the cabin, Alex mentioned it."

"You've been a great friend to my brother. And thank you for helping that night, really, for everything." She smiled. "I liked all the questions the other day, getting to know you."

"Ask away. What else do you want to know?"

"What division are you in? Or department? I'm not sure what they call them."

"Homicide." He didn't often bring up what he did because most people were scared off at the mere mention of the word.

"Oh." Her green eyes studied him as the song ended. "You must see some pretty horrible stuff."

"Yeah."

"How long have you been a detective?" She allowed him one more glimpse of her eyes before focusing on their joined hands and following him off the dance floor.

"Three years. I was in uniform for a few years before that." He steered them away from their friends to a vacant table near a corner bar. "Let me buy you a drink."

"I'll have a Coke."

He stepped away and returned with two. "What did we not talk about on Sunday? You grew up here in San Antonio?"

"I did. On the northwest side. You said you were born and raised here. Where did you go to college?"

Questions bounced between them, the conversation easy and comfortable. When she sipped the last of her drink, a pang of disappointment rattled in his chest.

"I guess we should join our friends." He didn't want her to feel trapped.

"They'll wonder what happened to me." She didn't act trapped when she caught his hand as they strolled to the other side of the room, dodging people carrying drinks and guys drooling on themselves over the brunette worming her way into Ben's heart.

A woman who'd had one too many beers clapped her hands together. "There you are, Marisa. Is this the Paul I've heard so much about?"

Every muscle in Marisa's body tensed. Ben wanted to whisk her back on to the dance floor, away from the uncomfortable questions.

She squeezed his hand. "Paul and I aren't together any more. This is my good friend, Ben."

He shook hands with the woman and greeted the other ladies at the table. Hearing her refer to him a good friend was more than he expected from the night.

Leaning in close so he could be heard over the music, he said, "I'll let you visit. I'll be at the next table."

"Ben." Marisa opened her arms. "I'm really glad we bumped into each other."

"Me too." He stepped into her embrace, not wanting to let go. "I'll check back after while. Maybe we'll take another whirl."

"I'm looking forward to it." Her green eyes twinkled.

Only a few paces away, he snagged an empty barstool and greeted his friends. Guys around him swapped tales and downed long necks. The few ladies that had showed up, rarely sat out a dance. Ben laughed at the appropriate times, grabbed a long neck from the ice bucket, and watched Marisa chat away.

"Hey, Ben." Bethany hopped up onto the empty barstool beside him.

He hadn't seen her since the set-up and wondered what direction the conversation would go. "How are you?"

"Pretty good."

As they chatted, Ben tried to keep from staring at Marisa. He wasn't very successful.

Bethany glanced over at the next table. "She looks familiar."

"She's a friend." He let his gaze linger on the topic of discussion.

"Thought you didn't know her?"

Ben scrambled to think of a truthful answer. "Turns out she's the sister of a friend."

"Y'all were dancing earlier?"

"Yep."

Bethany smirked and laid a hand on his arm. "Want to go back out?"

"No, thanks." Risking the evening's progress for a spin around the dance floor wasn't worth it.

Marisa tried not to stare as Ben chatted with the woman from the food truck park. Concerned that maybe there was more going on between the two of them, Marisa contemplated an early exit. She didn't know the others at her table well. There were a few from work and several of Lexi's friends. Trying to distract herself from the short blonde getting Ben's attention, Marisa chatted with those around her.

Ben was attractive and attentive. Any number of women in the room would jump at the chance to dance with him. That blonde sure wanted to.

Marisa tried not to notice when that woman touched his arm. Leaving meant Marisa didn't have to watch. She waved goodbye to the group at her table. "If Lexi shows up, tell her I cut out early."

Before embarking on the forever long drive in the dark back to the cabin, she stopped by the ladies' room.

When she walked back out, Ben waited near the wall. "Leaving?"

"I have a long drive back." She avoided eye contact and yanked her keys out of her pocket.

He matched her pace, walking alongside her out the door. "You driving all the way to the cabin tonight?"

She nodded, feeling less like talking with every step.

"Please talk to me. Don't freeze me out." He had no idea how frustrating he was.

"I'm not sure I'm ready, Ben." She unlocked her car and slid behind the wheel.

"At least let me—"

She slammed the door, ignoring whatever he was trying to say. He shook his head and walked away, and she started the engine and backed out of the space before she changed her mind and went running to apologize.

Headlights followed her out of the parking lot, down the road, and all the way to the highway. She swallowed irritation and turned up the radio. When she got to the outskirts of town, she sped up, wondering how intent he was on following. Halfway to Alex's, she pulled off at an exit and jumped out as he pulled up beside her.

As soon as he stepped out of the car, she got in his face. "What are you doing?"

"Making sure you make it home safely." His calm only infuriated her more.

"I didn't ask you to do that. I don't need you to do that."

"I'm sorry if I scared you, if you thought some creep was following you. I thought—."

"I wasn't scared. I knew it was you, but I don't like it." She lowered her voice when a couple walking out of the convenience store glanced her direction. "I'm not a child in need of a babysitter."

His jaw set, he stared at her.

She recognized his frustration and figured she could poke a hole in his calm exterior. "You counting to ten before you answer?"

"Twenty." Ben turned on a heel and climbed back in his car. He didn't drive away. He just sat there.

She knocked on his window, and it rolled down. "Are you just waiting for me to get back on the road?"

"Yes. It's important to me that you arrive home safely, but if you want me to leave, I will."

Marisa couldn't deny that fear weighed her down like a backpack full of textbooks. Paul could be anywhere, but she was not about to ask Ben to escort her to the cabin. "Do whatever you want."

The window slid back up.

She slammed the door of her car and pulled back onto the road. Headlights followed.

Frustration dissolved into tears. She tried to get them out of her system before facing Alex. He'd probably waited up for her. When she arrived at the cabin, she turned down the driveway and drove to the cabin, but the headlights stopped at the end of the drive.

The truck wasn't there. It was late. Alex was probably headed back from Kate's. Marisa didn't want him to see Ben anywhere near the cabin.

She parked, ran back up the drive, and climbed into his passenger seat. "You can't do this, Ben."

"Do what, Marisa? Care?" His voice soft and tender, he left little doubt of how he felt.

"Go home to your girlfriend. She's probably worried about you."

Illuminated by the dashboard lights, his expression hardened, and he shifted into drive. At a crawl, he made his way up the driveway to the front door.

"What are you doing now?"

"Taking you home."

"What? Since Alex isn't here, you think you can sweet talk me, sample the goods, then decide if it's worth it?"

He slammed on the brakes and shifted into park. "That's not at all what I was thinking. I'm not here to *sample*, as you put it." He took a deep breath and rested his hand on hers. "I care about you. You are complicated and engaging, strong and fragile, and I want you safe."

"That short woman?"

"Is not my girlfriend." He brushed his thumb along her knuckles.

Marisa leaned over and kissed his cheek, hoping he meant what he said about not sampling. "I'm sorry."

He pulled her close. "Goodnight, Marisa. I'll call you."

"I'll answer." She climbed out, and he stayed put until she was locked inside. Standing at the window, she waved and watched him drive away, just like the night of the party.

Ben bumped down the driveway hoping he could make it to the highway before passing the familiar blue truck.

Never calling her again would be easier on his stress level but not great for his heart. If they'd danced like they dated, they'd have never made it around the dance floor. She hadn't been joking when she said, "really slow."

On the two-lane road, halfway to the highway, a blue GMC passed, heading toward the cabin. Hopefully Alex hadn't noticed Ben's car or at least, wouldn't bring it up.

When Ben arrived back at the apartment, he texted Marisa: *I enjoyed dancing with you. Will call later in the week.*

*Why the wait, Detective?* Her reply caught him a bit off-guard.

Finding the right pace would be difficult. He answered: *Trying to take it slow. Have a good week.*

A happy face emoji popped up on his screen.

# Chapter 17

*Wednesday, May 4*

With his finger, Ben circled the day on his desk calendar. Wednesday. Wherever her new apartment was, Marisa would be moving in sometime during the day. He'd have happily offered his help, except no one had mentioned to him that she was moving. Accidental eavesdropping had earned him that tidbit.

He picked up his phone to text Alex, but a text from one and the same popped on the screen: *Busy Friday?*

Ben replied: *Besides work, No plans. Had moving day been changed?*

Alex's response had nothing to do with moving: *Same place as always at 7?*

*Sounds great. Anything else going on?* Ben stopped shy of asking about Marisa's move.

Alex gave no helpful information: *All good. See you Friday.*

~*~

"What do you think?" Marisa pushed open the door, so Kate and Alex could step inside her new apartment.

"Love it." Kate walked around, opening cabinets and closets. "Lots of storage."

"Nice place. You sure you don't want me to just bring stuff over?"

"You've done plenty. The movers will do all that on Saturday. Until then, I'll get this place scrubbed and ready for move in."

"Ben lives near here." Alex stood at the back door, looking toward the next complex. "Over there."

"Who?" Marisa made sure to note where Alex's gaze rested.

Ben hadn't yet called, but she hadn't given up hope.

Ben called Marisa before leaving the office, but it rolled to voicemail.

Before he left a message, a text from her popped on the screen: *Sorry I didn't answer. Can't talk now. Text okay? How are you?*

He texted back: *Good. I'd like to see you again. You free Saturday or Sunday?*

Her reply disappointed him: *Crazy, busy weekend. Maybe next week?*

*Okay. Hope all goes well.* He started the engine and headed home.

Had she moved? Was that why her weekend was busy? Tempted to ask, he didn't. He didn't want her to think he'd been stalking her. Overhearing that tidbit was nearly accidental, and she hadn't breathed a word about it.

He'd have to keep his eyes open for a moving truck.

# Chapter 18

*Friday, May 6*

Ben smiled at the bubbly waitress. "I'll have the ribs, please." He handed over his menu.

Alex closed his and slid it across the table. "Pepperoni pizza. And a root beer."

"Add a root beer to mine also."

"Will do." The waitress winked at Ben as she turned to go.

"Someone looks interested." Alex checked his phone, then slipped it back in his pocket.

Ben shook his head. "Not my type."

"You like being single?"

"What kind of a question is that?"

"You're what? Thirty? Haven't found the right girl or don't want to? Just curious."

"I don't intend to stay single forever."

"Then are you gonna call my sister or what?" A satisfied smirk spilled across Alex's face, though he didn't look up.

Stunned, Ben focused on the table. So many secrets made it hard to completely relax. "I don't know. She—She's pretty young. Besides, it hasn't been that long since… you know. Who put you up to this?" Ben stumbled over excuses.

"She's twenty-five, not exactly a kid."

"You trying to find her a bodyguard?"

"No harm in that, right? By the way, I saw a car just like yours the other night."

"Oh?" Ben silently pleaded for the waitress to walk up.

"Out near the cabin."

"Wow. I don't see many that same color."

Alex pushed a napkin toward Ben. "Here's her number. You don't have to tell her where you got it unless you want to. Not sure if it'll help or hurt. And no one put me up to it. I saw the two of you at the party, the way you looked at her from across the room."

"What are you talking about? I mean. She's beautiful, but I—"

"If I'm wrong, don't call her. But you'd be good for her."

"And why is that?" Ben pulled his wallet out of his pocket and slipped the folded napkin inside.

"For starters, you don't break the law. You uphold it."

Ben imagined Kate and Becca discussing his love life. "Can I ask a favor? A huge one?"

Alex squinted. "What?"

"Don't tell Kate."

"This is where we might have a problem. I don't like keeping secrets from her, two reasons mainly, because I'm horrible at it and she doesn't like it, not in the least."

"Don't say anything, please, to anyone." Ben didn't want Marisa thinking he'd said something about their relationship.

"She seemed pretty happy to see you at Kate's surprise party."

"Has she mentioned anything about the ex?"

"Not a word."

Ben leaned back from the table as the waitress set the drinks down.

"Food will be out shortly, guys."

"Thanks." Alex tapped on the table. "Anyway, the reason I called you…Would you be a groomsman?"

Ben swallowed back his surprise. "I'd ... I'd be honored."

"Thanks." Alex dropped his voice to a whisper; his gaze settled on the table. "I count you as a true friend, even though we haven't known each other long. Kate showing up at my door brought many good things. You're one of them."

"Funny, isn't it?" Ben fidgeted with his straw. He had a large circle of friends, but only a few close ones. Alex was definitely in that smaller circle. "Big shindig?"

"Yeah. Pretty big. Kate deserves the big, fancy wedding, and Travis wants to lavish her with whatever he can."

Ben wasn't surprised that Kate's dad was pitching for a big wedding. "If there's anything I can do to help, just let me know."

"Kate wants to have everyone that's going to be in the wedding over for dinner sometime before the big day. Probably won't be until June. Guess who else will be there?"

"Is this how it's going to be? Wink, wink, nod, nod every time your sister's around?"

"Maybe." Alex chuckled.

～＊～

"You got your cast off!" Marisa hugged Kate. "It smells divine in here. What did you make?"

"Enchilada casserole. Alex has been sharing his recipes."

"Speaking of, where is my brother?"

"Having dinner with Torres. Funny how they've hit it off. Alex talks to him as often as he talks to DJ." Kate set the food on the table. "He's such a sweetheart. Hopefully he finds a nice girl."

Alex's frequent conversations with the detective worried Marisa, but her brother wouldn't have stayed quiet if he found out any of the secrets Marisa had kept from him. Ben's silence enchanted her, too much so. But a nice girl—as Kate put it—Marisa would never be mistaken for.

"He seems nice." Despite her uneasiness, she hoped the line of conversation would continue.

Kate dropped her fork. "I was going to wait for dessert, but I can't. Will you be a bridesmaid?"

"Really, Kate? Are you sure?" After the trouble Marisa had invited into Kate's life, she was stunned to be asked.

Kate hugged her. "Of course I'm sure. Will you?"

"I'd love to." Marisa felt truly forgiven.

*What is Alex asking Ben tonight?*

# Chapter 19

*Monday, May 9*

Marisa ran down the stairs in her flats, heels dangling from her hand. The staircase was much easier to navigate without two-inch heels threatening to topple her. When she reached the car, she tossed her shoes into the passenger seat with her bag.

Red caught her attention. Tucked under the wiper blade, just like before, lay a red rose and a note.

*Hush little baby; don't say a word.*

The petals hadn't even begun to wilt. It hadn't been there long. She glanced around. Was Paul hiding nearby, watching?

She threw it on the pavement and ground the petals beneath her shoe. Whoever left it knew not only where she worked but which complex she lived in.

Determined to be more vigilant about watching her surroundings, she slammed and locked her car door. After another scan of the parking lot, she backed out of her parking space and headed to the office.

~*~

Ben crested the hill and slowed for the black Passat turning out of the complex next to his. He recognized the driver and smiled. In the complex next to his was a great place for her to live. Close by, she could call if she ever needed help or even if she just wanted to see him.

When they stopped at the light, he watched, hoping she'd glance in her rearview mirror. *Just one glimpse, please.*

She didn't disappoint. Delight exploded in her eyes as they locked gazes. She turned around to look back at him. Her expression captured everything he felt.

He waved as the light turned green—one of those goofy, wiggly-finger waves. She smiled in response, then followed the car in front of her through the light. Traffic separated them, and Ben lost sight of the Passat.

Glad that he'd chosen that time to run his errands, he grinned when his phone beeped. He pulled into a parking space and checked his messages.

Marisa texted: *Seeing you was a nice surprise.*

Ben couldn't have agreed more. *I'd like to see you this week.*

Her reply gave him hope of a great Monday: *Just say the word.*

# CHAPTER 20

*Tuesday, May 10*

Ben waited at the trailhead. He'd offered to pick Marisa up, but she suggested meeting. In the ongoing effort to take it slow, an evening walk along the trails seemed like a good idea.

He hadn't been there long when she pulled up. Gorgeous as always, decked out in workout leggings and a matching tank top, she grinned and waved. Seeing her in a tank made him all kinds of happy. The bruises had disappeared.

"You going to be able to keep up with me, Detective?"

That remained to be seen. "I'll do my best."

Walking fast enough to get their hearts pumping, they wound their way along the trail, picking up the conversation from where they'd left off after having drinks alone.

A mile down the road, she stopped. "You haven't asked me about why I was on your street yesterday. You know?"

"Heard that you were moving, but since you didn't bring it up, I waited. When I spotted you at the light, I guessed that you live close to me."

"I guess that makes whatever this is easier."

Ben laughed. "Easy doesn't describe you at all."

Marisa winked, then broke into a run. "Catch me if you can."

The chase was on.

Marisa flopped onto her couch. Exhausted, her heart still pounded from the run. He'd hardly touched her, just a quick hug when they parted. She'd intended to tell him about the roses, but enjoying herself, she forgot. Forgot wasn't the truth. She'd changed her mind, afraid that if he knew, things would change, and she liked the way things were headed. She erred on the side of quiet.

Living close offered more opportunity for evening runs together, maybe even dinner, eventually. It thrilled her and scared her.

She couldn't wait to see him again.

# Chapter 21

*Thursday, May 12*

Marisa opened the door to her apartment and froze. Drawers hung open. Boxes were dumped. Someone had trashed her apartment. She closed the door and pulled her phone out to call the police. Before hitting send, she saw a note on the table. The familiar handwriting made her nauseous. Paul's sloppy script was unmistakable.

*Thanks, baby. Found what I needed. See ya around. Let's keep this quiet. I'd hate for anyone else to get hurt.*

What he needed? She shook her head. It only made sense one way. He'd broken in to take back stolen items he'd hidden among her things. Marisa shivered at the thought of stolen property in her apartment. He could have set her up.

She dropped the phone. There was no way to report it without explaining everything that had happened and risking someone else getting hurt. She wanted that part of her life behind her, and she wouldn't put anyone else in danger. He's already hurt Kate. Paul had what he came for; Marisa convinced herself that she was of no value to him anymore.

Traipsing down the hall, she surveyed the mess littered in the apartment. It would take hours to clean it all up. When she stepped into her bedroom, she stifled a small scream.

A single red rose petal rested on her pillow.

Trying to scare her had worked, but she couldn't let it show. Paul thrived on weakness and fear.

At nearly two in the morning, Ben stumbled into his apartment, too tired to eat. After shedding his clothes, he collapsed into bed.

He hadn't gotten a full night's sleep the night before, and that wouldn't change until he and Miller wrapped up their latest case. He glanced at the time and set an alarm for six in the morning. Functioning on four hours of sleep would require gallons of coffee.

The phone still in his hand, he fell asleep.

Marisa woke from a deep sleep, her phone buzzing next to her. "Hello?"

Snores emanated from the other end of the line.

"Who is this?"

"Marisa." The word sounded more like a sigh.

"Ben?" She sat up. "Are you okay?"

"So beautiful." The last words dissolved into snores.

"Sweet dreams, Detective." She tucked back under the covers with the phone on speaker, listening to be sure he really was okay. After a few minutes, satisfied he was fine, she ended the call.

*Oh, Detective.* Hope danced in her thoughts as she drifted back to sleep. He even thought about her when he slept.

# Chapter 22

### *Friday, May 13*

Ben slapped at his phone, trying to make it shut up. When he woke up enough to get his bearings, he shut off the alarm and dragged himself out of bed.

Twenty minutes later, he was headed to the office. By the time he got to his desk, he was downing his second cup of coffee.

"Tacos." Miller held up a bag.

Ben dug into the bag. "I need more sleep. These short nights are causing crazy, vivid dreams. I'm too old for this."

"Shut up about old." Miller yawned. "We've got a homicide to solve. The sooner we do, the sooner you can get your beauty sleep. You need it."

Marisa stared at her phone, wondering if Ben noticed he'd called her in his sleep. Rather than point it out, she'd wait and see if he called or texted.

Once her work day started, she had little time to think about the call. After meeting an inspector at a home under contract, she hurried back to the office to search building permits for a client. After finding the building code information she needed, she talked to the client and made a follow-up appointment.

At one o'clock, she hurried out of the office to grab a quick lunch before she had to meet a structural engineer. While sitting in the restaurant, Marisa texted Ben: *Am I in your favorites?*

Ben glanced at his phone, stuck it back in his pocket, and then pulled it out again. Unsure how to answer Marisa's unexpected text, he stared at the screen.

"We got a tip." Miller ran over, keys in hand. "I'll drive."

Ben strode out of the building and buckled into the passenger seat, his mind on her text and not on the case, where it should have been. He replied: *Since day one. Why?*

Miller briefed Ben on the new lead as they drove, and he pushed her text to the back of his mind.

Marisa laughed at his delay in responding. He probably didn't know he'd called. She'd wondered whether he'd searched her in the contacts or if she was on the short list of easy to accidentally dial. But what he said—half asleep between snores—that made her smile.

"Marisa." Ted strolled up, a file in hand. "Have time to look over the Crowley file with me?"

Startled, she bobbled her phone but managed to keep it from falling. Hugging it to her chest, keeping eyes off her private conversation with Ben, she shook her head. "Not right now, Mr. Jenner. Can it wait until tomorrow?"

She didn't bother to explain that she had a meeting because he'd only insist on going with her, which she hated.

"Tomorrow works." He winked and headed back to his office.

Marisa made sure he was gone, then tapped out two other texts before racing off to meet the structural engineer.

The skies burned a golden pink as the sun sank below the horizon.

Ben dropped into the driver's seat, ready to be home. After an arrest, sleep was on his schedule—and maybe a hot meal, but he wasn't even sure about that part.

He checked his phone before backing out. Marisa had responded hours ago: *Next time you call to tell me I'm beautiful, maybe try a different time, not 2 am.*

Ben swallowed. He'd called her? He'd said that? Apparently, honesty left discretion tied up somewhere when he slept. So much for taking it slow. Before he scrolled through his call history, he read her other text: *But your sweet snores make great white noise.*

After confirming he had indeed called her at that ungodly hour, he laid his head on the steering wheel, trying to remember what else he'd said in his vivid dream.

He tossed his phone next to him and drove home. Avoiding further embarrassment required getting sleep before replying. And he'd be sure not to close his eyes with his phone in his hand.

# Chapter 23

*Saturday, May 14*

Marisa hadn't slept well since Paul had helped himself to her apartment. She hoped an evening walk would relax her, make it easier to rest. Halfway down the street, a scrawny calico sauntered out of the bushes. Flicking its tail, the feline squinted at Marisa, then proceeded to join in the walk. The cat kept up with Marisa all the way to the corner.

"You look hungry. Wait for me here." She ran into the pharmacy and found the pet supplies. After picking up three small cans of food, she grabbed a bag of dry food and a food dish. She made it all the way to the front before doubling back and picking up a water bowl and a collar.

Marisa was greeted outside the doors by a meow. The calico trotted alongside as Marisa made her way home.

"You can't come inside, but I'll put food out for you. And I'll give free scratches whenever you want."

The cat wove between Marisa's legs in agreement, leaving white and brown fur on her black yoga pants. Once they made it back to the apartment, Marisa set up the kitty station. Sporting a baby blue collar, the calico ate, purring the entire time.

Marisa was glad for the companionship. "I think I'll call you Kitty until I see what fits you better."

Ben sat on his parents' couch, a niece on one leg, a nephew on the other. While one told Ben a story about her dog, the other drove cars up Ben's arm. Family dinners were important to Mom, and Ben tried to make them as often as possible. It wouldn't be a stretch to say he even enjoyed them.

His sister-in-law, Gracie, sat next to him. Married to his oldest brother, she'd known Ben ten years and was like a big sister.

When the puppy story ended, his niece climbed down and ran off in search of candy.

Gracie glanced around then scooted closer. "I have a friend I'd like to introduce you to, if you're interested."

"I'm not." Ben hid the smile that Gracie would recognize as interest in someone else.

She cocked her head. "You don't know anything about her."

"Okay, then. What's her name?"

"Rachel."

"Not interested."

"Hmmm, if I didn't know any better, I'd say there was a particular reason. What's her name?" Gracie didn't miss much.

"Not Rachel." Ben chuckled at Gracie's surprise. "I'm not even sure if…"

"If you want to marry her?"

"Whoa." Ben shook his head. "I meant if she's interested."

She let loose her deep, melodious laugh. "You are. *That* is pretty clear. I'll be nice and keep quiet for now." She nodded toward the kitchen where his mom served up dessert. "Some people would inundate you with questions if they got wind of a special someone."

"I appreciate your discretion." He didn't even want to think about the never-ending stream of questions that would hound him if his mother discovered that tidbit.

His mother wanted only for her boys to be happy, but in her mind, happiness was synonymous with being married. Ben was the only unhappy one, and therefore she fretted over him.

After dessert, Ben said his goodbyes and ignored the poke from Gracie.

All the way home, Marisa dominated his thoughts. He wanted to swoop in, kiss her, and erase her past. Not even magic apples or singing mice could do that. He also decided he should watch fewer movies with his niece. They were clouding his thoughts.

When he got back to his apartment, he pulled out his phone and replied to Marisa's texts: *Sorry I interrupted your beauty sleep.*

She sent a smiling emoji.

He wished he hadn't waited so long to ask her out again: *Free tomorrow?*

Her response appeared a moment later: *Want to try and catch me on the trails again?*

*Absolutely. 10 am?* Smiling, he dared hope that maybe the relationship was progressing.

A thumbs-up confirmed the date.

# Chapter 24



Marisa dressed in her running gear. After pulling her hair up, she dropped onto the bed. Hesitation grabbed her. Tuesday's date had her thinking of the detective all week. His middle-of-the-night call had fueled those thoughts.

For all her poking and pushing and running away, he showed up again and again, repeating the same message. Maybe he did like her. What if he was just as nice as he appeared?

No matter how nice he was, he would eventually see her for who she was, then he'd be gone. Why delay the inevitable?

She picked up her phone and tapped out a text.

Ben waited at the trailhead. When his phone vibrated, he read the message from Marisa: *Have to cancel. So sorry.*

He wondered what came up. His gut said she'd chickened out. Two steps forward, then she ran a mile in the other direction. He sent a reply: *I guess I'll have to chase you another day.*

The trail awaited him. He ran a few miles before trudging back to his car.

# Chapter 25

*Monday, May 16*

Marisa gave Kitty a good scratch before hurrying to the car. In the front seat—inside the car—lay a stuffed cat and a note. Marisa locked herself in the car, tears stinging her eyes as she opened the note. She'd convinced herself that Paul left the roses and that it would all stop after the break-in. The stuffed animal in her car shattered that belief.

She read the note.

*I hope we can keep our relationship just between us. It's so much more romantic that way. And it would be an awful shame if anything happened to anyone close to you—like your friend, Lexi.*

Marisa dropped the note on the seat. Paul or whoever it was hadn't named anyone before. If reporting the stalker put Lexi at risk, Marisa wouldn't do it. She'd already put too many people in danger. She couldn't even tell Ben, but she wanted to. She wanted to be wrapped in his arms, to feel safe from Paul.

Her hand shook as she tried to open the glove box. After three attempts, it fell open. She shoved in the note inside and slammed it shut.

She breathed in deep, scanning the parking lot to ensure she was alone. Once her hands stopped shaking, she started the engine and headed to work.

Ben tugged his phone out of his pocket as he finished his run and read the text from Alex: *Dinner?*

After he started the engine, and cold air blasted through the vents, Ben replied: *Sure. Same place as always?*

Alex kept his response short and to the point: *Yep. See you in an hour.*

An hour later, Ben waved as Alex made his way to the table. "Kate didn't come?"

"She's with Marisa. They are out looking at dresses for the wedding." Alex picked up the menu, hiding his face. "Otherwise, I would have suggested we all have dinner together."

"So, I'm just the backup because you didn't have anything else to do?"

"Pretty much." Laughing, Alex looked over the top of his menu. "Have you called her?"

"Y'all going to live at Kate's after the wedding? What happens to the cabin?" Ben closed his menu. When his phone beeped, he checked his texts. A message from Kate with three photos of Marisa filled his screen with the caption: *Have a preference?*

In each photo, Marisa wore a different gown, but they were all mostly the same color. He clicked on the first and the image filled his screen. The vivid red dress only covered one shoulder, and the slit showed off her leg. Her hair pulled up, stray hairs dancing on her neck, she made him forget the questions he'd just asked. Seeing how she'd be dressed, he wished for the day of the wedding to hurry up and arrive.

Remembering that Alex sat at the same table, Ben turned the screen to be sure the images weren't visible to anyone else and moved on to the next photo. Strapless, the flowy dress won his vote until he scrolled down to the last one. Red hugged every curve, then flared near the floor. *That one. Please choose that one.*

He didn't dare type what he thought without risking saying something embarrassing. Trying to decide how to respond, his fingers hovered over the phone. Before he responded, another text popped on the screen: *Oops, sorry, Ben. Sent you that by mistake. But what do you think?*

He guessed it wasn't much of a mistake, more of a set-up, but he tapped out a reply: *She looks great in all three.*

When he glanced up, Alex grinned. Ben had spent too much time staring at the pictures of Marisa to feign indifference.

Alex chuckled. "You realize it's a group text, right?"

"I do now." Ben did not want to discuss Marisa with her brother.

Alex laid his phone on the table and scrolled through the pictures. "Which one? I know you have an opinion."

"Three." Ben hoped the topic would move along.

Smiling like the Cheshire cat, Alex danced his fingers over the tiny keyboard. "The mermaid one?"

Ben nodded, even though he had no idea if that was what it was called.

Alex's reply: *The last one.* popped up on Ben's screen.

Kate responded with a heart.

"You told Kate." Ben rubbed the back of his head. "Why?"

Alex shook his head. "I didn't. She brought it up. Apparently, I'm not the only one who thinks the two of you together is a good idea."

Ben wanted to say, "back off" and explain that things were tenuous, at best, and possibly non-existent. But he didn't. That would involve admitting to a relationship. Without Marisa's approval, he wouldn't reveal anything.

Alex could just assume that Ben pined for Marisa and hesitated about whether or not to ask her out.

Marisa glanced at her phone after changing out of the last dress. A series of texts filled her screen. She stared at Ben's answer.

Why had she stood him up? She wanted to see him.

Making sure not to reply to the group message, she texted only Ben: *Do you have a favorite?*

His reply made her want to see him even more: *You.*

# Chapter 26

*Wednesday, May 18*

Marisa stopped for barbeque on her way home from work. She caught sight of Ben as soon as she stepped into the restaurant. The line of his shoulders, the curve of his jaw, the tenderness in his eyes flashed in her brain daily. Currently, his shoulders sagged. He looked worn and tired. She stepped up behind him in line. Tempted to massage his stress away, she folded her arms.

From Alex, she'd gathered which complex Ben lived in with a pretty good guess at which building, but she wasn't quite ready to resort to stalking. Besides, stalking a police detective sounded like all kinds of a bad idea. If she really wanted to know, she could ask her brother for the apartment number, but she was the one who stood Ben up. He might be tired of her antics, but Monday night's text made it clear he was still interested.

She stood silently behind him in line, wishing she could sit across the table from him, losing herself in his brown eyes, drinking in his smile. Nervous, she decided that if he didn't see her, she'd let him go on his way without bothering him.

Ben stared at the menu above the counter, deciding what he wanted, while the woman in front of him ordered enough food to feed two little league teams. He loosened his tie and rubbed his freshly buzzed head. After a trying day, he wanted hot food and a quiet apartment.

The woman finished her order and tossed him an apologetic smile. She looked over his shoulder and added, "Such a nice gentleman. He's been very patient."

He glanced back.

Marisa smiled. "Hello, Detective."

"Oh, hey." He stepped up to the counter, all idea of what he wanted to order—poof—gone. "Go ahead. I need to figure out what I want."

*Serendipity.*

She stepped in front of him and ordered, but instead of paying, she turned and tapped his arm. "Your turn. It's on me."

"No. I couldn't."

"You don't have to eat with me, but I'm paying." In her tailored suit and red pumps, she looked a daring opponent. "It's my way of apologizing."

He wasn't about to reject an apology, so he ordered. "Two meat plate. Brisket and sausage. And a drink."

"For here or to go?" The teen behind the counter grinned, having heard the entire conversation.

"For here."

"Wise choice." The young employee handed Ben and Marisa cups and gave her the receipt with their order number on it.

After filling their drinks, they slid into opposite sides of a booth.

"How are you?" Ben pictured her in his favorite of the dresses and hoped it didn't show on his face.

"I'm good. I like my new place. So much better than staying at my brother's cabin."

"He still staying at Kate's?"

"No. Not since the engagement." She rolled her eyes. "He's always had old-fashioned ideas about love."

"How's the house business?"

"Going okay. After selling houses for a few high-profile clients, my name is getting out there." She jumped up when they called her number and grabbed both trays off the counter. "I wondered if I'd see you again. I'm sorry for standing you up."

"Everything okay?"

She barely met his gaze before lowering her eyes to her plate. "I got scared."

"Of me?" He'd been accused of being intense but never scary.

She shook her head. "Not you. Just … this, us."

He grinned. "Dresses looked nice. Which did y'all choose?"

"The mermaid one."

"Is that the …" He moved his hands in an hourglass shape, then fanned out near the lower edge of the imaginary dress. "Something like that?"

"Yes. I assume you're going. Or in it, perhaps?"

"A groomsman." Ben guarded his answers, trying to be casual, not wanting to scare her off. Again.

She stared out the window, watching a couple in conversation on the sidewalk. "Don't you wish love was contagious?"

He understood her question, the wistfulness. *Yeah.*

Ben gazed at her profile, hoping it wasn't a question she expected him to answer out loud. "Maybe, if you aren't busy …" He stopped when a tall, middle-aged guy with slicked-back, salt-and-pepper hair stepped up to the table.

"Hey, baby." He ran a finger down her arm.

Marisa whipped her head around. Anger blazed in her eyes. "Leave me alone, Paul."

"But I miss you." He poked at the top button of her blouse.

Ben jumped up, barely maintaining his cool. "The lady said to leave her alone."

"Believe me, she's no lady." Paul smirked. "I like your new apartment, by the way."

Marisa tossed her napkin on the table and stood up. "Come near me again, and I'll call the police."

Paul strolled away, laughing.

"Marisa—" Ben stepped closer.

"Just don't, Ben." She picked up her purse. "I don't need the two of you peacocking. Is that just how guys handle everything? I need to go."

He stopped himself from grabbing her hand. He could lecture and plead about filing a restraining order, but her body language made it clear she didn't want to hear it.

"Marisa."

She paused and looked back, her shoulders sagging, sadness in her eyes.

He wasn't giving up. "Thank you for dinner. Let's do it again soon."

# CHAPTER 27

*Thursday, May 19*

Marisa updated the status of a house, made an appointment with a client, and scheduled two showings. Only an hour into her day, she'd been busy since she walked in.

Lexi walked in carrying a lavishly wrapped box. "This was left at the front desk for you."

"Really?" Marisa refused to take it. "I wasn't expecting anything."

"Open it." Lexi pulled on the ribbon. "If you don't, I will."

Against her better judgement, Marisa tore off the paper and lifted the lid. A stuffed animal—a match to the cat she'd received before—lay torn open in the bottom. A note stuck out of the open seam.

"What in the world? Who would send you that?" Lexi reached for the note.

Marisa yanked it out of Lexi's grasp. "I don't know. Please don't say anything to anyone about this."

She waited until her friend walked out before reading the note.

*I'm not nice when I'm jealous.*

Marisa dropped the small slip of paper and shoved her office door closed. Jealous? Paul had seen her with Ben. Hugging her arms around herself, she leaned against the door, slowly inhaling and exhaling, trying to stop her body from shaking.

If Paul had wanted to scare her, it'd worked. She'd expected him to be mad that she'd turned him in, but she hadn't expected jealousy or stalking. Determined not to let his mind games put her job at risk, she picked up the note and snatched her purse off the desk before hurrying out to her car.

She shoved the note with the others in the glove box. Sure that he watched from somewhere close by, she shuddered. Checking her rearview mirror as she pulled out of the lot, she headed home for an early lunch.

As she drove, she considered her options. If she told Ben, he'd march her down to the station to file a report. Reporting what was happening put Lexi at risk. Marisa couldn't live with herself if anything happened to her friend. Calling Maddox wasn't the answer because he worked in a different county.

Marisa gripped the steering wheel. Her knuckles turned white, and her pulse throbbed in her fingers. The only option was to guard her surroundings and not let the notes bury her in fear. When she arrived at her complex, she scanned the lot. Then as she went upstairs, she stopped at each landing, tucked out of sight, and waited, listening for footsteps.

Spilling her secret to the one who'd kept all the others crossed her mind again. Maybe he would help her without calling the police. But she imagined his disappointment when he learned she hadn't reported the break-in or the notes, or even mentioned them to him. His job was to protect, and she'd made it clear his help wasn't wanted. Frustrated with herself, she couldn't bear to see it reflected in those soft brown eyes.

She'd wanted last night's dinner to be another step toward something more, but the way she'd stomped out didn't help that. Telling him about the stalking would end any possibility of a relationship. He'd think she was stupid for trying to handle it on her own. Was she?

~*~

Ben ran down the street, glancing at each black car that passed. He'd blamed the unexpected meeting for making her hard to forget, but that was a lie. If he hadn't seen her since that first day, she'd still be camped in his thoughts. Complicated and captivating, she confounded him. He'd tried standing up for her, literally, and it made her mad.

He didn't understand her, but if he had any chance of making her happy, he needed to change that.

# CHAPTER 28

*Saturday, May 21*

Marisa left the engine running, sitting in her car with the radio blaring while Ben jogged past. A faded, sweat-soaked image of Yoda stuck to his chest. He stopped and wiped his face with his shirt, revealing a toned six-pack. Doubling back, he slowed to a walk, passing in front of her car at a snail's pace. The temptation to honk made her giggle.

Once he was out of sight, she got out of the car.

"Hey." He grinned, clearly aware that she'd been watching him.

She spun around. "Have a good run?"

Even sweaty, he looked good. "How long have you been sitting in your car?"

"Long enough."

"Stalking's a crime, you know." He had no clue the icy effect those words had on her.

She wouldn't let her world be controlled by a creeper. "Want to come up and have a cold drink?" She held her breath.

"And stink up your apartment? Nah. I have plans, but you could join me. I could swing by and get you after I showered and got cleaned up."

"That's okay. Have fun." She waved and hurried up the steps, feeling his eyes on her back. *Don't look back.*

Ben wrestled with the temptation to chase her up the stairs and change his mind about the cold drink. *Of all nights to have plans.* He trudged back to his apartment. If he hurried, he'd only just make it in time.

After a quick shower, he pulled on jeans and a t-shirt and hurried back out the door. As he drove past her complex, he hoped for a glimpse, but he didn't even see her car.

After a short drive, he parked along the street and walked down to the food truck park. The guys from the office were easy to spot. No matter what they wore, they looked like cops. Miller's wife, Dana, waved as Ben approached and pointed to a spot near her husband.

Daniels clapped. "We bet on whether you'd show. And I win. You remember Brooke?"

"Good to see you again, Brooke. You bet on me? I said I'd come."

Robbins laughed. "What he's not telling you is that he bet you'd show up *alone.* Glenda, Ben. Ben, Glenda."

"Nice to meet you. Glad I could win you a bet, Daniels."

Of all the guys in Ben's unit, these three went out of their way to include him, the single guy, in monthly outings, that, of course, came with a healthy dose of ribbing and the occasional set-up.

"They have some great food trucks tonight." Miller pointed at the row behind him. "Grab food. We saved you a seat."

"Thanks." Ben headed toward the Korean taco truck.

Almost to the line, someone walked up behind him and leaned close. "Detective? Are you following me?" The enchanting brunette's breath tickled his neck. She brushed something off his shoulder.

He turned and ended up nose to nose with her. "Marisa? What are you doing here?"

"It's good to see you, too." She laughed. "I picked up dinner." A delicious aroma wafted from her bag.

Entranced by her gaze, he said what popped in his head. "Stay. With me."

"Detective?"

"For dinner. You'd be doing me a favor. I'm the only single guy." He nodded to the table. All those seated around it were staring in their direction. "Please."

"I suppose I owe you a favor or two." She looped her arm in his.

"You don't owe me anything, Marisa." He stopped walking toward the table when she tugged at him.

"Aren't you forgetting something?" She nodded toward the food trucks. "You haven't ordered anything to eat. I suppose I could share, but it isn't much."

He remedied his mistake and led her to the group. "Everyone, this is Marisa."

Flirtatious, she didn't act like someone weighed down by the past. She'd met the guys from work. Her brother approved. Their secret was becoming less of one.

"Torres, you are full of surprises!" Miller laughed.

Robbins patted the table, and Daniels pulled out his wallet, paying off his bet while Miller made introductions.

Marisa enjoyed the unexpected company, but none more than the man next to her. Hope swelled in her heart. After everyone said their goodbyes, Ben walked her to her car.

She leaned back against it, the detective in front of her. "I had fun."

"Me too." Stepping forward, he lowered his voice. "Marisa, I'm worried about you. Why did Paul say he liked your apartment? Has he been—"

"I'm not sleeping with him, if that's what you're implying." She bumped him with her door as she got into the car. "Goodbye, Ben."

Tears streaked down her face, a release she rarely allowed herself, but she didn't care. Blindsided by a question she wouldn't answer, she fumed over his implication.

Marisa cried all the way home. She wiped her tears as she walked up the steps to her apartment. Had she overreacted? What was he about to say when she cut him off?

Taped to her apartment door was a folded piece of paper. She pulled it off but waited until she was locked inside before she read it.

*Dinner with him again? I warned you.*

Marisa sank to the floor, and tears started anew. After the disastrous end to dinner, she couldn't call Ben, not that she was ready to risk Lexi to make the terror stop. Besides, the chances that Marisa would go out with Ben again wouldn't fetch great odds in Vegas. Her stalker had no reason to be jealous.

Ben slammed the door to his apartment. She'd completely misunderstood his intent, and he'd made her cry. Around her, the world tilted. It made him uncomfortable, but she tugged at him like a magnet on metal shavings.

When he finally went to bed, he tossed and turned. Too upset to sleep, he went for a run. The sidewalk near her complex swallowed his feet, bringing him to a grinding halt. He yanked his phone out of his pocket and tapped out a text: *I'm sorry. That's not at all what I meant. You'd call me if you needed help, right?*

He ran home before checking to see if the message showed as read.

# Chapter 29

*Wednesday, May 25*

Marisa called Kitty and unlocked the apartment. Usually the feline friend met Marisa at the door after work, demanding to be fed, but not that day. Inside, she dropped her bag on the end of the couch, changed out of her work clothes, and then went back out to fill the cat bowl. Kitty's collar lay in the empty bowl. A note stuck out from underneath.

*I won't share you.*

Marisa slammed the apartment door, sobbing. Her whole body shook. She sank to the floor and picked up the phone. Her finger hovered over Ben's number. She hesitated, knowing he'd make her report it to the police. After keeping the secret, reporting anything so long after it happened would make her look not only weak, but stupid.

A knock sounded at the door. Marisa peeked out the window, solidifying her decision to keep quiet. Lexi stood outside holding a pizza box.

Marisa wiped her tears and answered the door.

Lexi rushed in. "What's wrong?"

"I'd adopted a kitty. It isn't coming around anymore. It must've run away."

"I'm so sorry. I guess it's a good thing I brought pizza."

Marisa set plates and napkins on the table. "Thanks. Sorry I'm such a mess."

"We need to think of some way to cheer you up."

She snagged a slice of pepperoni and added parmesan to the top. "I'll be okay."

"Wish we could find that guy that bumped into you that night. Remember that?"

"Hmmm. The pizza is good." Marisa did her best to ignore the question.

Lexi eyed her. "Have you seen him again? Don't hold out on me."

"I've seen him around."

"You know what I remember about him? Those arms. I wonder what he looks like without a shirt."

"You crack me up. I bet you have no recollection of the woman on his arm that night." Marisa wasn't about to admit that, after the glimpse she'd had of Ben's abs, she wondered the same thing. "Pass me another slice. I'm starved."

She hadn't responded to his apology. As much as she wanted to, fear prompted hesitation. Seeing Ben again would anger whoever had left the note, the same person who'd taken her cat.

# CHAPTER 30

*Monday, May 30*

Ben traipsed through the department store trying to find a gift for his mom. "Don't give me gift cards. I never use them," she'd said. He hated shopping and hadn't the least inkling what she wanted. That wasn't true. She wanted him to get married and give her grandchildren. Perhaps a purse would serve as a sufficient substitute.

On cue, thoughts of marriage and grandchildren brought thoughts of Marisa. She never answered or even read his text. The frustration of his unanswered apology was made worse by the fact that the guys at work asked about her nearly every day. She'd made quite the impression.

His calls had been diverted to voicemail, and he'd left messages. She was worth whatever persistence it took. After leaving three messages, he quit calling, hoping that she'd either call him or that they'd bump into each other.

He walked through the racks looking at handbags. *Would any of these make a good gift?*

Marisa flipped through racks of dresses until she saw him walk past. Keeping distance, she followed him and chuckled at the bewildered look on his face as he surveyed the purses. Out of his element, he was fun to watch. *Who's he shopping for?*

She pulled out her phone. Rattled by the notes, she hadn't responded to his calls, but seeing him she couldn't help herself. She replied to the text she'd stared at several times a day for the last week: *Forgiven. Truce?*

Standing near the pantyhose, she waited. Her action depended on his reaction. A smile lit up his face and her phone beeped a second later: *Have dinner with me.*

He didn't give her time to worry that he was no longer interested. Staring at her phone, she pondered her response.

The beep caught his attention. She stood not far away, tucked behind a rack of pantyhose.

He tiptoed around behind her, hoping she stayed focused on her phone. "Tonight would be good for me."

She bobbled her phone, but he caught it before it hit the ground.

"You have your texts set so that they don't get marked read, don't you?" He handed her the phone, making sure he touched her hand twenty times in the process.

"Yeah. And dinner would be nice."

"Great, but first, I have to buy my mom a birthday present."

"What does she want?"

"What every mother of grown children wants."

Her eyes twinkled at the implication. "A scarf might be nice." She grabbed his hand and pulled him to the other end of the department.

She asked about hair color and eye color and what his mother wore. After he'd answer a hundred questions or more—at least it felt that way—Marisa ran her finger along the scarves and pulled three off the rack. "Which of these do you like?"

He shrugged. "Blue one's kinda pretty."

"Let's look over here." She stopped after one step.

He held out his hand. "Lead the way."

She hooked her finger around his pinky and strolled to another display.

Forty-five minutes later, a beautifully-wrapped scarf in his bag, Ben walked into the nearest restaurant, with Marisa on his arm. Not all Mondays were bad.

~*~

She slid into the booth, and he shifted in next to her. He continued to hold her hand while looking over the menu.

When the waiter walked up, Ben squeezed Marisa's hand. "What do you want to drink?"

They ordered drinks, and Ben added an appetizer before the waiter walked away.

"It's good to see you." Marisa felt safe for the first time in days. She tried not to think of what the stalker might send next if he saw her with Ben.

His eyes twinkled in that boyish way. "It's like Christmas."

The waiter set the drinks and appetizer on the table. "Food will be out in a just a few."

Ben let go of her hand. "Dig in."

Marisa heaped a scoop of the chicken mixture onto a lettuce leaf. "Love these."

Conversation flowed easily with him. She loved that. Quiet was a time to eat and enjoy companionship, never because neither knew what to say. The hard part was not telling him about the notes and the break-in. He'd want to know. He'd want to help.

"Everything okay?" Ben focused his detective stare on her. "You seem … nervous."

Marisa stalled, taking a sip of her drink. "I'm hoping I don't mess up this date too." She hated lying to him.

He didn't make her nervous.

Wheels turned behind soft brown eyes. "Maybe our next date will be less nerve-wracking."

Marisa's heart did a backflip.

Dinner progressed splendidly until the evening news filled every television in the room, and Paul was the lead story. His face filled the square over the anchor's shoulder. Marisa wasn't prepared for it. He'd been arrested again, this time in San Antonio.

Ben reached for her hand and flagged down the waiter with the other. "Could we get to-go boxes please? And the check."

"I'll bring them right out."

"Thank you." Marisa stared at the table, afraid people would sense her association with the man on the screen.

"Has he tried to contact you since he made bail?"

"I don't want to talk about him."

Ben brushed his thumb along her fingers. "I'll sleep a little easier knowing he's off the street at least tonight."

She fished her keys out of her purse with her free hand. "Girls like Kate need a bodyguard. I *don't*." Afraid Ben would read her expression, she grew uncomfortable under his gaze.

He didn't let go of her hand. His soft brown eyes darkened. "Kate escaped kidnappers, talked a guy out of shooting her, and laid Paul out flat when he attacked Becca. She doesn't *need* Alex. She *lets* him take care of her. She wants him to."

His meaning wasn't subtle, and it stung. It stung because Marisa wasn't letting him take care of her, even though he'd made it clear that he wanted to. But he didn't know the complexity of the situation.

Marisa yanked her hand away. "Never mind. You wouldn't understand. Let me out." She pushed against his shoulder, and when he stood up, she slipped out of the booth. "You can have my leftovers." Leaving him no choice but to wait for his check, she hurried out of the restaurant.

At least Paul hadn't seen her out with Ben. The notes would stop until Paul made bail, but even that thought didn't loosen the tightness in her chest.

She was almost to her car when Ben ran up beside her.

"Why do you do that?"

She glanced back at the restaurant. "You left without paying?"

"I tossed cash on the table and probably paid too much. Marisa, why won't you trust me?"

"I can't." She drove home, frustrated and scared.

Ben stood in the parking lot, watching her drive away. Any sane person would accept defeat and forget about her, but she made him crazy.

The flicker of hurt in her eyes, not quite masked by her flirtatious manner, deepened his curiosity. Her bravery and willingness to risk herself for others said more about her than the mood swings and tantrums. He hated using the word tantrums but couldn't think of a better one.

Paul must've contacted her. That would explain the fear, but not all of it. When a date went well, she panicked. The relationship scared her, letting Ben help prompted fear. He just didn't know why.

# CHAPTER 31

### *Thursday, June 2*

Curled up at the end of a sofa, Marisa sipped a latte while reading *The Blue Rebozo.* Dabbing her eyes, she sighed as she read. Her phone buzzed next to her.

Ben texted: *What are you reading?*

He hadn't texted or called since the night at the restaurant. His silence convinced her that not trusting him was the final deal-breaker. It probably didn't help that her ex had been arrested again. The text he'd just sent made her wish she'd been wrong.

She replied: *Are you following me?*

He chuckled as he sat down next to her. "You okay?"

"Yeah."

"Want to talk about the other night?"

Unprepared for the question, she snapped an answer. "No."

He closed up like a food truck at the end of the night. "Well, it was nice bumping into you."

"You too." She wouldn't beg him to stay.

Ben sat in his car, frustrated and confused. He couldn't win for losing with Marisa. He tried to be understanding and offered to talk about her feelings, but she'd shut him down.

He sent her a text: *I was looking forward to our next date.*

# Chapter 32

*Friday, June 3*

Marisa stopped far away from the box near her front door. The quiet meow from inside prompted her closer. She opened the card attached to the top.

*For my friend-*

*A little someone almost as cute. Hope this brightens your day.*

*-Lexi*

Marisa opened the box, and blue eyes squinted at her. "Hello, *Gatito.*"

A small orange and white kitten turned in a circle, wanting out of the box. Marisa carried her treasure inside. Tomorrow she'd pay the pet deposit. Tito wasn't going to live outside. He needed to be where she could take care of him.

A text from the detective popped up on her screen: *Miss you.*

# CHAPTER 33

*Wednesday, June 8*

A large spray of flowers welcomed Marisa as she walked into her office. She grabbed the note, harboring a tiny hope that maybe Ben had sent them.

*I'm sorry I upset you. Forgive me?*

She stopped reading and hugged the card to her chest. She'd hadn't replied to his text, so flowers were a huge surprise. She continued to read.

*One day when you least expect it, we'll finally meet. Until then…*

She threw the entire bouquet in the trash, dashed hopes and fear chilling her.

# CHAPTER 34

*Thursday, June 9*

Ben glanced back over his shoulder as he ran into the store. Marisa stopped at the pump just as he got to the counter. "Pump seven. I want to pay for her gas."

The clerk grinned and punched a button. "Hun, your gas has been paid for. Fill 'er up."

Ben chuckled as Marisa scanned the lot. "I'm grabbing a soda and snacks. I'll be back up in a sec."

Marisa filled her tank, then pulled into a space. She ran inside, hoping to get a description of who paid the bill.

Ben stood just inside the door, the cheesiest grin she'd ever seen plastered on his face. He'd never looked so playful.

"You could have pumped it for me."

He put on his sunglasses. "Good to see you, Marisa." Away he went, in his fitted slacks and pale blue dress shirt. When he got to his car, he glanced back over his shoulder. "Oh, by the way, my mom *loved* the scarf."

# Chapter 35

*Monday, June 13*

As Ben rounded the bend in the sidewalk, out for a late-night jog, he spotted a man leaning into Marisa's car. Sprinting, Ben closed the distance quickly. "What are you doing?"

The man jumped away and hid his face as he ran to a car parked on the street. Ben couldn't read the faded dealer plate.

He texted Marisa: *Someone was breaking into your car. I scared them off but didn't get a plate number. I'm in the parking lot now.*

She rushed down the stairs when she read the text. Concerned about what the stalker might have left, she approached the car, watching Ben, studying his body language. He'd have mentioned if it was Paul. Was she wrong about who'd been leaving notes?

Ben rubbed the back of his head. "I was running by and saw him digging around inside. We should call it in."

She held her breath as she glanced into the car. "Doesn't look like anything is missing. I'm not going to worry about it."

"Marisa, he broke into your car."

Her mind raced, trying to think of an excuse not to file a report. "Maybe I left the door unlocked. I can live without my loose change."

He hooked his pinky around her finger, a gesture familiar and gentle, a reminder of the night at the mall. "You won't change your mind?"

The plea is his eyes made her question the wisdom of her decision, but then she pictured Kitty, Lexi, and Tito. "I'm sure it's nothing."

Moonlight reflected in his brown eyes. "You know where I am if you ever need anything."

Marisa stepped closer and laid her hand on his chest—all of Lexi's comments running through her thoughts. "I'm sorry for the way I ran out during dinner."

He glanced at her hand and smiled. "Maybe we can try again one night."

"I'd really like that." Her lips parted, hoping for more than just a "goodbye."

His finger still hooked with hers, he stepped closer, tilting his head ever so slightly. Marisa inhaled. Anticipating the feel of his lips, she closed her eyes. His heart thumped against her hand, but he didn't move.

"I should probably go." He stayed still.

Her eyes open, she slid her hands around his neck. She wasn't ready to let him go. When he left, the fear would return. And that wasn't the only reason.

Warm arms circled her, and his breath tickled her ear. "Please, Marisa, let me help you."

She hated that he assumed she was keeping secrets. Even more, she hated that he was right. After holding on too long, she pulled back. "Goodnight, Detective." Before walking away, she hugged him again. "Please don't give up on me. I'm not trying to push you away." Her honesty scared her.

He tightened his embrace.

Before any more words she didn't want to say came spilling out, she slipped out of his arms and ran up the stairs. When she got to the top floor, she glanced over the railing, and he waved.

He hadn't moved.

# CHAPTER 36

## *Tuesday, June 14*

The next morning, with the aid of daylight, Marisa searched her car for what the man left, if he'd gotten the chance. She found a note tucked between the seat and the center console. Scrawled in red were words that scared her.

*I want to touch you. You won't have to wait much longer.*

She shoved it in the glove box with the other notes and hurried to work, checking her rearview mirror at each turn. Why did Paul insist on terrorizing her? If it wasn't Paul, who as it? She couldn't entertain those thoughts.

As she drove, she calmed down, telling herself that Paul had no interest beyond scaring her. If she maintained courage and didn't act afraid, he'd eventually leave her alone.

# Chapter 37

*Wednesday, June 15*

Ben stood in the corner store and scoured the rack of chips. "Come on. The only one you're out of is the kind I want."

Thankfully, the rack didn't answer back. A familiar perfume wafted by, and he closed his eyes. *Marisa.* He hadn't called or texted since he last saw her, but he also hadn't forgotten her final plea.

"You praying?" she whispered in her most reverent voice.

He bumped her shoulder. "Just tired and annoyed. They're out of my favorite chips."

"I heard. That is a shame. Anything I can do to make it better? I make a mean plate of nachos. Let me make you dinner."

Being a detective put him face to face with depravity every day. Some days were worse than others. The workday that just ended was off the charts. She didn't need to be subjected to him in his current mood.

Marisa pleaded silently for him to say "yes."

*Uh-oh, the creases are back.*

He wrinkled his forehead and rubbed the back of his head. "Can I get a raincheck? I wouldn't be good company tonight." Maybe he wasn't interested anymore but wanted to be nice about it.

"Sure." She spotted a bag hidden on a low shelf and stepped in front of him. Bending at the waist, she reached down to the back of the lower rack. Her fitted dress hugged in all the right places, and she knew it.

By the time she was upright, his back was to her. That ranked on her list of favorite things about him.

"This what you're looking for?" She dangled a bag of chips in front of him.

"Yep. Exactly what I wanted. Where did you …?"

"I guess you just didn't see what was right in front of you."

He grabbed a Dr Pepper from the cooler. "About tonight."

"No worries." She walked her fingers up his shirt. "The raincheck is redeemable any time, day *or* night."

He stepped closer and slipped an arm around her waist. Was he calling her bluff? Startled, Marisa wondered how to reel in her innuendo, but she didn't move.

"I accept." His other arm slid around her. "It would be disingenuous not to let you see both the good and the bad, and I wouldn't want you to think I was giving up. So, your place or mine?"

"What?" Stumbling over words, she pressed her hands to his chest, ready to push away. "I, uh—"

His cheek pressed to hers, he whispered so that the people nearby pretending not to watch the private conversation couldn't hear, which she appreciated. "Just dinner and conversation. I won't even kiss you."

In barely a whisper, she answered, "Your place." Nervous, she pushed on his chest, slipping out of his arms. "Let me get what I need."

After grabbing chips and cheese, she checked out, wondering if she was being brave or crazy for going to his apartment. She wanted to see where he lived, what his place looked like, and more than anything, she liked having him near.

"How about we drop your car off, and I'll drive you home after."

"Great idea." She almost changed her mind four times between the store and dropping off her car.

~*~

Holding the grocery bags, Ben unlocked his apartment and flipped on the light. "After you." Both stunned and pleased that she'd said yes, he eyed her as she studied his space.

She took the bags from him and wandered into the kitchen, seemingly at home. "Nice place. It's a lot bigger than mine."

"Mind if I run back and change?"

"Go ahead." She hummed as she unloaded items from the bags.

Ben yanked off his tie as he trudged down the hall. Humorless and worn out, he questioned the wisdom of his decision, but the melodious sounds coming down the hall convinced him it was the right choice. He wanted her close, and she deserved to see him at his worst before deciding if she liked him.

The oven beeped as he stepped into the kitchen.

"It just needs a couple minutes under the broiler."

"Thanks for doing this."

She caught him off-guard with a hug. "Sorry your day was horrible."

Ben buried his face in her hair and held her close, wanting to forget all the awful things he'd seen, but the moment was cut short when the oven beeped again. He let go, and she moved away.

They settled at the coffee table with plates full of nachos. Sitting next to him on the floor, Marisa chatted about growing up and having nacho night. She filled the quiet created by his funk without asking repeatedly if he was okay.

When her plate was empty, she jumped up off the floor and sat behind him on the sofa. Kneading circles on his tight muscles, she leaned forward. "Did you get the bad guy?"

He appreciated the simplicity of her question. "We did. Just not before—not in time."

"I wish I could massage the images away. I know how it feels to see something every time I close my eyes." Up his neck and across his shoulders, she massaged. "Have I told you about the time my brother caught me skipping school?"

Ben leaned back into her lap, mesmerized by her empathy. "You mean Alex?"

"Yep. Mr. Rules." She smiled down at him and laughed. "If Nico or Sam had caught me, they'd have paid for my lunch and taken me to the movies. Not Alex, though."

"He ratted you out?"

"Worse. He didn't. After a lecture, he drove me back to school and walked me into the building. Dork."

Ben couldn't help but laugh at the image.

Glad she'd fought the impulse to change her mind, Marisa had no regrets about coming. Seeing him so somber and quiet, a contrast to what she was used to, gave a glimpse of the pain he carried around. Because of that, the chasm between them didn't seem as wide.

When he relaxed at the touch of her fingers, the possibility that he might need her sparked hope.

She wrapped her arms around his neck, pressing her cheek to his. "This is kinda nice, but I should probably go home. You need sleep."

"I needed this—you. Thank you." Could he read her thoughts? He used the word she longed to hear.

She kissed the top of his head. "We should do it again."

"Absolutely." Ben held firm to his promise of no kissing, which disappointed her a bit.

# CHAPTER 38

*Saturday, June 18*

Ben dropped his keys on the coffee table and loosened his tie. Yawning, he wandered to the window and spotted Marisa powerwalking along the sidewalk. Dressed in exercise leggings and a t-shirt, she looked like she'd just stepped off the cover of a workout magazine. Her ponytail swung back and forth with every step. When she disappeared from view, he moved out to the porch for one more glimpse.

*Call her.*

They've texted back and forth every day since she'd made him nachos, which was new and nice, but he wanted to see her again. He waited until she'd had enough time to make it home before he picked up the phone and clicked her name in the list of favorites.

She answered on the first ring. "Ben?"

"Hi. I just got home, and this is really last minute. Are you free tonight?"

"Um, I'll be home about nine. Is that too late?" She had plans, but she hadn't said no.

"Yeah. Perfect. Text me when you're home." He paced, grinning. "I can't wait to see you."

"Until tonight, Detective."

～*～

Hours later, Marisa's thoughts still lingered on his call. She dropped into the passenger seat, trying not to let her excitement show. Telling Lexi about Ben could jinx it, so Marisa kept quiet.

"You are really done up for the movies." Lexi raised her eyebrows.

"You never know who we'll bump into."

"So true. Think that guy might show up? You know, the one from the food truck park that you've *seen around.*"

"That's not who I meant." Marisa didn't like the direction of the conversation. "You mentioned changing the color of your hair. Have you decided?"

Lexi launched into her thoughts on hair color. "The pink parts hardly look pink anymore. Maybe green or blue would look good. Anything but brown, no offense."

Marisa ignored the slam on brown hair. "You could pull off purple, too. It'd look great with your eyes."

At the theater, they each purchased a tub of popcorn and settled into their seats. Marisa sat through the movie, oblivious to the large screen. Her thoughts drifted to the detective.

～*～

Ben snatched up his phone at the first jingle of a ring. "Hello."

"Torres. I need a favor." Miller had never asked him for help outside of work.

"What's up?"

"My niece just called. She's drunk and needs a ride. But we're in Austin. Any chance you can pick her up and take her home?"

Ben glanced at his phone. *8:57 pm* "Yeah. What's her name? Where is she?"

"She's at a party near the university. At some guy's house. Her name is Sparkle. I'll text you the address."

"Seriously? Sparkle? Is this a joke?"

"I swear. I call her Sparky. My sister wanted her kids' names to be fun and different. I'll text you her home address, too."

"I'm leaving now."

Miller texted the addresses as soon as the conversation ended.

Ben shot off a quick text of his own before leaving: *Partner needs my help. Raincheck?* Cancelling on Marisa soured his stomach.

She replied with a sad emoji. All evening, she'd thought only of seeing him, which made the last-minute cancellation even more disappointing. When her friend, Lexi, stopped outside the apartment, Marisa decided staying home with nothing to do would be torturous.

"Want to go get a drink or dessert somewhere?"

"Sure." Lexi pulled back onto the street. "That coffee place okay?"

"Indy? Yeah. I love that place."

Busy on a Saturday night, the coffee house had several in line and very few open seats. Marisa and Lexi waited in line, then managed to snag two seats at the end of a table.

~*~

Ben clicked the seat belt into place because Sparky was much too drunk to work the buckle. He rubbed his face and shot off a text to Miller: *You owe me! Drunk doesn't begin to describe her.*

Miller responded: *Get some food and coffee in her before dropping her off. I'll pay you back.*

Ben tried to tune out the incessant giggling in his passenger seat. He drove down the street to the coffee house.

She clung to his arm, and they walked inside. As he struggled to keep her from wandering off, she bumped into a table, sloshing someone's coffee.

Embarrassed, he didn't look at the people. "Sorry. She's having a rough night." He tried to hold Sparky close while reaching for napkins.

"Don't worry about it." Marisa's voice stopped him cold.

The giggling started all over again. Sadly, Sparky wasn't too drunk to speak. "Hi. I'm Sparkle. Have you met my knight in shining armor?"

Ben's heart raced. "Marisa, it's not what it looks like. I'm doing a favor for my partner. He's out of town."

Green eyes focused on Sparkle, then Marisa leaned down and grabbed her purse.

"*Please*, Marisa." He stooped to begging. The last thing he wanted her to think was that he'd ditched her for a college kid named Sparkle, except that he had—but only to help out Miller, nothing more.

"You might want to quit talking." Lexi leveled an icy stare at Ben. "She doesn't look like she wants to hear it." She slid off the seat and marched to the door.

Marisa followed, never looking back.

After Ben had sobered up Miller's niece—at least enough to leave her alone—and dropped her off at her house, he texted Marisa: *She's my partner's niece, underage and drunk. I'd much rather have spent the night with you.*

He pressed send, then reread what he'd sent. Typing as fast as he could, he followed that with another message: *I'm not spending the night with anyone. I meant I'd rather have spent time with you. Please understand.*

# CHAPTER 39

## *Sunday, June 19*

Marisa waved as she and Lexi parted ways outside the bookstore. After an afternoon of shopping, they'd had dinner, then coffee. Marisa had only thought about the detective a few hundred times. She still hadn't replied to his text. Hurt and disappointed, she wanted to believe him, but Sparkle's knight-in-shining-armor comment stopped her whenever she picked up the phone.

She opened her car door and dropped her purse in the seat. A note on the windshield caught her attention. She glanced around the parking lot and ripped the note from under the wiper blade. Dropping into the driver's seat, she locked herself in the car before reading it. One word screamed at her.

*Soon.*

Marisa glanced in her backseat before starting the engine. She blinked back tears and set her jaw. Hyper-aware of her surroundings, she navigated out of the parking lot and headed home.

Locked in her apartment, she sank to the floor near the door and checked the time on her phone every few minutes. After that note, how would she ever sleep again?

She picked up her phone and searched for Maddox's number. Acknowledging the foolishness of keeping the notes and gifts secret, she tried to figure out a way to reverse direction. When the notes seemed an annoyance, keeping them a secret to protect others made sense. Finger poised over the call button, she argued with herself. Kate had already been hurt. Was Marisa willing to risk Lexi too—over something Paul probably thought was a grand joke?

Choosing not to risk her friend's life, she dropped the phone.

Why couldn't she admit everything to Ben? Why couldn't she let him be her knight in shining armor?

# CHAPTER 40

*Monday, June 20*

Ben drove home, irritated by her lack of reply. He'd stayed busy all day, trying to keep Marisa from dominating his thoughts, but it hadn't worked.

Wildflowers on the side of the road—straggly looking things, barely surviving the heat of summer—reminded Ben of what he'd seen his dad do when he'd gotten crossways with Mom. *Flowers.*

Ben needed to buy Marisa flowers. It'd worked on the first date, at first. He didn't want to wait for the florist shop to open in the morning. He wanted to deliver them when he got home.

He parked outside a local grocery store and ran inside. Flowers filled black buckets all around him. *So many choices.* After sniffing and searching, trying to decide, he skipped the sunflowers and opted for one flower instead of a bouquet—a single yellow rose.

By the time he got home and changed clothes, the sun hung just above the horizon. He jogged down the street, clutching the stem.

Since he didn't know which apartment was hers, he tucked the rose under the wiper blade of her Passat and texted Marisa: *Left you something on your car. I'm sorry.*

He sprinted back to his apartment and smiled when his phone buzzed. *Forgiven. Please don't ever leave anything on my car again.*

He appreciated the forgiven but wondered about the other part.

A second later, she texted again: *And next time you go pick up a drunk college girl, maybe you should take someone with you, Einstein. You could've asked for my help.*

Did Marisa have any clue how much irony dripped off that last sentence? But, if there ever was a next time, he would ask. *I'll remember that.*

# Chapter 41

*Wednesday, June 22*

Marisa hadn't heard from Ben since he left the rose. She was glad he'd texted saying he left it, but even knowing it was from him, seeing the rose on her car unnerved her. It added one more reason not to tell him. He'd feel horrible.

Wanting to see him again, she decided it was her turn to initiate a date. She wanted much more than that, but she had to start somewhere. While she waited in line at the checkout, she texted him: *Hello, Detective. I'm making dinner. I'll pick you up at seven.*

That would give her enough time to prep food and give him enough time to get back from the office.

She couldn't shake the fear that settled on her after the last note. Ben's apology had been a sweet surprise, and she didn't want to be alone. Making him dinner put a winning mark in two columns. She needed to tell him what was going on, all about the notes. Excited and a little nervous, she drove home, waiting for a response.

~*~

Ben tucked his notebook in his shirt pocket. The crime scene was a mess. After hours on the job, his day was just beginning.

Miller jingled keys in his pockets and surveyed the disarray. "Call the lab. Have them put a rush on the results."

Ben pulled out his phone and saw the missed text. Frustration and disappointment vied for first position. Though he wanted to see her, he couldn't. He had a job to do.

He shot off a quick text: *Can't. Working a case.* Before he made his call, he sent Marisa another text: *I really wish I could.*

*Another night then.* She added a heart after her text.

# Chapter 42

## *Thursday, June 23*

Ben walked out of the pharmacy and opened his chips before backing
out. If he continued getting junk food after work each day, he might
as well quit working out. He uncapped his Dr Pepper and took a swig.

Marisa walked out of the fast food place across the street. Instead
of getting in her car, which he didn't see in the lot, she headed toward
the panhandler on the corner.

The older man, covered from head to toe in grime, grinned as she
handed him the bag and cup. He set it near the lamppost. Opening
his arms, the vagrant said something, and Marisa nodded. He hugged
her. She gave him a light tap on his back and waved as she walked
away.

Ben stared, surprised by Marisa yet again.

She hurried up the sidewalk toward her apartment as the sun dipped
closer to the horizon. She didn't like walking in the dark, not after the

notes, and would have already been home if she hadn't stopped to get food for the guy on the corner.

Maybe she'd suggest meeting Ben for walks on the trail after work. Or she could just join a gym, but time with Ben appealed much more.

She yanked out her phone to call him, hoping she could see him, but put it away and quickened her steps as footsteps approached from behind.

Ben started to back out of his parking space but stopped when a man ran up behind Marisa. Instead of passing her by, he hovered a few paces behind her. After looking away only long enough to pull back into the spot, Ben jumped out of the car. The sidewalk across the street was empty. He scanned for where she might have disappeared as he crossed the street, dodging cars, trying to get to her.

"Marisa!" Ben forced himself to calm down and focus, taking in his surroundings. He walked or drove through the area every day. What was close, but hidden from sight? A paved road that served as a back entrance to a hotel lay mostly hidden by the scrub trees and high grasses. The way the pavement curved, part of the road wasn't visible from the sidewalk where he stood. He started that direction, and shuffling caught his attention. He ran toward the sound and spotted her just around the curve. The man who'd walked up behind her had his arms around her, pinning her arms to her side, or trying to.

Marisa struggled against him. "Let me go!"

Next to them was a black car with the rear door open. Ben raced toward them. She fought and wrestled, freeing an arm. The man— focused on trying to force her into a car—didn't notice the free arm.

She slammed her elbow against his nose, evoking a shriek from the would-be kidnapper. While his hands covered his face, she spun around and kneed him in the groin. "I said 'Let me go'."

"Hey!" Ben yelled as he closed the distance.

The car engine revved, and the man muttered curses and slammed the car door. The black sedan sped away. Ben watched faded dealer plates disappear from view.

"You okay?" He ran up to her, his anger held in check by admiration for the way she'd handled herself.

"I'm okay." She stepped up close and rested her head on his chest. "Thanks for—"

He wrapped and arm around her and pulled out his phone.

She grabbed his hand. "Who are you calling?"

"The police, Marisa. You were attacked. He was trying to drag you into a car."

Her jaw set, she glared at him. "There is no law that says I have to. You can't force me to report it."

"Not reporting it would be stup—" He rubbed the back of his head. "Please, Marisa. Let me call it in." He hadn't caught himself soon enough, and disdain for his word choice burned in her eyes.

"No." She turned and marched back toward their street.

Ben chased her, catching her arm. "Stop. I won't call." It went against everything for him not to report it.

～∗～

Marisa shook her arm free, dusted off her leggings, and eyed Ben. Scared and rattled, she needed a topic that put her in control. "Sorry you had to work late last night."

"Me, too." He loosened his tie.

She wrapped her arms around his waist. Playing a tease made it easier to hide her uneasiness about the attack, and anger fizzled quickly looking into his brown eyes. "How did you know to run down this street, Detective?"

Clearly irritated, Ben pointed to the pharmacy parking lot. "I'll drive you home."

She wanted to feel safe from her stalker. Telling Ben was the first step toward making that happen, but when he told her what to do, it angered her in a completely irrational way. Maybe it wasn't irrational. It reminded her of all the others that had forced their will on her. While she understood Ben's intentions, the dictates made her crazy. Calling her stupid didn't help either.

"You always so dictatorial? I'll walk, thank you."

"Marisa, please. Would you like a ride to your apartment? Nothing would give me greater pleasure." Ben dipped into a low bow, which came across as humorous, his intention for sure.

She liked him all the better for it. Without a word, she crossed the street and slid into his passenger seat. Letting silence tease him during the two minutes it took to drive up the street, she tried to figure out a way not to be alone again. When he pulled into her complex, she leaned across the seat and whispered, her lips brushing his ear. "Go change. I'll be at your place in ten minutes, and we'll see about that greater pleasure part." She hopped out and ran up the stairs.

Ben drove home and shed his work clothes, changing into athletic shorts and a t-shirt. He prepared himself for he wasn't sure what. Marisa's sudden mood change made him more than a bit nervous.

A knock sounded at the door.

He swung it open. "Listen, Marisa, I don't—" He stopped, noticing her load of grocery bags. "Let me help."

"Thank you, Detective."

"What is all this?" He poked through the bags.

"Dinner. The one I didn't make you last night."

He salivated as she pulled out thick steaks, fingerling potatoes, and zucchini spirals. "I'm not sure what to say."

"Thank you is a good start. Here." She handed him an ice-cold bottle of nut brown ale. "You relax while I cook."

He hovered near her as she dug through cabinets. "What do you need?"

Face to face, she walked her fingers up his t-shirt. "I need you to get out of the kitchen and let me cook."

Fighting the urge to kiss her, he dropped into a dining room chair. "Thank you."

Marisa prepped the steaks while the potatoes roasted. She heated a pan for the spirals, turned the potatoes, and seared the steaks. She worked quickly, ignoring the curious stare from Ben. As she slid the steaks in the oven, he broke the silence.

"This is nice."

She flipped the steaks and stirred the zucchini. "Set the table. It'll be done in a couple minutes."

Plates rattled behind her in response.

"They're ready." She set a plate in front of him, eager to see the delighted expression on his face. She wasn't disappointed.

He devoured his food, mumbling compliments between bites, which she relished. What was the saying about the way to a man's heart?

"Thank you for coming to my rescue earlier." She took a deep breath, preparing to tell him all about the notes. It would shatter all ideas that the attack was random, and he'd insist that she report it. But it needed to be done.

"You were impressive." Ben finished the last of his beer. "But, Marisa, don't walk by yourself at night."

Her relaxed demeanor changed. "It wasn't dark yet, and I can take care of myself."

He leveled a gaze at her and grinned. "Clearly, but I'd be happier knowing you weren't out at night like that. Why won't you just listen to me?"

"And I live to make you happy." She threw down her napkin and picked up her purse.

"Stop. Don't be childish. I wasn't trying to pick a fight."

"Childish? Seriously?"

As she reached for the doorknob, thunder rumbled outside, followed by the pitter patter of rain.

"Stay until the storm lets up." He stood between her and the door. "Please."

Her chest heaved. Fury danced on her skin like heat on the hood of a car in summer. He'd put his foot in it for sure.

"Get out of my way."

Ben put up his hands. "I'm sorry. I shouldn't have said it that way, but your reaction doesn't even make sense to me."

The pitter patter changed to pounding, and she moved away from the door. "Did my brother put you up to looking after me? Keeping an eye on his baby sister?" She perched at the edge of the couch like she was ready to bolt at any moment.

"No. He hasn't. Why would you think that?"

Trying to follow her train of thought was next to impossible.

"So you worry about me?"

"I have since the day we met, Marisa. Yeah, I care." He sat down in his arm chair, flustered. Fighting on a full stomach gave him indigestion.

She crossed her arms and stared at him. "What do you want, Detective?"

He couldn't believe she'd asked him that. "Want? You're asking what *I* want?" He leaned forward in his chair but kept his voice even. "I've been very clear on that point. What do *you* want? It seems to me you're the one that needs to contemplate that question. You've pushed and pulled so many times I've lost count, and you're asking what *I* want."

She launched off the couch and ran out the front door, leaving it wide open.

In his stocking feet, he followed as she raced down the stairs. "Please, wait a minute."

At the bottom of the stairs, she stopped, boring into him with an icy stare. "No." She slammed the car door and backed out.

As if in cahoots, the weather worsened, the rain coming down in sheets. Ben stayed planted in his square of sidewalk and watched her taillights turn onto the street. He wiped the rain out of his eyes.

*What do you want?*

The answer was easy. He wanted her.

Tires squealed as a pick-up careened around the corner. The rear-end fishtailing, the truck sped up. Ben yelled as it plowed into the back of Marisa's car.

He bolted toward the street in a panic. "Marisa!"

When she stepped out onto the pavement, raging mad, breath returned to Ben's lungs. The phone to her ear, she was already reporting the accident while an over-bearing, belligerent punk yelled at her for driving too slow on a public street.

Ben reached for her as he ran up. With a wave of her hand she swatted him back.

"Are you okay?" He stood between her and the other driver.

"Did you witness the accident?"

"Yes."

"Good." She returned to her phone call. "Yes, there was a witness."

Ben paced next to her.

Sirens approached, and she hung up. "Go put some shoes on."

"As soon as the officers arrive, I'll run in."

"I'm fine. I don't need you to babysit me."

Ben took off for the apartment, furious. He showed concern and got called a babysitter. She came on strong, all giggles and innuendo, but at the mention of help, all he got was an icy stare.

He yanked off his wet socks, pulled on shoes, grabbed his phone and wallet, and made it back to the car as the officers rolled up. The guy from the pick-up stood nose to nose with Marisa, screaming at her, his arms flailing.

Tears streamed down her cheeks, a sight Ben had rarely seen. Officers hollered for the man to step back. Ben flashed his badge and hurried up to Marisa as the other driver directed his rant at the officers. She buried her face in the curve of Ben's neck.

Ben wrapped his arms around her. "You okay?"

She nodded without looking up. "But my car isn't."

Holding her close, he stayed quiet and hoped that the earlier exchange would be forgotten in the embrace. He'd have stood like that, even in the rain, all night if that was the only way to be near her.

A young uniformed officer stepped up beside them. "Excuse me, ma'am, I need to get your statement."

Ben stepped aside as the officers talked with her, filling out the report. In turn, he gave his witness statement. As they loaded her car onto the tow truck, Ben pulled her aside. "I can give you a ride to work tomorrow. Want me to call your brother?"

The Marisa that melted into him after being yelled at disappeared. "I'll figure it out myself."

He waited while the tow truck loaded her car, hoping she'd be more open to talk when they were alone. But as soon as the police and tow truck left, she turned and darted off toward her apartment, leaving Ben standing on the sidewalk alone.

He trudged home, trying not to worry about her.

~*~

Marisa closed herself in her apartment and sank to the floor. What was wrong with her? A man who was everything she desired and needed made it clear that he wanted to protect her, and in response, she'd acted like a child.

She typed out a long text, blinking away tears to be able to see the screen. Would he forgive her? After her last tantrum, would he even read her apology?

*Ben, I'm sorry. You haven't deserved the way I've treated you. I don't know how to explain what I was thinking when I stomped out or when I left you on the sidewalk. When you turned the question back on me, I was embarrassed. You were right. I've behaved childishly. I'm afraid of letting you get close. Is there any chance you can forgive me?*

She sent the text and waited. Minutes went by, but he hadn't read it.

~*~

Ben trudged back into his apartment and headed straight for the shower. Soaking wet and frustrated, he hoped he'd be able to relax under the hot stream of water. In his head, he replayed the events of the evening. He had no idea what had set her off. If his mother was privy to the tug of war that defined his relationship with Marisa, his mom would plead with him to walk away.

Remembering the night outside the apartment when Marisa had asked him not to give up on her, he struggled with what to do. She was young, and she clearly didn't know what she wanted.

Logic said it was time to walk away. The thought alone left a dull ache in his heart, but the back and forth wasn't fun.

Out of the shower, he pulled on shorts and a t-shirt before wandering into the kitchen to tackle the dishes. His head a little clearer after the tumultuous evening, he resigned himself to letting her go. She didn't want to be caught.

After the dishes were done, he dropped onto the couch. As wound up as he was, sleep wasn't going to happen for a while, so he picked up the controller. Before starting a round, he picked up his phone and noticed that she'd texted him over an hour before.

He set the phone down. Reading it would only get him stirred up. He stared at the phone as his match started. Not reading it would make him crazy.

He opened her text and read it. Could she sense from down the street that he'd fallen off her hook?

But one sentence stood out from all the rest. *I'm afraid of letting you get close.*

If she couldn't get past that, the relationship had no future.

He tapped out a text and hit send before starting a new round. *I forgive you.*

Marisa's phone beeped, and she grabbed it off the nightstand. The short response was so much less than she'd hoped for. She sent a follow-up message: *Maybe we could walk tomorrow evening? I'd need a ride to the trailhead.*

She squeezed her eyes closed, willing herself not to start crying. He'd taken so long to respond and said so little.

Seconds later, her phone beeped again.

*I'm not sure that's a good idea.*

Marisa pulled the covers over her head and sobbed. What had she done? More importantly, what should she do?

# CHAPTER 43

## *Friday, June 24*

Miller waved a piece of paper in front of Ben. "Torres, did you hear anything I just said?"

"Sorry. What? Marisa was in an accident last night. It's got me scattered today." Ben didn't want to explain that it had gone sour.

"Take the day off."

He shook his head and focused on the job. "Show me the lab results." He'd made a decision, and unless something drastic changed, he planned to continue in that mindset.

Marisa's office manager stood in the doorway. "Marisa. I heard about what happened to your car. Why don't you take the rest of the day off?"

"I'm just finishing up paperwork on the Wheeler house. My car is in the shop. Hopefully it won't take a month for it to get fixed."

"I insist, Marisa. Let me drive you home." She pointed to the door.

Marisa followed, given little choice in the matter.

When she arrived at the apartment, her front door hung open. She ran down the stairs and picked up a rock. Hesitantly, she pushed open the door. "Hello?"

"Marisa!" Her sister squealed and wrapped her in a hug.

Marisa dropped the rock behind her, hoping Lucia hadn't noticed it. "I thought you were flying in tomorrow?"

"Changed my plans. Got a rental and drove over to surprise you. I picked up your apartment key from Alex."

"He didn't mention that. You staying here?"

"Nah, I booked a hotel." Lucia handed Marisa a sealed envelope. "Oh, this was on your door."

"Let me change really quick." Marisa ran down the hall and opened the note.

*I'm so excited about our time together, I decided to forgive your unfaithfulness—for now.*

Not wanting to even think about it, Marisa tucked the note out of sight and changed out of her work clothes. She wasn't back in the living room a full minute before Lucia started asking questions.

"You okay? Something bothering you?" Even living miles away, Lucia hadn't forgotten how to read Marisa like a book, which bothered her to no end.

"I'm fine. Why?"

Lucia sat cross-legged on the sofa, a pillow hugged to her chest. "You dating anyone?"

"Why?"

"What's his name?"

"I'm not dating anyone." The words were so true they stung.

Lucia ran to the refrigerator and pulled out a bottle of nut brown ale. "You don't drink beer. Who'd you buy this for?"

Marisa remembered the surprise on Ben's face when she'd handed him the cold beer. "A neighbor. We had dinner."

"When?"

"Lucia, really. Why all these questions?"

Her sister eyed her. "But something's wrong."

"I'd rather not talk about it."

"After what happened with Paul, we talk about it. You worried us, Marisa. What's going on?" Lucia didn't even know the half of it.

Marisa resigned herself to letting her sister in on the secret. "Promise not to tell Alex."

"Maybe."

"Alex has a detective friend. He lives near here, and we've bumped into to each other a few times." That wasn't a complete representation of the truth, but it wasn't a lie.

"Why are you upset?" Lucia crossed her arms and looked so much like their mother, Marisa almost wanted to cry.

"He told me not to walk at night."

"Wise advice."

"You too?"

"It's a matter of safety, Marisa. It's not safe to walk alone at night. It stinks, but it's true."

Marisa filled a glass with water and downed half of it. "Will you let me finish? *Please.*"

"Okay."

"At dinner, he called me childish."

Lucia stifled a laugh. "That's what I'd call this. He sounds like he cares."

"Do you want to hear the story or not?" Marisa didn't appreciate the interruptions. Explaining what she'd done was hard enough.

"Go on."

"I messed up. He's a wonderful guy, who has been intentional about asking me out, protecting me. I like him, and it scares me. I keep waiting for him to show a side I haven't seen, to change the way Paul did." She lost it when Lucia wrapped Marisa in a hug.

After a few minutes of quiet, Lucia asked, "Have you apologized?"

Marisa nodded, wiping her eyes. "But it was too little too late. He's given up on me."

"Are you giving up on him?" Lucia's question was what Marisa needed to hear.

She shook her head. "No. It's my turn to chase. I'm just not sure what to do. I asked him out, and he said it wasn't a good idea."

"Ask again."

Marisa texted Ben: *Dinner tonight? I'll cook.*

⁓✳⁓

Ben read Marisa's text and was momentarily tempted to say yes. But, saying yes meant canceling plans with his family and given all that had happened, he wouldn't do that.

*Already have plans. Sorry.*

He didn't want her to think he was upset with her.

Another text popped up seconds later: *Will you give me a ride to Kate's tomorrow?*

Needing time to think about it, he didn't answer. All her invitations were making it hard to stick to the logical route.

# Chapter 44

*Saturday, June 25*

Ben held the phone to his ear as he fished keys out of his pocket. "Torres."

"This is Alex. You coming tonight?"

"Yes. As I said before and the time before that and the time before that, I'll be there. I took the day off, Alex. I'm coming." He planned to attend to the pre-wedding dinner, even though being around Marisa would be awkward at best, and possibly torturous. "Can I help with anything?"

"Yeah, I need a favor."

"What's up?"

"Any chance you could pick up my brothers from the airport? I'm trying to help Kate get ready for tonight. She's crazy nervous about everything being perfect." Though Alex tried to sound light-hearted, stress echoed in his voice.

"Only one problem. I don't know what they look like. You want me to hold a sign that says *Ramirez* in the San Antonio airport?"

"That brings me to the second favor."

From the tone of Alex's voice Ben guessed he wouldn't like the next request. "What?" He rubbed the back of his head.

"Marisa needs a ride. Take her with you. Her new place is—"

"What's the apartment number? Does she know I'm coming?"

"Three forty five. I'll call her. The flight arrives at three. Her car is in the shop. She had a small fender bender."

*Small fender bender?* She handed out convenient bits of information that didn't fully depict the truth.

"No problem. I'll run by and get her." Ben couldn't avoid picking her up without explaining everything that happened to Alex, and Ben did not want to do that. He should probably have responded to her text. "Text me after you talk to her."

He needed to be showered and dressed in twenty-five minutes, and he was ten minutes away from his apartment. Racing home, he wrestled with his excitement. He wanted to see her, there was little doubt about that, but the teasing and holding him at arm's length wasn't what he wanted.

And who knew what landmines awaited him.

Marisa answered the phone, still wrapped in a towel. "Hello?"

Her brother skipped the hellos and cut straight to the point. "Ben's on his way to pick you up. You're going with him to pick up Nico and Sam."

"I'm not ready." Her heart raced.

"Then get ready. He'll be there at two."

She had to play her part to keep her brother from picking up on her excitement. "I thought *you* were coming to pick me up. You said four o'clock."

"Kate needs my help, besides Ben lives right there by you. You're practically neighbors."

Panic grabbed her. "What has he said to you?"

Alex chuckled. "Get dressed, Marisa. You have thirty minutes."

She tossed the phone on the bed and gathered what she needed for the party, all the while, deciding how to win Ben's affections.

Ben walked up the stairs. Outside her apartment, he raised his hand to knock, but the door swung open before he had a chance.

"Hello, Detective." Her long, dark hair, normally sleek and straight, hung loose around her shoulders in natural waves. She'd never worn it like that before.

He'd give her a ride to the party and try to enjoy the evening. The back and forth between them left him feeling like a ping-pong ball. "Please, just call me Ben."

"I'll think about it. Let me just grab my purse and clothes." Her long, tanned legs, accented by her white shorts, carried her down the hall. "It's nice of you to do this. I could've picked them up, but my car is in the shop," she called out from the other room.

"I know that, Marisa. I saw the *fender bender* happen." He glanced around the sparsely furnished apartment. "I'm sorry I used the word childish." He swallowed the other words he wanted to say.

Accusing her of playing catch and release wouldn't set the right tone for the day.

An orange tabby kitten tore up the hall, back arched, ready for battle.

"Hey, there, little guy." Ben picked up a ribbon with a crinkle toy attached and dangled it above Marisa's little roommate, who balanced on his hind legs batting and swatting the ribbon. Then, without warning, he flipped to his back and grabbed the toy, rabbit-kicking and biting his captured prey. Ben reached down, and the cat attacked. Ben scooped up the fuzz ball and scratched him behind the ears to avoid getting a scratched-up hand. The kitten squinted blue eyes and purred.

Marisa stopped at the end of the hall, mesmerized by the scene before her. Ben nuzzled the kitten, who purred in response. Everything about this guy, she liked.

She'd subconsciously wrecked things when she started to believe he might actually care. That fact that he was still around confounded her, but realizing how much it ached to have him pull away, she made a decision.

Watching his cuddle moment with the kitten warmed parts of

her heart she thought were permanently frozen. He wanted to take care of her. She'd scraped by the last three years on her own, convincing herself that she didn't need taking care of. But it was deeper than that. She didn't want to need anyone. She'd been hurt. Everyone she needed left or pulled away. If she let him play the role he wanted—protector—would he disappear soon after? Was that all he wanted?

She knew it wasn't.

She wanted him to care about her, not the nice-girl version or the naughty-girl version. And she wanted to know that he'd stick around. Seeing him with her kitten sparked a risky idea. *Be yourself. Trust him. Let him get close.*

*Don't give up on him.*

The real Marisa like to shake things up, see how people reacted. Would he still want that person? How he responded could change everything.

She dropped her bag near the front door and draped her garment bag over a chair. "What have you told my brother about *us*?"

Ben coughed, and the kitten jumped from his arms. "Besides the night he gave me your number, nothing."

She'd learned something new already. "Did you ask for it?"

"I already had it. Keeping our dates a secret wasn't easy."

"You felt bad?" She slowly moved toward him, without breaking eye contact.

His sentences tumbled out and tiny beads of sweat appeared on his forehead. "He's a friend. So, a little. I don't know."

She crowded his personal space, standing close enough that their shoes touched. "You met Tito."

His grandmother would have said it the same way, with a long e sound, her tongue glancing off the consonants as if they were barely there.

He spilled the first words he could string together. "Short for *gatito*?"

*What's with all the questions?* Interrogation was his job.

Delight danced on Marisa's high cheek bones. "You're the first one that's correctly guessed his name."

*Of course Marisa named her kitten the Spanish word for little cat.*

"I've heard how Bureau got his name. I went out on a limb."

The Ramirez family had an interesting way of naming pets, and Marisa, in particular, had an interesting way of… everything.

She nodded toward the bag. "I'm taking stuff I need for tonight, so I can change at Kate's. Do you mind giving me a ride out to Schatzenburg?" She grabbed a canister of kibble off the table.

"Not at all. Nothing would—" He caught himself a little too late but didn't finish his quip. When she bent down to fill the cat bowl the same way she did when she'd retrieved the chips, Ben turned around, convinced nothing she did was without intention. "We should probably leave soon."

She startled him when she leaned over his shoulder and whispered in his ear. "I frustrate you, don't I?"

He spun to face her. "Do you practice moving silently through the apartment?" He rubbed his face.

"Do you find me annoying?" She inched closer. "Stupid? Cheap?"

"No. I don't think that you're—I don't think that." He didn't realize he was backing up until he bumped into the door.

Perfectly shaped eyebrows arched over glittering green eyes. Wearing white canvas tennis shoes, she stood three inches shorter but towered over him. Her smile proclaimed victory, but he was still foggy on the battle itself.

"Good."

Something had shifted. He didn't know what, but he liked it. "I find you unforgettable, brave, and maddening, in all the best ways." He'd said way too much if he wanted to cool things off, but put on the spot, he couldn't help himself.

Her eyes went wide, and delight danced a pirouette in the vivid green.

Thrilled by the possibility of what her delight implied, he leaned in close. "We should go. I'll carry that bag."

"It's a little heavy."

It was a lot heavy.

~*~

Marisa followed him down the stairs, relishing his response. Watching him back up, flustered, amused her more than it should have. Almost always controlled with an air of quiet authority, he'd definitely dropped his guard in that conversation, if only for a little bit. And she liked him all the more for it. When he backed against the door, honesty spilled out, and she loved his answer. Guessing her cat's name, under pressure no less, won him loads of points too.

She danced a finger along one of the lines on his dress shirt. "Thank you."

"For what?"

"Paying for my gas, saving me from the bad guy, staying with me while they cleared the accident, giving me a ride, but mostly, for being honest."

He dropped the bag in the backseat. "Why am I being interrogated?" The air of authority was back in force.

"Oh, Detective." Marisa rubbed non-existent wrinkles out of the front of his shirt, enjoying the feel of what lay hidden underneath. "We should probably hurry. You don't want to be late picking up my brothers. They'll be thrilled to meet you."

Her words sounded like a veiled threat. *What is she up to?*

The ride to the airport was quiet. Too quiet. The silence rattled Ben. He wasn't sure what to expect when he met her brothers. He liked the saucy, flirty, strong Marisa, but wasn't sure what she'd say or do next. Eight years his junior and more independent than a two-year-old after fists full of candy, she captivated him.

In the airport parking garage, she jumped out before he had a chance to open her door, then grabbed his hand as they walked into baggage claim. When he glanced at her, she looked away. Nothing in the world made him want to let her go.

He stopped near the luggage carousels. She continued toward the walkway, their fingers still intertwined. As they slipped apart, she glanced back over her shoulder and winked.

He filed her behavior under drastic change. Letting things cool off was no longer his plan.

Marisa dodged people as she hurried to greet her brothers. They looked enough like Alex that Ben might've been able to pick them out of a crowd, but he was happy she'd come along, for many reasons, even if he didn't understand most of them.

In turn, her brothers each lifted her off the ground in a hug. Animated, she waved her hands talking, then pointed to where Ben waited. He smiled as they walked toward him.

"Nico, Sam. This is Alex's friend, Detective Torres. He likes people to call him Ben." Marisa grinned, a teasing glimmer dancing in her eyes. The disconnect was gone; what showed on her face danced in her eyes.

"Thanks for getting us." Nico hurried toward a carousel as his bags emerged from the back.

Sam slapped him on the back. "Alex sounded a little frayed. I think Kate's got him running in circles."

"And he loves every minute of it." Ben had seen firsthand what lengths Alex would go to for Kate. Planning a dinner party hardly compared.

Marisa slipped her arm through Ben's, gripping his bicep. "You really think that?"

"It's what I've observed." Conscious of her brothers' looks, he moved away from her and picked up one of the suitcases.

Marisa smirked. "Everyone follow the detective."

He wasn't sure if she was flirting with him or toying with him. Whichever it was, he didn't hold the upper hand.

*Putty, that's what you are.*

Marisa chatted with her brothers as they walked to the car, letting her fingers brush against Ben's hand until he looped a finger through hers. She rewarded him with a smile.

On the way out of town, her brothers talked about how much the city had changed in three years. Story after story about their growing up years filled the time. She'd heard most of the stories before, more than once.

As they neared the hotel, she focused on the detective. "They like you." She kept her voice low enough that her brothers couldn't hear over their own conversation.

He rubbed the back of his buzzed head. "That's good, I guess."

"Oh, it's very good."

~*~

As Ben pulled into the hotel lot, Nico pointed toward the covered driveway near the double doors. "Don't park. Just drop us off."

Nico and Sam piled out of the backseat and grabbed their bags from the trunk.

Marisa rolled down the passenger side window. "We'll come get you in about an hour." She turned toward Ben. "Won't we?"

"Yeah. Sure." He waited until her brothers disappeared inside before he pulled away.

As he navigated the back roads to Kate's place, Marisa was quiet, until she wasn't. "Ben, if you don't like it, I can stop."

His head throbbed, and he tried to decide how to answer. "It's not that I don't like it. I'm just not used to—"

"I know, and that makes it so fun." She turned to face him, adjusting her seat belt. "I interrupted you, sorry. You were saying?"

"I'd been the one doing the chasing. But now..." He tried to imagine how she'd interpret his words.

"And you don't like that."

"On the contrary. I chased because it was my way of showing that I was making the effort to see you, trying to win your affections."

"But you stopped chasing." Her words held regret more than sadness.

He hesitated to state his hopes. "With the tables turned, I want to assume your reasons are the same."

She trailed a finger down his arm. "They are."

*What happened?*

He'd pretty much just told her he wanted her, not that he hadn't before. But she'd said almost the same, which left him almost giddy, like a crushing schoolboy who'd been kissed.

At Kate's, Ben grabbed Marisa's bag and swung it over his shoulder. She opened her own door, but he held out a hand.

One finger, tipped in red, slid up his palm before she clutched his hand. "Chivalry isn't dead, I guess." She pointed into the backseat. "My dress is in the garment bag. I need that too. Otherwise, I'd have nothing to wear."

"I'll get it." He retrieved her clothes and followed her to the back door.

Alex pulled it open before they even knocked. "Come in. Any trouble?"

*Trouble? She is—in the best kind of way.*

Ben dropped the bag and opened his arms as Kate walked toward him. "None at all. It was good that Marisa came with me, though." He'd gotten used to Kate's hugs. And though he'd never had one, Kate felt like a little sister—Marisa, on the other hand, not so much.

"Thank you. I wouldn't have been ready if Alex hadn't stayed." Kate pulled Ben close again.

He glanced around. "Everything looks perfect. Anything I can do?"

Marisa hung back, but her gaze bored holes in the back of his head.

"No, don't think so, but if I think of anything, I'll let you know." Kate turned toward Marisa. "I'm so glad you made it. Sorry to hear about your fender bender."

"I wouldn't miss it." Marisa embraced Kate, making their seven-inch height difference more noticeable. "Where should I put my stuff? I hope you don't mind me getting ready here."

"I don't mind at all." Kate pointed down the hall. "Use my room."

Marisa stifled a grunt as she heaved her bag onto her shoulder. Ben had made it look easy to carry.

"I can get it for you." He stepped up next to her, his voice quiet, soft.

She ignored him, lugging her bag into the hall.

He stepped in front of her. "Give me the bag, Marisa." The gruffness of tone contrasted with the playfulness in his eyes.

Very aware of Kate and Alex watching the exchange, Marisa resisted the urge to kiss him and kept her voice at a whisper. "Yes, sir." She cocked an eyebrow and dropped the bag near his feet, barely missing his toes.

He leaned in close before bending down to pick it up. "See? It's not so hard to let me help."

"Really, Detective?" She followed him down the hall.

He set her bag on the bed and hung the dress on the open door. "I should head back out there, so you can do whatever it is you need to do."

Marisa stepped up close. "You afraid they are talking about us?"

"I'm afraid of a lot of things." He smirked and slipped past her, then marched down the hall without looking back.

She watched his retreat until she noticed her brother's grin. Alex winked at her, and she closed the bedroom door, toppling her dress to the floor.

In Kate's room, Marisa put on her make-up, changed clothes, and styled her hair. Keeping tabs on the time, she made sure to stay out of sight until it was time to go get her brothers from the hotel. She'd given a lot of thought about what she should wear to the dinner, knowing the detective would be there. She smiled at her reflection, anticipating that boyish stare.

Ben waited outside, checking the time. He didn't want to be late picking up her brothers. Pacing near his Jetta, he swung the keys in a circle around his finger.

The back door creaked. Marisa slipped out the door, floral fabric dancing in rhythm to her steps. His keys clattered to the ground. There were no sunglasses to block his stare, nor did he care to.

Without a word, he rushed over to the passenger side and pulled open the door. Her loose-fitting dress brushed her curves as she moved. The scent of pomegranates washed over him as he helped her into the car.

After he buckled into the driver's seat, he recovered the use of his tongue. "You look—Wow." For all his looking, he hadn't noticed her shoes. White, strappy heels showed off red toenails. "Right down to your toes."

"You're staring at me, Detective." She ran her finger down the side of his cheek. "Shouldn't we go?"

He grinned stupidly, stalling his car twice before he made it to the main road. She was all kinds of distracting, and he was reveling in every minute. "I'm not sure what changed, Marisa. I mean, you're still like you were the first day we met, but something's changed."

"I opened my eyes."

"What?" He didn't understand her meaning.

She smiled. "I meant every word of that apology. And I know you forgave me, but I thought you'd given up on me."

Guilt pounded in his chest. He had. "Marisa, I—"

"It's okay, Ben. You hung around much longer than any sane person would have."

"What are you trying to say?" He winked, trying to make sure she knew he was teasing.

She waited until he stopped and kissed his cheek. "Thank you. I'm crazy about you, too."

Nico and Sam were waiting outside and jumped into the backseat as soon as Ben pulled to a stop.

"Sorry we're a couple minutes late." He shifted and started back toward Kate's.

"Alex texted that you were on your way." Nico poked his sister. "What's Kate like? Will we like her?"

"First of all, you have no choice but to like her. Alex is going to marry her. And second, she's fantastic. You'll love her." Marisa leaned between the seats, looking back at her brothers.

Sam met Ben's gaze in the rearview mirror. "What say you?"

"I haven't known either of them long, but watching the two of them together over the last few months, through some pretty rough stuff, I'd have to say she's perfect for him."

"But is she nice? Or is he blinded by *love*?"

"Kate's great. I really do think y'all will like her." Ben took advantage of the minutes between needing to shift and rested his hand on Marisa's. "Marisa is right. You should trust her judgment."

That comment earned him a delighted smile.

Lucia drove up just as they arrived at Kate's. Ben hung back, giving Alex's brothers time to meet Kate, letting the family have a few minutes before other guests arrived.

"I'll be inside in a bit." Walking down the driveway, he breathed in deep, hoping the evening would go smoothly. Meeting Marisa's entire family made the whole situation more complicated.

Killing time, he texted Gracie: *It's possible she is interested.*

His sister-in-law's reply made him laugh: *Squee! Details?*

Ben wasn't about to jinx the progress. *Not yet.*

She responded: *I'm happy for you.*

He strolled around to the front porch and made it to the top step before he heard the swing move.

Marisa's bare feet brushed along the porch. When had she shed her shoes? "Sit with me?"

"Marisa—"

"I'm just inviting you to sit for a minute, not asking for a commitment."

He sat down next to her, not completely opposed to the latter.

She stared down at his hand, her pinky finger barely brushing against his. "Until we figure this out—if there is a this—can we keep it between us? I know I was teasing earlier, but—is that okay?"

"What about your brothers?"

"They've seen me tease before."

"Is that all this is?" Ben laid his hand on hers.

Brown curls danced on her shoulders as she shook her head. "No, not for me."

"What changed?"

"It's never been teasing, Ben."

He raised his eyebrows and chuckled. "I meant about keeping it between us. From when I picked you up to now."

"If there is something, I want it to be because I'm me, not because you're friends with Alex and Kate. When we got back and everyone was here, I worried that maybe—I need to know that's not the reason."

"If you want to keep it quiet, I will." He squeezed her hand. It hopefully made for fewer questions.

She glanced down at his hand and forced a smile, clearly misinterpreting what he'd said. "Good."

"And, Marisa,"—he brought her fingers to his lips.—"you are the only reason."

She met his gaze. "I want to believe that." Secrets and hurt still lay buried in her dark eyes, but she'd tell him when she was ready.

Content, he'd have stayed there next to her on the swing for hours, but DJ and Becca's car heading up the street signaled an end to the private conversation. "Other guests are arriving. If Becca sees us holding hands, it'll crush her dreams of you dating Phillip."

Red lips curved into a wide smile. "Jealous, Detective?"

Ben winked as she pushed open the front door.

During dinner, Marisa watched Ben talk and laugh with her brothers and everyone else around the table. The feeling she had when she'd spotted him cuddling Tito multiplied. He fit seamlessly with her family.

When everyone finished eating, the ladies cleared plates from the table.

Lucia pulled Marisa aside while Becca and Kate served dessert. "Your detective is good looking."

"You promised, Lucia. Please don't say anything." Marisa kept her voice to a whisper.

"No one needs me to say anything. I'd guess he hasn't given up. It's written all over his face. And yours." Lucia flashed a wicked grin and strolled away before Marisa could think of a snappy response.

Not scooting close to Ben and holding his hand while chatting proved to be the hardest part of the evening. Next to him was where she wanted to be.

At the end of the evening, as people said goodbyes, Lucia hugged Marisa. "I'm taking Nico and Sam back to the hotel. Enjoy the rest of your night."

Instead of protesting, Marisa said, "Thank you."

On the way back to San Antonio, she stared out the window. The car grew quiet. Marisa hesitated to break the silence, knowing she needed to tell him about the stalker. Fear that the news would change how he felt kept her quiet.

"Hard to believe they're getting married in three weeks." Ben let go of the stick shift and reached for her hand.

"I just knew everyone would love Kate. She's great for Alex. He needed someone like her."

"I think she needed him, too. And I don't mean to take care of her."

"It takes a lot to admit that you need someone or that you want to be needed." She inhaled ready to spill the truth. "Ben—"

"Marisa."

The words tumbled out at the same time.

He tapped her hand. "Go ahead."

She took the opportunity to delay telling him. "No. You go ahead. Please."

He flashed her that irresistible smile. "Whatever changed, I'm glad. And on that note, would you be my date for the wedding?"

"Yes. I'd love that."

"It won't be a secret after that."

She kissed his hand. "It'll be fun to see the reaction."

"You working tomorrow?"

"Tomorrow is Sunday. But, no, I don't have any appointments tomorrow." She answered, unsure of where the line of questioning was headed.

"On Monday, do you need me to give you a ride to the office? Since your car is in the shop?"

"Thank you, *Ben*. Yes. That'd be great. Is six too early?" She didn't always go in early, but getting in before the office was busy allowed her more time to get things done.

With him driving her to work, she'd be safer. Maybe telling him could wait a day or two.

He pulled into her complex and parked. Before giving her an answer, he jumped out and ran around to open her door. "I can be here by five 'til."

After she stepped out, he hoisted her bag onto his shoulder and followed her up the stairs. At her door, she unlocked the apartment, then took the bag from him.

"You want to come in, Ben?" She wasn't ready to say goodbye.

Although he loved the thought of snuggling up next to her and chatting over a cup of coffee, she needed time to be absolutely sure of what she wanted. If it was more than a game, she'd still be chasing on Monday morning.

"Can I get a raincheck?" He squeezed her hand. "I enjoyed today."

"I did, too. And, yes. Just say when." The door closed, and she peeked out the window.

He lingered outside her door a moment before trotting down the stairs.

As he ran down, he laughed at himself. He'd wanted her to call him Ben, and now that she did, he missed being called detective.

Monday morning couldn't arrive fast enough.

# CHAPTER 45

*Sunday, June 26*

His thoughts dominated by Marisa, Ben woke up early and decided a run would clear his head.

After running a few miles, he unlocked his apartment. Sweaty and nasty, he was still thinking about her.

He could only know if she'd really changed if he spent time with her, so he picked up his phone and texted, hoping it wasn't too early.

Marisa smiled at the message on her screen: *I want to see you today.*

She had no doubt Ben remembered the question she'd asked him in his apartment, and so she texted: *Are you sure that's what you want?*

He replied: *Can I pick you up in thirty minutes?*

She jumped out of bed after sending a reply: *I'll be ready.*

While putting on makeup, she tried to decide what to wear. As early as it was, maybe they'd hike before the sun blasted heat down on every visible surface. Where did he want to go? She dressed in shorts, an off-the-shoulder top, and her canvas tennis shoes—an outfit suitable for almost any activity, even walking. But, just in case he had something else planned, she switched to a large purse and tucked a sundress and strappy sandals inside.

She smiled when footsteps sounded in the breezeway but waited for Ben to knock and peeked out the window before opening the door. "Hello, Detective."

"Ready?"

"Where are we going?" She tangled her fingers with his when he offered his hand.

"I thought we might go to the zoo, ride the train, and then find a quiet place to have dinner at the end of our day. That okay?"

"Sounds fun." She loved the part about dinner. Spending all day with him appealed to her for a hundred or more reasons. "I haven't ridden the train in ages."

"We can walk the Sunken Gardens as well, if we have time." He opened her door when they got to his car.

She caught his hand when he slid behind the wheel. "I'm glad you texted this morning."

~*~

As they walked through the zoo, Ben spent more time watching Marisa's reaction to the animals than he did watching the animals themselves. Elephants could have stampeded down the sidewalk, and he might not have noticed.

Together, they strolled the walkway, her finger looped on his pinky. Being led around by his little finger cemented his feelings and fueled his desires.

When they got to the lorry exhibit, she grinned. "Let's go in and feed the lorries."

"Is that what those birds are called?"

"Yep."

"Never knew that." He'd do just about anything to make her happy, so he bought two nectar cups.

As soon as they stepped inside, they were immediately accosted by the brightly-colored creatures.

He held out his cup. "You can hold both of them."

She handed him her bag and held a nectar cup in each hand.

Birds alighted on her hands and head, slurping nectar out of the tiny containers. Ben snapped a series of pictures, not that he'd need them to remember the moment.

When the birds emptied her cups, they fluttered around. He ducked when one of the birds landed on his head, hoping for more treats.

Marisa laughed and shooed away the beggar. "Don't worry, Detective. I'll protect you." She wrapped her arms around him. "You're safe with me."

Ben leaned close and whispered in her ear, "I feel like I'm falling." It might have been the cheesiest and truest thing he'd ever uttered.

Her green eyes sparkled, the pain that used to hide in the sea of green less noticeable but not gone. She kissed his cheek and pulled him toward the exit. "Now I want to see the butterflies."

When they passed a restaurant, Ben stopped. "What do you say we have lunch first?"

"Sure." She stepped closer. "I'm really enjoying myself."

He wrapped his arms around her, and if the preschooler sitting on the bench licking on a drippy popsicle hadn't been staring at them, he'd have kissed Marisa right in the middle of the walkway. Because of the audience, he delayed that first kiss.

Once inside, they read over the menu, her hand still in his. He ordered them lunch, and they found an empty table.

"I regret all the times I torpedoed our dates." She picked at her salad.

Ben reached across the table and took her hand. "When you texted the other night, you said you were afraid of letting me get close."

"I was afraid that if you knew me and all the stupid choices I've made, you'd walk away."

He needed to know that she'd chosen to move beyond her fears. "And now?" He waited for her answer, knowing it would affect how he acted the rest of the day.

She tightened her grip on his hand. "Ask me anything. I'll tell you whatever you want to know. You're still here, and I can't explain what that means to me." She met his gaze. "I won't run away. I'm not giving up on you."

He kissed her fingers. "Eat. We have butterflies to see."

Hours later, after a stroll among the butterflies and a walk through the Sunken Gardens, when they climbed onto the train, Ben steered the conversation in a more serious direction again. She promised she wouldn't run away, but she couldn't while they were on a moving train.

"The other night, you asked me what I wanted."

She looped her arm through his and snuggled close as the train wove through Brackenridge Park. "I shouldn't ha—."

"Let me finish." Ben shot her a sideways glance. "I want a partner. Don't tell Miller. He'd be hurt."

Marisa rested her head on his shoulder and tightened her hold on his arm. As they wove through trees and bumped along the tracks, she didn't speak.

Summoning every ounce of patience available, he waited.

Inside the dark tunnel, a whisper tickled his ear. "I want you."

He squeezed the hand wrapped around his arm, and neither said a word until the train pulled back into the station.

Ben tapped her leg. "Want to ride it again?"

"I'm a little hungry."

"Then we'll go eat."

After getting off the train, Marissa excused herself to the ladies' room and changed into her sundress and sandals. Changing in the park bathroom wasn't exactly optimal but worth the reaction she expected.

When she walked out, Ben pulled off his sunglasses. His jaw hung open a few seconds before he spoke. "Wow. What other surprises do you have in that bag?"

She grinned. "I wasn't sure what you had planned today. I wanted to be properly dressed."

"Well, you look amazing." He caught her finger with his pinky. "You did even before you changed."

Marisa stopped at the passenger door and let him open it. The smile it earned her was worth it. She smoothed her dress as he climbed behind the wheel. "Where to next?"

"What do you think about one of the Brazilian steakhouses for dinner?" Ben turned out of the lot.

"Delicious." She watched him while he shifted and navigated traffic.

The turn the relationship had taken in the last twenty-four hours anchored her to the truth she'd been afraid to admit for so long. She wanted things to work out with Ben. With each wall she let down, he raced closer.

At the restaurant, they followed the host to a table tucked in a corner, the perfect spot to finish off their day.

Marisa glanced around the restaurant. "It smells divine in here."

"Depending on how my workday goes tomorrow, maybe we can get together for dinner or something."

"Working? On Monday?"

"I'm covering shifts Monday and Tuesday."

"Dinner sounds good. I'd like that."

With plates in hand, they made their way around the salad buffet. While Ben was still adding to his plate, she headed back to the table. She stopped when Paul stepped in front of her.

"Marisa." Icy, his tone instilled fear.

"Leave me alone, Paul." She managed to keep any waver out of her voice.

"That's not very nice. I mean, we were close … once. Looks like you've moved on." He stared over her shoulder. "Protective—if I remember correctly."

She didn't need to turn around to know he was talking about Ben.

～＊～

Ben's blood ran cold when he noticed Paul blocking Marisa's path to the table.

Drawing in a deep breath, keeping his temper in check, Ben touched her back as he stepped close. "This man bothering you, Marisa?"

Paul bore daggers into Ben. "She didn't think that before."

"Leave us alone, or I'll call the police." Marisa clutched Ben's hand and pushed past her ex.

Paul, whose sneer made a tempting target, bumped Ben as he passed. "Good luck. She's a feisty one."

Marisa's grip tightened around his fingers.

Ben ignored Paul and pulled out her chair. "He's not worth it."

Paul sauntered away, the smug grin still etched on his wrinkled face.

Ben hoped that man would get sent away for several years when the case was decided, but it would be a while before the case went to trial. Until then, with Paul out on bail, Ben hoped her ex had the sense to leave her alone.

She reached for his hand, which he considered a small victory. She hadn't bolted out of the room. "I'm sorry, Ben."

"Look at me."

She glanced up, her eyes red but dry.

"*You* didn't do anything wrong." He pulled her hand to his lips. "And I happen to like your brand of feisty."

Her fingers tightened around his hand. "I'm not running away." Whether she was promising him or trying to convince herself didn't matter. The words were music to his ears. She was still next to him, hopefully trusting him. "You don't deserve that. It's because of my past."

"It's not your fault Paul is who he is." He flipped over his card, letting the waiter know he wanted meat. "Let's eat."

During the rest of dinner, they chatted and ate, savoring the cuts of meat, enjoying the never-ending offerings. Touching his arm and sharing stories, she settled back into the intimate companionship they'd shared earlier.

When they'd had their fill of meat, they made room for dessert and split a crème brûlée. Her spoon loaded with a sugar-topped bite of sweet goodness, she held it out, offering it to him. He opened his mouth. That bite tasted better than all the rest.

Ben paid the check, trying to think of ways to extend the evening.

As they walked out to the car, he slipped an arm around her waist. "Thank you for saying yes this morning. I can't remember when I've had a better day."

"I don't want it to end." She'd snatched the words off the tip of his tongue.

All the way home, when he wasn't shifting gears, Ben held her hand. "So, think you'll go out with me again?" He hoped she caught his attempt at humor.

"Uh, yeah." She laughed. "In case I haven't been clear, I like you, Detective."

Ben squeezed her hand before reaching for the gear shift. When they arrived at her complex, he walked with her up to her apartment.

When she got to the door, instead of unlocking it, she leaned back against it. Moonbeams danced in her eyes. "Thank you for dinner and … everything." She licked her lips.

She wanted to be kissed. An invitation hovered in her eyes, in her stance, in the tilt of her head. She gazed at him, her lips parted ever so little. And Ben wanted to oblige her, to feel her body against his, and much more than that.

He stepped closer and slipped an arm around her waist.

She arched her back and pressed into him. "You want to come in?"

Her question asked much more than that. While the thought of what lay hidden beneath her dress set his insides ablaze, his desire stemmed more from the connection he felt with her. Like the sun on a wintery, grey day, he craved her, wanted her, not only in his bed, but in his life. His heart pounded with anticipation. As he leaned in close to answer with a kiss, the moonlight glinted off the green in her eyes, a feature that reminded him of her family ties and the cabin.

*Sampling the goods.*

Ben couldn't sleep with her, not yet, but his ability to walk away would diminish the moment their lips touched.

"Stay. With me." Her words danced on the breeze, teasing him.

"Not tonight, but I'll be right back here bright and early." He pulled both of her hands to his lips. "Sweet dreams, Marisa."

Marisa slipped her hands out of his and looped her arms around him, letting her fingertips dance along the nape of his neck. All of him said yes, except his lips.

"I don't understand you, Detective. I might just have to hang around until I do."

"Please do." He pulled her close. His arms said he wanted to stay, but his lips said, "Goodnight."

She turned, still wrapped in an embrace, and unlocked the door. Before stepping inside, she leaned back into him. "Until morning."

She slipped out of his arms and closed the door before the buttons fell off her dress.

# Chapter 46

*Monday, June 27*

Ben laid the bouquet of sunflowers in the passenger seat and drove to Marisa's apartment, hoping he'd catch every light just right. Who knew buying flowers that early in the morning would take so long?

When he got to her door, he hid the flowers behind him and knocked.

She opened the door, her hair pinned up in an unruly twist, her face stained with tears.

Panic gripped him. "What's wrong?"

She stepped back and motioned him in.

He was all the way in the apartment before he remembered the flowers. "These are for you."

Her lips moved like she wanted to smile. "Thank you. I'll put them in water."

"Why are you upset?" He followed her to the kitchen.

"After what Paul did—stealing stuff from the houses I had listed—I was put on review at the office while the higher ups investigated." She inhaled and clamped down her jaw as she slowly exhaled. "It'd been so long, I thought everything was fine, but I was dismissed. I checked mail this morning. The letter must've arrived on Saturday. It said that even though I'd broken no laws, my behavior was inconsistent with their expectations." She wiped her eyes.

"I'm sorry. You checked mail this morning? How long have you been up?"

"Don't ask." She stepped toward him and hovered her hand near his shirt. "Please don't say anything. Please. Not right before the wedding. Alex will only worry about me. They all will."

"I won't." He leaned down to pet Tito, who wove himself between Ben's legs. "Listen, I don't have to be in the office for a while. Want to grab some breakfast?"

"You want me to go out of the house looking like this?" She stared at Ben like he had popcorn coming out his ears, but wearing sweats and a threadbare t-shirt, she looked just as stunning as the day they'd met, as enchanting as last night.

He wiped tears off her cheek. "Seriously, Marisa? You're gorgeous, no matter how you are dressed."

She blinked at him like he'd just told her she won the lottery. "I'll put shoes on."

All the way to the restaurant, Marisa closed her eyes, reliving the moment over and over. Gone was the little boy awe, replaced with something passionate and mesmerizing. At her worst, he called her gorgeous, but his words didn't feel like an assessment of her looks.

At each stop sign and stoplight, he glanced her way. "It'll be okay."

"I know." And she did. She didn't know how or when, but she believed him, except when she thought about telling her oldest brother.

At the restaurant, the hostess showed them to a table and flashed a sympathetic smile as Marisa slid into a booth. Ben sat down next to her, and she leaned her head on his shoulder. The most natural thing in the world, she rested on him, content to just be with him.

The waitress hurried over from across the room, smirking, until she stepped up to the table. Her expression changed when she saw Marisa upset.

"What can I get y'all?" The waitress focused on Ben.

"Two coffees and two specials, one with extra bacon." He handed over the menus, then turned his attention to Marisa. He brushed her cheek again. Perhaps he recognized the power in that simple gesture. "After breakfast, why don't you drop me at work? Keep my car for the day. If you can drive a stick?"

"I can. Is this your way of guaranteeing that you'll see me again later?" Playful and snarky was part of who she was. Being herself around him came easier after the all-day date.

"You can see right through me." He put his arm around her.

"How could I have been so stupid? I drank in his attentions like a parched fool. I thought I'd captured his affections, but he was just using me." She wiped her face but didn't dare look at Ben. Dropping the truth before coffee was likely the worst idea she'd ever had. "It was horrible when he put my friends in danger, but now even my livelihood is gone."

The conversation had ventured into territory that frustrated Ben. It dredged up all the regrets he had about not protecting her from Paul's abuse. Seeing Paul last night hadn't diminished how Ben felt about Marisa. It had multiplied it. He didn't harbor judgement against her, but the idea of abuse haunted him. He tensed, picturing Paul's hands pawing at her, leaving bruises.

"I'm sorry. You probably don't want to hear about that." She dabbed her eyes with the napkin. "I understand if you've changed your mind about me."

He gazed at her, with her tangled mess of brown hair, glistening green eyes, and flawless skin. Flashes of her braving a trip to the police station, knowing the risk, and of her hugging the panhandler after buying him dinner—those images framed Ben's view of her. Marisa was the girl Ben wanted to take home and introduce to his parents.

"My mind is made up." He kissed the side of her head. The scent of pomegranates filled his senses. The thought of waking up to that on his chest each morning made him smile.

"You aren't anything like him. Not a bit. He was old and showy, slick and loud."

"Let's ignore the old part. When I was a senior, you were still in elementary school. And maybe we should watch a Spurs game together before you assume I'm quiet."

"I don't even know how old you are."

"Thirty-three."

She almost grinned. "Wow. You are old."

The waitress set their coffees on the table. "Food will be out in a sec."

"Thanks."

Once the waitress was out of earshot, Marisa shifted. "Who's going to hire me after this?"

"We'll figure it out." He wanted to take care of her. He wanted her to let him.

"*We?*" She drew invisible circles on the table with her finger.

"You and me, together." He thought of what she'd whispered in the dark tunnel.

Plates appeared in front of them as the waitress swooped in. "And the extra bacon." She set it in front of Ben. "Anything else?"

"We're good for now. Thanks." He slid the bacon to Marisa. "I'd take off the whole day if I could."

"I know you would, Detective, but I'm not the only one that needs you." She squeezed the hand resting on her shoulder. "Our city needs you out there."

They ate in silence, what he wanted to say coming together as a coherent thought. Once he'd cleaned his plate, he leaned back, watching her finish the stack of pancakes.

She smiled and broke off a piece of bacon. Holding it by his mouth, she popped it in when his lips parted. "I wish I'd met you before any of the others."

The rest of the restaurant disappeared. *Ask her.*

"Marry me. I mean—will you marry me?" All the back and forth didn't matter anymore. He wanted her in his life. "I love you, Marisa."

She choked on her coffee. "You're not joking." Scanning his face for any signs of teasing, she found only the same look he'd given her in the apartment.

"Not in the least. I don't have a ring, yet. I will, though. I know this is not taking it slow, and it sounds crazy." He held out his hand.

She slipped her fingers into his hand and nodded until she could string together a answer. "Yes. I'll marry you. But…"

"But what?" He pulled their joined hands to his lips and kissed her fingers.

"I want you, but not a wedding." She held her breath.

"So you don't want to get married? Are you asking me to live with you?"

"No, not at all. I mean … the dress, the fancy ceremony, the big reception … I don't want any of that."

"Okay. But why not?"

Focused on their joined fingers, she dropped her voice to a whisper. "My parents died the day after I graduated high school. Without them around to be part of it, I don't see a need for all the hubbub."

"No hubbub, then."

There was no question what she wanted—she'd told him—but she feared that somehow, she'd mess it all up. "Can we get married today?"

With the way she'd behaved, he might not want to rush into it, and she couldn't blame him.

"If we get the license today—I can meet you when I break for lunch—we can get married in three days. Whatever you want, Marisa. In a few days or in a year, it doesn't change the way I feel."

"I know what I want. I'd rather not wait." More than anything she wanted to taste his lips, sealing the deal, feeling his words. "Will you finally kiss me, Detective?"

Ben slid out of the booth, a grin stretching his cheeks. "Once we're married."

Her fingers still tangled with his, she waited next to him while he paid the check at the register. She'd never had anyone not kiss her. It had always been quite the opposite.

But kisses lingered in his gaze and danced in the brush of his fingertips. He had kissed her, but not in the ways she was used to. She wouldn't have painted him as the type to not kiss until the altar.

In the car, as he merged into traffic, she broached the topic again. "Why?"

～✳～

"What?" He glanced over his shoulder as he changed lanes.

"Kisses. Why the wait?"

He'd said it as a joke, returning her banter, but her expression changed his mind. "Is it a prerequisite?"

He longed to be what she wanted, and showing her that his love hinged on more than her beauty and her body became his priority. Her astonishment at his remark prodded him to show her love without kisses.

"No, but … I mean, it's different."

"I just proposed over bacon. We are well past different."

"Have you ever kissed anyone?"

"Yes, Marisa, I have. But you aren't anyone. What I did before doesn't matter. What you did before isn't an issue. This is about us."

"If you don't want to …"

He couldn't risk taking his eyes off traffic long enough to look at her. "I want to. Oh, how I want to."

A sweet gasp of anticipation wrapped around her words. "Oh, Detective."

At the station, he pulled up to the curb in front. On the sidewalk beside the car, he handed her the keys.

"This is where we met." She laid a hand on his cheek. "What if we surprised everyone? Please, can we not say anything?"

"Your brother's going to kill me."

"He gave you my number."

"He did indeed." Ben laughed. "Pretty sure this wasn't what he had in mind."

"Alex probably thought a strong, upright officer of the law like you would be good for me." She straightened his tie and left her hands resting on his chest.

*Good for her.* Alex had said the exact words.

Ben held happiness in his arms. He wanted to be the best for her, and she was what he needed. She challenged him, delighted him, and though she hadn't said the words out loud, she loved him.

"My brother was right. But let's not tell him I said that." She traced a heart over Ben's. "I've never been happier."

"Torres? You ever going to say goodbye and actually go into work?" Miller jingled keys in his pocket as he laughed. "Good to see you again, Marisa."

She smiled then whispered to Ben, "Just text me when you want me to come and meet you for *lunch*. You have my number with you?"

"I do. In my favorites."

She winked and ran around to the driver's seat.

Miller slapped Ben on the back. "Looks like someone had a busy night."

Ben set his jaw and breathed through the anger raised by the implication. "No. And the conversation is off-limits."

Miller clicked his tongue then laughed too loudly. "Torres, I've never seen you like this. I do believe you are smitten."

"Don't want to talk about it." Ben pushed opened the door, willing the hours to pass quickly.

~*~

Marisa ran through the grocery store buying what she needed for lunch. If she hurried, she could get food packed and make herself presentable before they met to get the license.

At the apartment, her friend, Lexi, waited by her door. Marisa unlocked it, juggling grocery bags.

"Hey, let me help you with those." Lexi took half the bags from Marisa.

"You aren't at work?"

"When you didn't show up this morning, I asked around and heard about what happened."

"Yeah. They were very clear about not coming back to the office. Said they'd ship me my stuff. The office manager must've known on Friday. That's why she sent me home early."

"Why don't we go have an early lunch in a bit? I took the day off."

"I can't. I have plans. Another day?"

Lexi poked through the bags. "What are you making?"

"Some stuff for lunch." Marisa braced for the next question, scrambling to think of an answer.

"For someone special?"

"Maybe."

"The guy from the food truck park? The one that was with the drunk girl?"

Glad her head was hidden by the refrigerator door, she allowed herself the smile bubbling from inside. "Hmmm?"

"Marisa! You didn't answer my question."

"I'm afraid talking about it might jinx something." She'd been honest with her friend but didn't give away the secret.

Ben paced outside the courthouse, checking the time on his phone. It wasn't even one yet. Away from her, he'd had ample time to sort fact from feeling. He rehearsed what he'd say when she arrived.

He glanced left and right, boring holes in the sidewalk waiting for her to show.

Her perfume encircled him as she wrapped her arms around him from behind. "I came through the building."

"You came." His prepared monologue reduced to two words.

"You think I was going to disappear with your car?"

"I only have a few minutes. We caught a case. Miller is covering an interview now."

She pressed a manicured finger to his lips. "We don't have to do this."

"More than anything, I want to." He pulled a small loop of paper out of his pocket, a diamond shape drawn as a placeholder. "I'll get you a real one."

"See, this is where the no kissing part is so hard." She nuzzled his neck.

They ran up the steps hand in hand.

After only a short while, with the license between them, Marisa's heart pounded as he drove the few blocks back to the station. When he stopped, she met him on the sidewalk just like in the morning. "Oh, in the backseat. I packed you a lunch."

Mischief crinkled near his eyes as he pulled her closer. "You are one surprise after another."

She leaned in so that her lips left their red color on his ear. "Like one of those surprise balls, the more you unwrap, the better the gifts."

"I'll take leave Thursday *and* Friday so that we have time for unwrapping."

"I can't wait." She pressed a hand to his chest. "You know I love you, right? Have I said that?"

"No. But I sort of read between the lines."

"I love you, Detective." She kissed the paper ring on her finger. "Text me when you're ready to come home."

When his day finally ended, Ben smiled as she pulled up to the curb, and he dropped into the passenger seat, letting her drive them home.

She leaned over and kissed his cheek. "How was your day?"

"Tough." He tilted his head back, eyes closed, trying to forget the job.

"If you want quiet, I can do that. If you don't, I can do that, too."

"I want to wrap my arms around you and enjoy hot food. I haven't decided what I want first."

"Kate called me."

"You spill our secret?"

"I did not. She wants all of us to go dancing tomorrow night."

Ben glanced down at the phone buzzing in his lap and put a finger to his lips as he answered. "Hey, Alex. What's up?"

"You free tomorrow night? Kate wants to go dancing. Thought it would be fun to go as a group."

"Tomorrow night? I'm free."

"Marisa will be there. Y'all seemed chummy on Saturday."

"Dancing sounds fun."

"Since she lives near you, think you can give her a ride?"

"Sure, I can do that." Ben winked at Marisa.

"I'll let her know you'll pick her up. What time should I tell her?"

"I'll call her."

"Need me to send you her number?"

"I still have it. Just text me the details." Ben wanted to put an end to the conversation before he said the wrong thing.

"Have you called her?"

"Bye."

As soon as Ben hung up, Marisa exploded with laughter. The secret would be that much harder to keep, next to her, dancing with her, in full view of their friends and her family.

"Need a ride tomorrow night? Your brother suggested I check with you."

"He's not going to kill you, he's going to hug you."

When they arrived at her apartment building, she pulled into a parking space and jumped out. Before he even pulled on the handle, his door flew open. Her grin dared him to object.

"You are a whole list of never before. Never before have I been a passenger in my own car with a woman behind the wheel. Never before have I had a woman open my car door. Never before have I proposed or even told a woman that I loved her."

"Stop waxing poetic and come inside." She ran halfway up the stairs and stopped. "Crap."

"What?" He brushed her cheek as she joined him near the bottom stair.

She pointed at a car. "Lucia's here."

"Neighbors can't have dinner together?"

"She'll know something's up and start asking questions—lots of them. I'm an open book to her."

"Then I propose another first. Let me make you dinner. I've never cooked for a woman before."

"Not even your mother?"

"I didn't mean her. Growing up, I cooked some."

"So you've never cooked for a date before?"

"Exactly." He climbed back into the passenger seat. "Let's go to my place."

Marisa drove the short distance to his apartment and followed him up the stairs. Inside, after he'd changed out of his work clothes, she joined him in the kitchen and perched on the counter. "You called me a lady."

Ben smacked his head on the cabinet door as he whipped around. "What?"

Grabbing his t-shirt, she pulled him to her. Lipstick covered the mark the cabinet left on his head. "Sorry. When Paul walked up to the table at the barbeque place, you referred to me as a lady. Thank you."

He took her hands in his. "I wish you could see yourself the way I see you."

Her insides buzzing with excitement, she needed to do something. "Put me to work. How can I help?"

He rustled around in the bottom of a drawer and acted as if he hadn't heard her question. When he popped up with an apron in hand, she laughed.

"Tie this for me, will ya?" He slipped it over his head.

"Should I even ask why you have a frilly apron?" She tugged on the strings before tying a bow.

"I plead the fifth."

"What are you cooking?" She expected macaroni and cheese.

"Jambalaya would take too long. I'll make that for you another time."

"I don't want to hear about what I'm not going to eat. What's on the menu for tonight?"

"Tonight, I'll make you enchiladas, the way my grandma used to make them."

"Please let me help." She slipped off the counter. "I've only ever cooked for someone, never with someone."

"You never cooked with your sister, one of your brothers, or your mom?"

"You know what I mean."

"Pan for the ground beef is in the lower cabinet. I'll get the chiles boiling for the sauce."

For the next hour and a half, they danced around each other in the small space. As she laid plates on the table, he trailed his fingers down her back. Letting her help, giving her space in his kitchen by his side, he promised her a lifetime of the same. Did she understand? For years, he'd wanted a wife. All the while, he'd needed her.

She turned and danced a finger down his cheek. "This is perfect. Tonight, making dinner together."

"I couldn't agree more." He filled two plates with food and set them on the table.

She blew on her first bite before tasting it. "This is amazing, Ben." A thin string of cheese dangled from her chin. "With skills like this, how are you still single?"

"I told you I didn't cook for women … or with them."

"Why not?"

He set his fork down, prepared to share his flaws, risking the walk down the aisle. "Saying it out loud will make me sound like an ass."

Wide green eyes fixed on him. "I'll love you anyway."

"Maybe it was different in your house, but in ours there were definite roles. Mom stayed home, cooked, cleaned, took care of me and my brothers. Never once did Dad touch the laundry or cook dinner. I grew up thinking that was the way things were supposed to work."

"But you cooked?"

"Mom's ideas were different from Dad's—at least where her boys were concerned."

She pushed his chair back from the table and sat in his lap. "Keep talking."

"And there was none of this. To dad, taking care of mom meant making sure the account had enough money for her to get groceries and keeping her car running. External things. Feelings were something to avoid, red flags warning of dangerous territory."

"Did I raise red flags?"

"From the moment I laid eyes on you." He closed his eyes, transported to the station on the day they'd met. *Trouble.* That's what he'd thought. "Told you it made me sound bad." He waited for her ribbing.

"Your dad did something right, raising a man that looked me in the eye."

"He may have kept his feelings hidden, but no one ever wondered how he felt about mom. He adored her, still does. We boys were taught to treat women the same way we wanted people to treat our mom."

"And I love that." She lifted his chin. "So how is it *supposed* to work?" She didn't have the answer, but she had no idea how to make enchiladas from scratch either.

"I don't know. But I'm hoping something like making dinner."

"Figuring it out together? Or does your grandma have a recipe for marriage, too?" Her grandmother did, but she wasn't quite ready to share it with Ben. Yet.

With his traditional cultural ideas came a strong protective edge, something she'd craved but resisted for a very long time. Admitting it, she opened her heart, and he stepped in. Glad he'd paired that edge with a healthier idea of gender roles, she rested her head on his shoulder, excited about their future. "So I get to talk about my feelings?"

"Any time you want."

"Will you fix everything?"

"If I can."

Chuckling at his completely expected answer, she rested her forehead on his. "And if you can't?"

"Is that when I'm supposed to listen and hold you?"

She swatted his arm and slipped back into her own chair. "Let me finish eating, then it's my turn to bare my soul."

As Ben washed out the sink, she dried the last plate. There had already been more baring than he was used to, and skin wasn't even part of the conversation. But he anticipated hearing more. Waiting tortured him, like a kid struggling with each bite of vegetables knowing dessert was promised at the end.

"Wine?" He tried not to let his eagerness show.

"Please."

He sat next to her and handed her a glass. "I seem to recall a promise to bare your soul."

She shifted. Legs draped over his lap, she eyed him over the rim of her glass. "Is it too late to change my mind?"

Wine droplets splattered on her legs when he choked mid-sip. After a brief coughing fit, he started to get up. "Sorry. I'll get you a rag."

"No. I'll wash it off later. I didn't mean about getting married." She pulled a strand of hair into the corner of her mouth. "After you opened up, I wanted to do the same, but this is hard."

"You don't have to tell me anything, Marisa."

"Yes. I do. If I'm going to marry you, you need to know what you're signing up for. And for the record, this is the first time I've ever bared my soul. Usually I just—you don't want to hear that." She wiped at tears.

Softly and slowly, he kneaded circles in the balls of her feet.

"When I graduated from high school, I felt so grown up. Ready to face the world on my own." She sipped her wine, as if it fueled her ability to speak. "The next day, when Mom and Dad died, that became my only option. I continued with my plans, went to school, and pursued my degree. Lucia lived here, and I saw her often. Alex was here, too. But siblings aren't the same as parents." Exchanging the wine glass for a throw pillow, she hugged it to herself. "During college, I learned to get by on my own. Alex and I were pretty close. I leaned on him more than my other siblings because by my sophomore year, the others had all moved away."

Massaging her feet, Ben let quiet pauses remain between them, undisturbed.

"When Alex's wife died, he retreated from the rest of the world. I didn't have anyone. So I figured life out on my own. Please, you can't ever say any of this to him. He'd never forgive himself, and I'm not blaming him."

Ben handed her a tissue. "I can keep a secret."

"My choices were horrible. The last three years have been a series of bad relationships. With the first, it happened slowly. I felt trapped for a while." She buried her face in the pillow before shaking her head and making eye contact with Ben. "But when I got free of him by moving away, I wasn't the same anymore." Her chest heaved as her head dropped back to the pillow. "After that, those guys seemed more what I deserved."

He launched toward her, pulling her into his arms. "What you deserve is someone who will risk everything to love you, to protect you."

"I want to marry you. I love everything about you. But if we do this, you can't leave me." She rested her head on his shoulder. "Ever."

"It was a forever question, Marisa." He kissed her hair. "And I know it won't all be roses, but it's the fertilizer that makes the flowers grow."

She exhaled but didn't move. "No more secrets."

"I'm not keeping secrets from you, Marisa. About you, now that's a different story. If you really want to know how the apron ended up in my kitchen, I'll tell you." His mind raced, trying to figure out what she meant.

"I'm being stalked." She didn't lift her head.

Ben closed his eyes as the room started to spin. "How long?"

"Since April, not long after they arrested Paul."

"Think that's who doing it?"

"Yes. Maybe. I don't know. My apartment was broken into, and the note left was definitely from Paul, but I'm not sure about the others."

"He broke into the apartment and you didn't say a word? And last night?"

She sat up and faced him. "I can't explain why. My choices were all kinds of bad. I was trying to protect Lexi, and I didn't want you to leave me. Please don't look at me that way."

Ben rubbed his face, trying to dispel his frustration. "Protecting you is easier if you trust me. I don't understand why you need to do it all by yourself."

"But not anymore. Right?"

His heart melted, and he pulled her to his chest. "Not anymore. In the morning, *we* will file a report."

"If you think that's a good idea."

"We have to." Ben cradled her face. "I have an extra bedroom. You can stay here."

"No, Ben. Not until Thursday, please." She stood up, moving away from the couch. "Our relationship is different, and as much as I tease, I want it to be different. Please, can we wait three days?"

He tried to hide the panic building in his chest. "How can I protect you?"

Images of Paul at the restaurant and Marisa tugging down her sleeve burned in his memory.

She rested a cool hand on his cheek. "I'm careful. I stay aware of my surroundings. I even quit walking alone close to sunset."

"Let me at least walk you home tonight."

"Detective, I'd be disappointed if you didn't."

# Chapter 47

*Tuesday, June 28*

Ben ran up the stairs praying under his breath that she was okay. Walking away from her door last night tortured him, but sleeping in the apartment breezeway wasn't a viable option.

She peeked out the window after he knocked, and he relaxed a bit. She was being careful and smart about it. He needed to trust her.

"You ready?"

"No, but I'm going anyway." She clutched a manila envelope to her chest. "I'm supposed to talk to Detective Mike Fuller."

"I know him. He's a good guy."

"I'm nervous. Waiting this long to file a report makes me look stupid."

"You are anything but stupid. Don't even say that."

Marissa's grip on Ben's hand was so tight as they walked into the station, she almost expected him to wince.

When called back to an interview room, she glanced over her shoulder, making sure he was with her.

"I meant *we.*" He rested a hand on her back.

An older man, with grey hair and kind eyes, sat across the table from them. "I'm Detective Fuller." He tapped his pencil on a yellow pad. "So tell me about what's been happening."

Marissa dumped the notes out onto the table and arranged them in order. Giving dates as best she could remember, she told him about the roses, the break-in, the notes, and stuffed animals, even the enormous bouquet of flowers.

"So this has been going on a while."

"The threat to my friend kept me quiet." Marisa pulled a strand of hair into the corner of her mouth. "But he insisted I should report it." She glanced at Ben.

"He was right, but I understand wanting to protect someone." Fuller's kindness helped her not feel quite so stupid.

～＊～

Ben stared at the last note, his twisting gut threatening to send his breakfast back up. "When did the last note arrive?"

Fuller and Marisa stared, surprised by his interruption.

She reached for Ben. "Um, it was a Sunday evening. The day after you had to pick up that girl."

"So, the guy on the sidewalk a few days later wasn't random, was it?" He remembered the faded dealer plates.

Marisa teared up and shook her head. "But I didn't know that guy at all."

"What about the guy behind the wheel?"

"I didn't see him." Fear flickered in her eyes. "If you hadn't come…"

Ben caressed her hand.

Fuller leveled a gaze at Ben. "Can you describe the car?"

"A black sedan. A Camry. Older. Paper plates, but unreadable." Ben explained what he saw and how events unfolded on the side street. Then he recounted the other time he'd seen the same car, when the man drove off after breaking into Marisa's car.

She clutched Ben's hand while Fuller scrawled notes on the yellow pad.

By the time all the facts were in the report, Ben wondered how he'd be able to leave her long enough to go to work. As they walked out to the car, he broached the topic. "Marisa, want to go with me to the office?"

"I'll be in the way. If it makes you feel better, we can swing by my apartment, so I can get what I need for dancing tonight, and I'll spend the day at your apartment. Tito will be okay without me."

"Thank you." Glad that she hadn't insisted on staying at her own place, he kissed her hand. "Leaving you at all is difficult."

She stopped and pulled his arms around her. "I'm scared, Ben. Seeing it all laid out on the table rattled me. I'll spend days at your place and only sleep at mine."

"I'll be at your door every morning and walk you to the door each night."

"I like that plan."

He held her. "Two nights."

"Then you won't be able to get rid of me. Ever." She climbed into the passenger seat.

~*~

After Ben had been gone several hours, Marisa shifted on the couch. Without much to do and bored of cable television, she scanned Netflix for something to watch and texted Lexi: *I was silly to think I could jinx this. He's perfect.*

Hearts in four different colors popped up as a reply followed by: *I'm a wee bit jealous. Be honest, without a shirt . . . is he heart-stopping? Never mind I don't want to know.*

Marisa laughed at her friend's antics: *I don't know and wouldn't tell anyway.*

Lexi sent a sad emoji. Then she messaged: *What does he do? Work at a gym?*

Marisa smiled as she tapped out the answer: *Police detective.* A wash of pride choked her up.

She waited several minutes before reply showed up: *Well, duh.*

*Should have guessed that by looking at him. Will text more later. Work.*

Marisa snuggled against a throw pillow and closed her eyes. Emotional exhaustion caught up to her, and she zonked.

Ben texted her as he walked up the stairs: *I'm home.*

He tapped the door but got no response. *No one else knows she's here.* He swallowed back panic and unlocked the door. When he glimpsed her curled up on the sofa, he shut the door quietly.

They didn't have to leave right away, and he wanted to let her sleep as long as possible. Even though he wanted to drop into his chair and stare, he scribbled *in the shower* on a napkin and laid it on the coffee table. His keys lying next to it would serve as the clue he was home.

Washed and rinsed, Ben closed his eyes and buried his face in the stream of hot water.

Marissa stuck the napkin around the edge of the curtain. "Was this an invitation or purely informational?"

Ben jolted at the unexpected interruption. "Marisa Ramirez!"

"Need a towel?" She handed in a washcloth.

He slid the curtain away from the edge and peeked around it. "You want to tease? Fine." That was a game he would enjoy playing with her.

"Don't you dare come out from behind that." She turned her back to the tub.

He snaked his arms around the curtain and caught her around the waist.

The curtain between them, she wriggled, squealed, and giggled. "Benjamin Torres!" Her playfulness fueled his enjoyment.

"It's just Ben, and if you keep squirming, this shower curtain will come down. Where would that leave us?"

She stilled. "What are you going to do to me?" Leaning back, she ran her finger along his forearm.

"I'm giving you a turn in the shower." He lifted her into the tub, setting her down facing the spray of water. Reaching toward the counter, making sure certain parts stayed hidden behind the curtain, he snatched up his towel and wrapped it around his waist. "Enjoy."

"Detective." Soft and sultry, her voice dripped with tease.

"I'm not turning around, Marisa." A wet t-shirt landed near his feet, and he stepped around it. "So not turning around."

"Maybe between jobs I should write a book... about you."

He shook his head. "It'd be boring."

"Water droplets glided down his toned back chasing her gaze lower, lower. She sighed at his magnificent form." Her words dissolved into laughter.

"Very funny." Ben set a clean towel near the tub and exited the bathroom. "I'll leave you to your writing."

After her impromptu shower, Marisa scrambled to get ready. She relented to the curl in her hair, opting not to fight the natural wave. She didn't have enough time to straighten it. She reapplied makeup, then changed. "Almost ready."

"Sorry about getting you wet. I wasn't thinking about hair and stuff. But, for the record, I like it wavy."

She walked out of the bedroom and looped her arm through his. "You surprised me, Detective." She leaned her head on his shoulder. "In the best way possible. I loved every minute of it."

"Kinda gathered that from the squeals and giggles. My ploy to stop your teasing may have backfired."

"You know what I love?"

His muscular arms tugged her to him. "What's that?"

"I knew you wouldn't." She trailed her fingers along his chest. "Know what I love?"

"What?"

"Your writing." He winked and led her out the front door.

She still battled the thoughts that he'd tire of her, but she needed him. She wanted him. Trusting him took an exhausting amount of energy, but being with him refueled her.

When Marisa and Ben arrived at the dance hall, Alex, Kate, DJ, and Becca were already there.

"Anyone else coming?" Marisa hovered close to Ben without touching him. She couldn't wait to be in his arms on the dance floor again.

Kate and Becca eyed Ben when he leaned close to whisper to Marisa.

All smiles, Alex celebrated his perceived victory. "Only us. Phillip was going to come, but since Lucia left today, he decided he didn't want to be the odd man out."

Becca sipped her club soda, then patted Marisa on the arm. "He could've danced with you. He is all kinds of good-looking."

"Hey!" DJ flashed his signature grin and grabbed Becca around the waist. "For that comment, you owe me a dance."

She pulled him to the dance floor, laughing. "Come on, lawman."

"Mind if we dance?" Kate leaned back into Alex. "We're practicing for the wedding."

"Go ahead. We'll be fine." Ben draped an arm around Marisa's shoulders. "I'll keep her company."

Marisa waited until she and Ben were alone before she turned to face him. Trailing her fingers down his pressed-cotton, paisley shirt, she said, "Whispering that you can't wait to shower with me again is not fair."

His eyes twinkled. "Dance with me."

"Yes, sir."

~*~

Ben led her away from the tables, the rhythm of the music spurring couples around the dance floor. "How many dances before people raise their eyebrows?"

Marisa clasped his outstretched hand, pressing against him as he put his hand on her back. Effortlessly, she moved with him, the music pulling them around the sawdust floor.

"No comment?"

"Kate called me earlier today. Can you please explain to me why she calls you Torres?"

"I'm not sure. She has since the beginning."

"Hmm. Interesting."

"You going to make me beg for information? Kate called you and what? Obviously, you were talking about me."

"She asked if I'd dance with you tonight."

"Kate called just to ask you to dance with me?"

"I think she was fishing for information."

"And?"

"I promised to shower you with attention, so you wouldn't feel sad about being all alone." Marisa pressed her cheek to his. "I don't want you to be sad. Or alone."

Ben squeezed her hand as the song ended and escorted her toward their friends. DJ, Becca, Alex, and Kate sat on stools around a table. When Ben pointed to an empty stool, Marisa shook her head and pointed to the bar. He nodded and followed her, ignoring the eyes of his friends boring into his back.

Decked out in red boots, jeans, and a fitted white blouse, she sashayed through the room with him in tow, his pinky hooked on her finger. As if she had a beacon focused on her from the ceiling, she attracted eyes wherever she went. Men, even those with a woman on their arm, gawked as Marisa walked by.

Ben pulled out his wallet. "What do you want?"

"A kiss." She winked as she ran a finger down the front of his shirt.

"To drink?"

"A bottle of water."

Instead of returning to the others, he tugged her toward a corner. They stood next to the bar-height table, watching the dance floor, out of sight of their friends.

He shifted behind her, his mouth by her ear, so he could be heard over the music. "I want to, you know."

"What's that?" She cast him a backward glance. Each time her hair moved, fragrance tickled his senses.

"Kiss you. You have no idea how much I wanted to say yes Sunday night."

Her giggle set him on fire. "It was a wee bit obvious."

A man—tall, blond, and accustomed to hearing "yes" as an answer—stopped in front of Marisa with his hand outstretched. "Excuse me, would you care to dance?"

As if closing a sweater against the cold, she laced her fingers with Ben and pulled his arms around her. "No. Thank you."

The arrogant blond shrugged and sauntered away.

She shook her head. "That guy has no idea."

Jealousy dissipated as Ben focused on being her refuge, not that she needed it. The fact that she wanted it stirred him more.

She pressed her back into him. "I hear your wheels turning, Detective. Talk to me."

"You could have your pick. Why me?" He tightened his arms around her waist. His question surprised him. He hadn't given it a second thought before that moment. So taken with her, he'd never wondered why the interest was returned.

"I should be asking you that question."

"Don't go changing the subject."

She twisted, her body close to his.

With a look, he promised care and affection. His actions made payment on his promises. He showed up again and again, spotlighting her value, until she began to believe him. That and a hundred more reasons were why she loved him.

"Because I love you, silly."

"Please, Marisa. Indulge me. I want to know. There are hundreds of guys like me in this town."

She wrapped her arms around his neck, her lips by his ear. "No, Ben, there aren't. Not here, not in Austin, not anywhere."

His eyelashes tickled her cheek.

"When you looked at me in the station that day—no one had ever looked at me like that before, at least not that I ever noticed."

"How did I look at you?"

"You didn't leer. That caught my attention. When you followed me out and drove me all around because you saw that I was afraid, it made a huge impression. You protected me without asking anything in return, not even my name."

"That's my job."

"No it wasn't. And you left thinking you'd never see me again."

"True."

"So aside from your dashing good looks—your workout routine hasn't been a waste of time, by the way. I watched you run for a reason. Want to know what my neighbors said about you?"

"No. I want you to finish the why."

"You protected me when you had no reason to. Knowing everything I'd done, you still treated me with respect, called me a lady. You chased when I didn't think of myself as a prize. But the biggest reason—you loved *me*." She stopped, her throat tight with emotion. "Even the messed-up parts."

"I do love you—beautiful mess and all. And if you want to slow this down, wait a few months until the wedding, I'm okay with that. I really am."

"Are you kidding?"

"I'd have begged the judge to let me marry you yesterday. I just don't want to rush you into anything."

She cradled his face in her hands. "When I said 'yes,' I meant it. I want to be your wife. I want to be yours." She brushed the tip of her nose against his. "And you aren't the only one looking forward to unwrapping, especially now. Every time I close my eyes, all I see is you in that towel."

He sighed and buried his face in her hair. Not kissing her red lips took all his willpower. He raised his head, face to face with her again. "Marisa..." He stared at her mouth.

She pressed a cool finger to his parted lips. "Not yet."

He brushed her cheek, more in love than minutes before.

"They'll come looking for us soon." She picked up her water bottle and grabbed his hand.

"What if I don't want to keep the secret anymore?"

"Please." Her eyes went wide, a sudden fear darkening the green.

He wanted the whole world to know how he felt, but making her happy mattered more. "My lips are sealed."

Marisa poked him in the ribs. "I already know *that*. I'm just waiting until Thursday."

"Alex and Kate are probably giddy that we've hit it off so well." Ben winked as they approached the table.

When Alex saw them, he focused on Ben, patting him hard on the back. "Aren't you glad you came?"

"I guess." Ben was a terrible liar, a great quality in a future spouse.

Marisa slid her hand in his back pocket. With his back facing away from the group, no one noticed except Ben. Based on the squared shoulders and red tint to his ears, he noticed.

She grinned. "See. He doesn't look sad."

Kate laughed as Alex caught her by the hand and pulled her toward the dance floor. "I knew you'd be good for him."

When Marisa and Ben were the last two at the table, he planted a single kiss on her neck.

"Watch it." She tapped his lips.

He grinned. "Did you hear what she said?"

"Am I?"

The music slowed, and Ben pulled her onto the dance floor. "Absolutely. From the first day I met you."

She danced her fingers through his soft buzzed hair. Remembering that day, how taken she was by his boyish stare, she closed her eyes. "You seemed in a hurry to get away, but then you came running back."

"I spent sleepless nights worrying about you. I called Maddox. But until that day at Kate's, I didn't know your name." He brushed his lips on her ear. "It's my grandmother's name."

Every word he spoke, peeled back layers of her heart. She loved him in ways she didn't know how to tell him, for things he didn't know he'd done. Unable to contain her emotions, she spilled her heart.

"This is probably the wrong thing to say and the worst place to say it, but after meeting you, I couldn't sleep with him. It took every excuse I could think of, but I didn't. When he leered, I thought of the look your sunglasses didn't hide." The loud dance floor wasn't where she imagined telling him that truth. She hadn't even decided if she should. "That look offered hope of something other than what I knew, not even necessarily from you. I don't even know if I'm making sense."

The song ended, but he continued to hold her, swaying, his face still buried in her hair. His silence tore her apart.

"I'm sorry I said anything." She envisioned her words chiseling away at the foundation they'd laid.

He leveled a gaze at her, his eyes rimmed in red. "Did he hurt you because you wouldn't?"

"Near the end, after the accident, he was suspicious of my every move. It was hard to know what would set him off." She wiped the dampness off Ben's cheek.

"I'm sorry I didn't protect you."

"You did in so many more ways than you know." The desire to kiss him was only overcome because of the eyes staring their direction. "Now, what are we going to do about our audience?"

The last couple on the dance floor, they'd attracted the attention of their friends and pretty much everyone else in the dance hall.

"Why do we have to say anything? We were dancing. Isn't that what they asked us here to do? Let them think their little set-up is working. By the way, I took tomorrow off too."

"I can't wait." She hooked a finger through his belt loop and followed him off the dance floor.

It was late by the time they got back near their apartments, but Ben passed her place. "Will you come up for a little while? If you're not too tired." He wasn't ready for the night to end or to leave her in her apartment alone.

"Of course. I might even have a glass of wine."

"Wild." He tousled her wavy hair.

In the apartment, she poured them each a glass of wine. "I had-fun. We should go dancing more often."

He clicked the remote, and music filled the room. "We don't even have to go out."

Wine glasses abandoned on the coffee table, Marisa and Ben swayed to the music.

"Tonight's been perfect." Marisa closed her eyes and held him even tighter. "Almost magical."

"Yeah." He kissed her on the temple before letting her go. "Be right back." He hurried down the hall to the bedroom.

Marisa walked to the window. With her eyes closed, she relived the moments at the dance hall.

"Marisa."

She turned around.

Ben was on one knee in front of her. "Will you marry me?" He held out an open box, a white gold solitaire nestled inside.

"Yes." She stuck her hand out. "Oh, Ben, how am I going to wait until Thursday?"

Two sleeps was a long time to wait for her happily-ever-after.

# Chapter 48

*Wednesday, June 29*

Ben rolled over and picked up his phone. How had he slept so late? Being on the phone with Marisa until the wee hours of the morning might have had something to do with it. He texted her: *You awake?*

Marisa opened the small window over the sink, trying to get the smoke out of the apartment, then yanked on an oven mitt. The pan of bacon she slid out of the oven was too overdone too eat. Packing for her move to Ben's, she'd left the surprise breakfast in too long.

The smoke alarm began shouting its complaint, and Marisa ran to the front window. After flipping the lock, she tugged on it, but it wouldn't budge. *Stuck.* Desperate to get the alarm to stop, she reached for the doorknob. She needed a cross breeze. Before even unlocking the bolt, she peeked out the curtain. The breezeway looked like it always looked, empty.

She pulled open the door and peeked her head out. *Calm down. No one is out there.*

With the door open, smoke dissipated some, and she managed to stop the alarm. As she stepped down off the chair, her phone played a special jingle, announcing a text from Ben. Her back to the open door, she scanned the room until she spotted Tito, making sure he hadn't made a mad escape.

She smiled as she read the message from Ben, then tapped out a reply: *I made you breakfast but burned it. Sorry. Come whenever.*

Before she hit send, someone shoved her from behind. She stumbled forward and landed on the floor of her apartment, barely missing the edge of the coffee table. Her phone flew out of her hand. Tito jingled past her. The door slammed.

She tried to get up, but sweaty hands shoved her face first into the carpet.

*Who is doing this?* Coherent thought slipped farther away. Fear clawed at her. *The stalker. Paul?*

The intruder straddled her back and yanked her hands behind her. Duct tape pulled at her flesh as he wrapped tape around her hands, binding them together. Her heart thudded in her chest. Would Ben come looking for her?

The man—she guessed it was a man—stretched dark fabric over her eyes while she wriggled and fought. Once blindfolded, she stopped fighting. She needed to figure out an escape plan. When he tugged at her arm, she stayed still, refusing to get up. A yelp jumped out of her when he yanked her up by her ponytail.

On her feet, she ran blindly away from him. He caught her, and all she managed to do was knock the pan of bacon off the counter. She struggled against his every step, but he dragged her back to the bedroom.

Marisa yelled as he tossed her on the bed and was rewarded with duct tape slapped over her mouth. Bound, blindfolded, and gagged, she fought her attacker as best she could, but the click of a switchblade stilled her. The cold blade laying against her cheek, she held her breath as he slid his hands inside her shirt.

Whoever had her pinned face down on the bed didn't utter a word, only soft groans as he rubbed his hands on her body. The clasp on her bra opened, and Marisa tried to think of something else, anything else.

Soft brown eyes were her escape. *I need help, Ben.*

Ben stared at his phone, waiting for the response to appear when the dots stopped dancing. No text came. She had to have seen it.

Curiosity poked at him. Why hadn't she sent the answer? He didn't worry that she didn't want to see him. They'd moved well beyond that guessing game. But it didn't make sense.

He jumped out of bed, pulled on shorts and a t-shirt, and sent a follow-up: *Headed your way.*

No response came. No bubbles appeared. Trying not to worry about the lack of response, he hurried out of his apartment and took off down the sidewalk. He hadn't even reached her parking lot, and a familiar orange tabby dashed up to him, the bell on his collar jingling.

"Tito?" He scooped up the escaped feline. Fire burned in Ben's gut.

She never let Tito out of the apartment. Something was wrong. Marisa was in trouble. Still holding the fur ball, Ben dashed toward her apartment. *Please let her be okay.*

He hurried up the stairs, scanning each landing. On the third floor, he set down the ball of fur and drew his gun. He made his way to her door and quietly tried the knob. *Locked.*

Marisa winced when the intruder picked up the knife. The fabric of her shirt made a horrid noise as he cut through the threads of the sleeves, then the back. After snipping the straps of her bra, he peeled away the layers, leaving her topless. Terrified, she restarted her struggle. She couldn't let him do what he clearly wanted to do.

Weight lifted off her back. She slid backward trying to get her feet to the floor. A sharp slap on her backside startled her. The assailant dragged her back onto the bed by her ponytail and rolled her onto her back. Her unbound legs were her only means of escape, and that hope dwindled as her shorts slid down and twisted around her ankles.

On top of her again, the man breathed in her ear. "Finally, you're mine."

The voice. Who was on top of her? Panic muddled her memory. His clothes still between them, Marisa strained to get him off, her shoulders burning from the weight of him on top of her. Persistent beeps sounded on his phone. He ignored them a minute or two, then cursed under his breath as he climbed off her.

"Stay there." Desperation strained his voice. "Don't move."

He'd moved farther away. Footsteps sounded in the hall.

Ben tapped out a 911 to Miller and peeked in the window, but with the blinds down and the curtains drawn, couldn't see in. Ready to break down the door to get to her, Ben breathed in deep.

The scent of burnt bacon assaulted him as the door flung open.

A man wearing a ski mask barreled out of the apartment. Ben dodged, but not far enough. The impact hurled him into the wall, and pain shot through his side. After catching his balance, he chased the man down the stairs.

Breathless taunts echoed up as the man ran down the steps two at a time. "I'm not done with her. I'll make you pay next time. She wants me, you know."

Heart pounding, Ben raced to close the distance. The parking lot would give him the advantage. He ran in the area often, knew the landscape and the shortcuts. As he hit the bottom stair, his side burned, but he stayed focused on the green shirt racing away.

An engine revved, and a car backed out of a space. The masked man jumped into the passenger seat, and the car's tires squealed as the driver turned out of the complex, jumping a curb in the process.

As soon as footsteps sounded in the hall, Marisa shook her feet until her shorts untangled, freeing her ankles. She slid off the bed and felt her way around to the far side by the wall. She crawled into the corner and huddled on her side, praying the man wouldn't return.

Jingling pierced the quiet of the apartment. Fur brushed her legs, but Tito couldn't help her. She wriggled and twisted her hands, trying to loosen the tape. Desperate to free her hands, she scraped the tape along the bottom edges of the metal legs on the bed.

When Alex had set it up for her, he'd sliced a finger. If she could find a sharp spot, she could tear the tape. Blindly rubbing her wrists along the metal, she tried several times to snag the tape. Pain marked her success.

As she yanked off the duct tape, footsteps sounded not far away. Tito jiggled away, and the noises in the apartment were drowned out by the rush of blood pounding on her eardrums. *He's back.*

Hands behind her, acting as if she was still tied, she waited.

Ben called Miller as he ran back up the stairs. "We'll need a CSI unit. The guy got away."

"I'm almost there. She okay?" Miller maintained calm.

"Don't know. I gave chase. Headed back up to her apartment now."

"Ben." Miller's tone promised a conversation Ben did not want to have.

"We'll talk when you get here." He hung up before his calm broke.

In the apartment, he made his way down the hall, clearing each room. When Tito darted into the bathroom, Ben closed the door. "You'll be safer in there."

He listened. The silence in the apartment worried him. "Marisa, where are you?"

Peeking into her bedroom, he tried to prepare himself for what he might find. His greatest hope had come from the attacker's taunts. *I'm not done with her.* Ben clung to the threat as hope that she was still alive.

Evidence of the motive lay strewn on the bed and floor. He surveyed the room, panic doing backflips in his chest. *Where is she?* After a quick scan of the empty closet, he forced himself to calm down. She had to be somewhere in the apartment. He dropped to his knees and glanced under the bed. Limbs were barely visible in the far corner. The sight of her huddled in fear tore his heart to pieces.

"Marisa, it's me." He made his way around the bed.

When he touched her leg, she launched toward him, slapping and beating on his chest, yelling from behind her tape.

He caught her arms and pressed his cheek to hers. "It's me. Ben. Let me take off the blindfold."

She grabbed his neck.

Crouched in the tiny space, with Marisa clinging to him, he wrestled with the knot in the black fabric. "I've got you. We need the blindfold and tape as evidence. You got your hands free?"

She nodded against his shoulder.

～*～

The blindfold fell away. Marisa blinked, and Ben's face came into focus. She tore the tape away from her mouth without letting go of him. "If you hadn't come."

"I'm here." He brushed the hair out of her face, his normally soft brown eyes wide and dark. "You okay?"

*I am now.*

"He didn't—he left before…" She glanced down and crossed her arms over her chest. "I don't know who did this."

"He got away. There was a car waiting." His focus riveted to her face, he helped her to her feet, then pulled her close. "But we'll find him."

"I think maybe someone warned him by text." Barely dressed and upset were not how she wanted Ben—or anyone else for that matter—to see her, but his arms buffered against the reality of what had just happened. She didn't know who had done it. The touch wasn't familiar, but Paul seemed the most likely candidate. The voice wasn't Paul's. She couldn't place the voice.

"Tell that to the police. They are on the way." He stepped back, his eyes scanning her.

She crossed her arms again.

"Just making sure you're okay." He touched her wrist. "There's blood."

"I think I cut my hand getting the tape off." She showed him a scrape, then spotted the blood on his clothes and his torn shirt. "It's you. You're hurt."

Heavy footsteps sounded near the front door.

Ben called out, "Hello?" To her, he whispered, "I'll stay in front of you until I can get the quilt around you."

She lifted his shirt and pressed her hand against his wound. "He had a knife. You need a doctor." The leap from blood to death was short given her mindset.

"Right now, I need to stay with you."

"I can't lose you." She planted kisses on his neck. "I need you."

"Calm down. I'll be okay." He whispered in her ear. "Save the kisses for later."

*Later.* She hoped that was a promise.

Ben turned them so that he blocked the view of Marisa from the doorway, limiting who saw her dressed in only lace panties.

Miller moved into the room. "Torres?"

"She's okay."

"Whose blood is that on the stairs and in the hall?"

Ben recognized other voices down the hall. "Mine. He must've cut me with something."

"CSI unit just pulled up." Miller held up his hand, preventing someone from entering. "Andrews, in here. The rest of you out there." He pointed at Ben. "You need to get looked at."

"In a bit. Door was locked when I got here." Ben glanced back over his shoulder toward the doorway. "And wide open after he ran out."

Miller barked orders. "Dust out there. Start with the lock inside the front door." He made eye contact with Ben, and silent information passed between partners. "I'll check back in a minute."

Andrews stepped into the room, surveying the scene.

Ben hadn't seen Bethany since the night at the dance hall. "She freed her own hands. The tape is on the floor. Blindfold and tape from her mouth are on the bed."

Based on her expression, she recognized Marisa. Hopefully Bethany didn't harbor ill feelings.

Marisa tensed when she picked her head up off Ben's shoulder. Before he could whisper not to worry, Miller appeared in the doorway, and she burrowed closer.

"Can I wrap that quilt around her?" Ben rubbed her back.

Andrews pointed toward the dresser. "She can get dressed, but we'll need to collect what she's wearing. Just leave it on the bed."

Ben kissed Marisa on the forehead before stepping away. "I'll step out for a moment, give you privacy."

"Stay." She touched his back. "Right here, please."

He stopped, still facing the door. "Okay."

"Call me when she's ready." Bethany slipped out of the room.

His heart pounded as Marisa shuffled behind him, resting a hand on his shoulder for balance. When her hand left his shoulder, drawers opened and closed.

Marisa leaned against his back a few moments later. "I'm dressed."

Ben reached back and ran his hand down her cotton t-shirt. "Marisa's ready."

When another drop of blood hit the carpet, he pressed his hand back to his side. With the panic easing, he noticed the pain that reverberated through his side with every breath, but he tried not to let Marisa see that he was hurting.

Bethany pointed down the hall. "Let's talk out there." As they made their way to the kitchen, she furrowed her brow at the sight of Ben's bloody shirt.

Marisa stood near the table, clutching Ben's hand.

"Marisa? That's a beautiful name." In a soothing tone, absent of bitterness, Bethany addressed Marisa. "My name is Officer Andrews. You can call me Bethany. I'll need to ask you some questions." Bethany had a reputation for being gentle and disarming with victims. Turning to Ben, she added, "Torres, mind stepping away for a minute?"

Marisa clutched his t-shirt. "What made you come to the apartment?"

"I came to get you, but then Tito met me on the sidewalk. I knew something was wrong."

Marisa hoped that Andrews couldn't force him to leave. "I want him to stay with me."

"He needs the EMTs look at that cut."

He kissed her cheek. "Just tell her everything you remember."

"You won't leave without me? If you have to go to the hospital, I'm going with you." Marisa didn't want to let him walk away.

"I'm not leaving." He cradled her face. "I'll stay close. Call me, and I'll be right back."

"Promise?"

"I love you." He couldn't have answered with a better yes.

Andrews waited until he walked away. "Seems like Officer Torres is sweet on you."

"Yeah." Marisa stared at the ring on her finger. "We're getting married, but we haven't announced it yet. Please don't say anything."

"Of course. Would you like to sit down?"

"No." Marisa paced behind the chair.

"This is what will happen. I'm going to ask you a few questions, but then we'll have you go down to the station for a follow-up interview. Okay?"

Marisa nodded. She just wanted to tell what happened and get out of the apartment.

"I'd also like to call in an advocate who works with Sexual Assault survivors."

"I don't want to talk to anyone like that."

"You can wait and decide later. I need to start out with contact information."

Marisa rattled off her phone number.

Bethany watched Marisa's every move. "Will you be staying here?"

"Ben's apartment, but I can't remember his address."

"I can get that from him. Whenever you're ready, tell me what you remember about today."

Arms crossed, Marisa gave a barely coherent account of what had happened. She wanted Ben back by her side. She didn't know why, didn't want to figure out why, but the petite blonde made Marisa want to run away.

While EMTs treated and bandaged his cut, Ben explained to Miller and Fuller what happened, how he'd found Marisa. "I haven't touched anything on the bed. Our cat is in the bathroom; don't let him escape."

"A cat?" Miller shook his head.

"CSI guys left him in there." Fuller patted Ben's shoulder. "Why don't you go get that stitched up, and we'll stay here with Marisa?"

Miller shook his head, wagging a finger at Fuller. "You're wasting your breath, Mike. He's not leaving her."

Ben hated that the attacker was out there, free, and even more than that, Ben couldn't imagine being away from Marisa. Being halfway across the apartment made him antsy. "Jack's right."

Fuller tucked his notebook back in his pocket. "While Marisa's at the hospital, someone there can tend to you."

The reminder of what she went through crashed against what still awaited her. Ben glanced toward the kitchen, worried about how Marisa was coping with the nightmare.

"Let Andrews do her job." Miller motioned for Fuller to walk away.

He walked off down the hall, calling to one of the CSI guys.

Ben dropped his voice to a whisper. "I never called Bethany after dinner that night."

"Tell me something I haven't heard a couple dozen times."

"I wasn't trying to be rude."

"Dana quit asking when Marisa met you for dinner in May." Miller shifted so that his back was to the end of the hall. "You okay?"

"He said he's not done with her and that next time I'll pay. Don't breathe a word of that to Marisa, please. I've met the ex. It wasn't him." Ben rubbed the top of his head. "Whoever it is, I'll die before I let him hurt her."

"Love's a pain in the ass like that." Miller patted him on the back and kept his voice low. "Noticed she has a ring on her finger."

"Please don't say anything. Not yet." Ben glanced toward the door. "Will you let Fuller and Andrews know to keep it quiet?"

"Sure thing." Miller nodded toward the kitchen.

Marisa poked her head around the corner. "Ben, I need you to talk to her."

"What's wrong?"

Tension hung in the air like a fog. Bethany wouldn't even look at him.

Marisa grabbed the back of a chair. "I don't want to go to the hospital."

Ben pulled her close. "They need to collect evidence, Marisa. From under the nails, your clothes, and ..." He kissed her on the temple. "Go. I'll go with you."

Eyes pleading for backup stared at him. "They have my clothes, and I don't *need* a kit run." The first hint of tears pooled in her eyes.

"CSI can collect from under her nails here, can't they?" Choosing to defend her choice of not going to a hospital ran counter to his police training, but forcing her would be wrong. He wouldn't. Loving her meant trusting her.

"If that's her choice, we'll have to do it that way." Andrews didn't sound irritated, but the look that crossed her face made it clear she disagreed.

Ben understood the desire to collect every thread of evidence, but listening to Marisa and letting her make that choice was much more important.

Bethany tucked away her notebook. "Thank you for talking with me, Marisa. You remember what we talked about? You'll need to go down to the station for a follow-up interview."

"I remember." Marisa clutched Ben's hand. "What about you?" She lifted the hem of his shirt.

"I need stitches, but we'll go once everything is wrapped up here."

Andrews motioned that she wanted to speak to him, and he reluctantly pulled away.

"Let them scrape your nails. I'll be right back." Ben squeezed Marisa's hand as two CSI guys stepped up.

Bethany waited in the hall, clicking the end of her pen repeatedly. "I need your address. She said she'd be staying with you."

Ben recited his address. "That all you need?"

"Since she refused a trip to the hospital and didn't want a kit run, we'll just have to see what we can pull off what we've got." Andrews kept her voice low. "You should have *made her go.*" Without waiting for a response, she hurried away.

Ben swallowed his irritation with Andrews, reminding himself she meant well, and walked back across the room.

Marisa stepped in front of him, curiosity burning in her green eyes. In her sweats and t-shirt, she exuded a look of comfort neither of them felt. "What did she want?"

"My address."

"I refused because I know they won't get anything." She pressed her hands to his chest. "But she didn't believe me."

He ran his hands down the sides of her shirt. "She wasn't here, but Bethany *is* trying to help."

"But if you hadn't shown up when you did, I'd be on my way to the hospital." Shaking, she closed her eyes. "I don't know who did this, but when they find him—"

"It'll take everything in me not to put a bullet in his head." Ben made sure no one else overheard.

"When can we get out of here? I don't want to be here."

"As soon as the guys are finished, we'll go to the hospital and the station. Then we'll go back to my place."

"Ben…" Marisa grabbed his shirt.

He buried his face in her hair and took a deep breath. The emotion in her tone plucked at the tendrils barely holding him together. "Not yet. Not with everyone here. We'll talk later." With more still to do, he couldn't afford to break down. His paper-thin walls would be easily pierced by emotion-tinged words.

She stared at her hand splayed on his chest. "I can find somewhere else to stay. You don't have to—"

"Marisa, listen to me." Ben cradled her face. "I want to. I want you with me."

"I should have said something earlier. I waited too long."

"No. Stop. Nothing about this is your fault. Nothing. He's the only one to blame." Ben berated himself, thinking of all he could have done differently but tried to believe what he'd told her.

Miller cleared his throat. "EMTs need her to sign a waiver. Then why don't y'all get out of here? Go get patched up. I'll stay."

Hours later, when they finally got back to Ben's apartment, Marisa curled up on the couch and hugged a throw pillow to her chest. Exhausted and worn out, she worried about Ben.

He whispered with his partner at the door before saying goodbye, then joined her. "Want me to make you something to eat?"

"I'm not hungry." Marisa huddled at the end of his couch in her sweats and t-shirt. "You need a shower."

"Yeah. And a new shirt." He shook his head as yanked off the disposable shirt he'd been given by the nurses.

She tensed, not wanting him out of her sight, but keeping him from a shower was stupid. Eyes closed, she focused on breathing in and out, slowly.

His soft voice reached out to her. "If you want to be back there while I shower, lay on the bed or whatever, I—I might spend more than thirty seconds getting cleaned up."

"Sure."

He shuffled around the kitchen. "I need help with the Saran Wrap—to cover my stiches."

"I'm coming." She loved that he made her feel needed.

While he showered, she curled up at the foot of his bed. Exhausted, she hugged a pillow that smelled like Ben. The running water acted as a lullaby, and she closed her eyes.

While dreaming of colorful lorries sipping out of nectar cups and butterflies dancing in the air, the attacker's voice twisted the dream into a nightmare, transporting her to back to her bedroom. Jolting from the fright, she opened her eyes just as Ben touched her hair.

She grabbed his hand as he pulled it away. "That wasn't because of you. Nightmare."

"I made you tea. Let's go out to the couch." When she'd taken her spot at the end of the sofa, Ben handed her a cup of hot tea and sat down next to her, leaving a noticeable gap. "What else can I get you? What do you need?" He fussed like a worried grandmother, his tension and concern evident in every glance and gesture.

"I don't want what happened to change anything."

"My feelings haven't changed. But however long you need to wait, I'll will. No matter how long, I'll be here."

"Please, Ben, I need to hear it."

He slid closer and grabbed her hand. "I love you, Marisa. I want to marry you." Ben pushed her hair back off her shoulder. "Even more now than I did this morning, if that's even possible."

"If we push the ceremony back one day, that's okay?"

"Of course. We can push it back six months." His words were tender, but his body was taut. He rubbed his head. Whatever he'd wanted to say, he hadn't spilled. His tight shoulders and set jaw added weight to her already heavy heart.

She needed the Ben that held her in his lap and bared his soul. "Look at me."

Brown eyes full of pain and frustration bore into her.

"Talk to me. *Please.*" She waited for him to fall apart, needed it. "Your wall only keeps me out."

He pressed his forehead to hers, eyes closed. After a deep sigh, he whispered, "I want to be strong for you, do whatever I can to make you feel safe." He lifted his head and traced the curve of her face with his thumb. Anguish filled his voice. "But I don't know what to do."

Hearing his voice crack, Mari wanted to pull him to her chest and shush him, but she needed him to open up, needed to see him raw and emotional.

He shifted his focus, staring across the room, clutching her hand. "I've never been as angry or afraid as when I saw you like that." His chest heaved, and he stopped to wipe his eyes. "It's never been that personal before, not in that way. But what I went through doesn't compare to what happened to you." His gaze snapped back to her. "How? I don't know how you're breathing."

"I don't need you to be strong, Ben."

"I feel helpless, like I failed you."

"You came when I needed you. Right now, with you here, I feel safe. This is when you hold me." She cradled his face and kissed the tears on his cheeks. "I need you to be *you.*" She shifted and curled up on her side, resting her head in his lap.

He rubbed her back, then stopped. "If you don't want to be touched, I understand."

Tears escaped despite her best efforts to keep them prisoner. "Be the same Ben you were last night. *Please.*"

The memory of dancing with her, holding her, flooded over him. She needed him to be real; he needed her close, needed to feel her heart-beat.

"Sit up a second." He stretched out on the couch, and she nestled against him as soon as he opened his arms. Pain zipping through his side, he tensed.

"Oh, your cut." She sat up.

"I'm fine." He pulled her back to his chest and picked up the remote. "Chick flick or adventure?"

"*The Princess Bride*?"

"As you wish." He kissed the top of her head before clicking play.

A few minutes into the movie, her eyes started to droop. He pulled a blanket off the back of the couch and draped it over them. By the time Fezzik and Inigo were rhyming in the boat, Marisa slept, burrowed against his chest. She hadn't yet cried. It was coming. Beyond the tears, healing waited. But sleeping on him, with every breath, she stitched back together his shattered pieces, weaving in hope that they would both heal. Stroking her hair, he closed his eyes, letting the temporary calm permeate his tense muscles.

An hour later, he startled awake, grabbing at air. "Marisa?" The front door was still locked, so he ran down the hall.

The shower was running, and sobs echoed in the bathroom. Ben slid to the floor, helpless.

His phone beeped a text notification. *This is Bethany. Miller gave me your number. I wasn't sure Marisa wanted to hear from me. How is she?*

He tapped out a reply: *Upset right now. Was better earlier.*

Bethany responded: *It'll take time. Call or text if either of you need anything.*

He jumped up when the bathroom door opened. Wrapped in a towel, Marisa poked her head out.

"Oh. Sorry." He retreated a few steps down the hall.

"Stop." The frailty of her voice stabbed at him. "It doesn't matter. You've seen it all anyway."

With his back turned, he said, "It does matter. Aren't we still us? I'm the same Ben I was last night—determined to wait—but I saw enough to make standing here facing away from you nearly impossible." He closed his eyes and crossed his arms, shielding himself from the temptation.

"I love you, Ben." The door to the guest room closed.

He paced in the hallway, trying to remember how to pray.

Hours later, after finally eating, Marisa brewed herself a cup of coffee.

"If I give you a list, would you mind getting stuff from my apartment for me?"

"Of course. And I'll bring Tito over if you want."

"Am I moving in, then?" She turned to face him, hoping the answer would be yes.

Ben didn't step closer, didn't reach for her. "I'm not going to tell you what to do, Marisa, but I want you to stay here with me."

"Did you change tomorrow's appointment?"

"We got the last slot on Friday, but I can move it again if need be."

"I want you, even more now than before, but..." She stepped into his arms. "I'm not ready to go outside." The Marisa he knew huddled somewhere deep inside, wanting him to stand guard while she clawed her way out from under the blanket of fear. "He's out there somewhere."

Tears landed on her shoulder. "I should have been there sooner. I saw the dots, but the text never popped up. I waited too long, and I should have been ready for him at the door. I'm sorry I let him escape."

"He's the only one to blame. You said so. Please, he has to be."

Ben smothered her in an embrace and nodded. "Make me the list, and I'll get your things."

She sat down at the table, but her hands shook when she tried to write. After a few attempts, she gave up and dictated a list.

"I'll be fast. Lock the door behind me." He rushed out.

She locked the bolt and paced. *Hurry back, Ben.* Her phone lit up in her hand. "Ben? Is everything okay?"

"I'd feel better if you stayed on the phone with me. I might have questions about the list."

A parking spot right near the base of the staircase was waiting for him when he pulled into the lot. That would make it easier. "I found a great spot. Headed up now."

"I bet Tito will be happy to see you."

Ben pushed open the door and jingling sounded in the bedroom. The little orange tabby blinked like he'd woken up from a nap. "I think I woke him up."

"I'm sorry to make you do this. It's probably awkward."

Chest tight, Ben made his way to her bedroom. He grabbed an overnight bag and gathered the things on her list, starting with her underwear drawer. "Can't say that I mind much. Mind if I bring along a few extras?"

The faintest of laughs sounded from the other end of the line.

He double checked the list, asked which hair products and make-up she needed, then ended up gathering it all into the bag so he wouldn't miss something she had to have. "I think I've got everything on the list. Just need to gather the fuzzy one."

"His crate is in the hall closet."

After a short battle, the kitten was locked in the crate. Ben had a pile near the door, ready to load. Two trips was all it took to get it to the car.

"I'm back in my car and headed your way. Hear Tito complaining?"

"Poor kitty. Thank you, Ben."

"Love you, Marisa. Just parked outside. Be up in a sec, but don't hang up."

~*~

Marisa peeked out the window and smiled as Ben came into view.

Seconds later, he tapped on the door. "It's me, Marisa."

She opened it but didn't hang up.

He stepped inside, dropped her bag near the door, and handed her the kitty carrier. "Be right back. Gotta grab the food and litter. Stay on the line."

Marisa released Tito, who bumped his head against her chin, purring. "I love you too, Tito."

"I can hear that." Ben's teasing relaxed her, made the horror of what happened seem farther away.

Once Ben was inside with the last load and the door bolted, she breathed a little easier and ended the call. He shuffled her things to the guest room, then made her another cup of tea and brought her pillows. "If you need anything, just say the word. I'll stay right here."

And he did.

Long after the sun set, Marisa lay curled up on the sofa, Tito near her feet and Ben sitting on the floor in front of her. He'd stayed within arm's reach for hours. When fear gripped her, she touched him, a reminder she was safe.

"That officer—Bethany—she was the one I saw you out with that night. Wasn't she?" Marisa recognized the short blonde and hadn't missed the way she said his name or the way she looked at him.

"Andrews? Miller's wife set us up for dinner once, that night you saw us."

"Did you go out a second time?"

"I'd already met you, even saw you that night with Andrews next to me." Ben leaned his head on her arm. "Short answer, no. I didn't ask her out."

"The way she touched your arm when you picked up my purse, I assumed more was going on." Marisa trailed her fingers through his buzz cut. The brush of the soft hairs relaxed her in a way she didn't have words to explain.

"That night, all I could think about was my green-eyed mystery woman."

"She touched your arm again at the dance hall."

"Marisa." Ben pulled her fingers to his lips. "There was nothing going on."

"Not for you. But I'm not sure you always realize when women are interested. You are a piece of eye candy."

"Then we're perfect for each other."

She held on to his words like a lucky charm, choosing to believe it was the truth. "Will you stay next to me while I sleep?"

"Let me grab us some blankets. If you're comfortable on the couch, I'll sleep on the floor right here."

"Thank you." She tried not to think of how she didn't deserve him or how Bethany seemed like a nice girl. "I love you, Ben"

"And for that I'm glad." He brushed a finger along her cheek. "Love you, too."

# CHAPTER 49

## *Thursday, June 30*

Ben's shoulder ached. He'd slept on the floor but held her hand most of the night. She'd awakened several times in a fright, clutching his hand, calling his name. With the sun gleaming in the windows, she slept more peacefully. Covered in tears and kisses, his hand still rested against her cheek; his other rested on his weapon. He shifted to a sitting position without pulling away.

Friday was too soon. He'd ask her to wait for both of them. Busy calculating how much leave he had, how many days he could spend locked away in the apartment with her, he jumped when her phone buzzed. Ben let Alex's call roll to voicemail.

Tito dropped a toy near the couch. Ben tossed it across the room. After attacking it and batting it around, the kitten brought it back. The process repeated several times until Tito got bored.

"Good Morning." Marisa let go of his hand. "Thank you for staying close."

"Listen, what if we push back the appointment another week? It'll give us a few more days like this."

"You mean the wedding?" She crossed her arms. "Why?"

He reached for her hand. "It's not at all that I don't want to marry you. You know that, right?"

"I do, but I don't want to wait." She shifted behind him and draped her arms over his shoulders. "Please, Ben. I'm not broken. I know what I want."

Ben twirled the ring around her finger. "I don't think you're broken."

She pressed her thumbs into his tight shoulder muscles, kneading, massaging. "Detective, I can't wait another week for you to kiss me."

Sultry and flirtatious, the Marisa he'd met and dreamed of whispered in his ear and dropped kisses on his neck.

He closed his eyes as his body responded to her breath on his neck. "Ay, Marisa."

She slid off the couch and sat in his lap, facing him. "That man, whoever he is, will not own me. I choose. I choose when and where. I choose you."

"How am I not going to kiss you after that?"

She giggled a delightful chirp of happiness, the first since the horror, and put her finger to his mouth. Without closing her eyes, she kissed her nail, only a finger and a whisper of air between their lips.

When a knock sounded, her smile fell away as she jumped up and raced down the hall.

Ben checked the peephole and took a deep breath. "Just a minute." He hurried to the guest room. "It's your brother."

"I don't want to see anyone, and please don't tell him what happened."

Ben nodded and pulled her door partway closed. Then he opened the front door prepared to do battle.

"Is Marisa here?" Alex raked his fingers through his hair.

Ben stepped aside. "Come on in. Want a cup of coffee?"

"I want to know where Marisa is." Alex didn't raise his voice, but his tone carried the force of a charging cavalry. "She texted yesterday and said she was with you. I haven't been able to get a hold of her since then. A neighbor at her place said something happened. Police were there."

"Alex, do you trust me?"

"What the hell is that supposed to mean? Where's my sister?"

"She's in the guest room, but she doesn't want to see anyone right now." Ben stepped in front of Alex as he moved toward the hall. "I *won't* let you in there."

Alex glared at Ben, fury flooding his green eyes. The knob rattled, and Alex looked past Ben down the hall. The anger died away as tears appeared. The guest room door scraped softly as it closed.

"Is she okay?" Alex walked away from the hall.

"She is."

"Are you sleeping with her?" His question carried more heartache than accusation.

"I'm not." Ben leveled a gaze at his friend. "I intend to keep the promises I've made to her. There isn't much I can tell you; maybe one day she'll explain. But, *please,* trust me to take care of Marisa."

Alex nodded as he opened to the front door. "You love her?"

"More than anything in the world." Ben glanced down the hall, hoping she'd heard what he said.

"Tell her she can call day or night when she wants to talk." Alex left without another word.

Ben ached for his friend, but protecting Marisa, her secrets, and her dignity took priority.

～*～

Marisa wrapped her arms around Ben from behind. "I shouldn't have asked you to do that. I just—I don't want him to know what happened. Ever."

"I'll take your secrets to my grave."

"Please don't say it that way." She closed her eyes. "You said more to Alex than I expected."

"I didn't spill our secret, but I had to ease his worry. And I wasn't going to lie to him, not about that." Ben glanced down when his phone rang.

"Talk to your mom." She buried her face in the soft cotton on his back.

"Hello.…Monday? I'm not sure." He rubbed the top of his head.

Marisa tapped him on the shoulder.

"Mom, I'll call you right back. … I will. I will." He ended the call as she stepped away.

She popped a pod in the single serve coffeemaker. "What's going on?"

"Mom's hosting a family get together on the Fourth of July."

"We should go."

"Are you sure?" His willingness to pause the rest of the world until she felt like herself again wasn't missed.

Marisa hoped they'd be happy about the marriage. "I do want to meet your family."

"They're going to love you."

"Will they be too disappointed about not being at the wedding?" She dropped onto the couch and patted the seat next to her.

"Nothing that grandkids won't make up for."

"What if I don't want children?" She walked her fingers up his shirt as she asked, watching his reaction closely.

～＊～

He'd always thought he'd have kids, but there was no question what he wanted more. "Then I'll tell them to go bug my brothers, and we'll get another cat."

"I do, though." She patted his chest. "I want kids—but not right away—and maybe another cat."

"Me, too, but I must insist that you let me name them."

She tickled his sides, but he didn't even flinch.

He smirked, gazing at her. "I'm not ticklish, but I'm guessing you are."

She tucked her arms around her waist. "Maybe."

He ran his fingers through her hair. "I won't tickle you. Not now, at least."

"A little later, I'll go with you to my apartment to get what I need for tomorrow."

"You don't have to go back there. I'll pack up that entire place, and you never have to set foot in there again."

"I choose. That's my motto."

"Well, my holstered buddy and I will go with you."

"Holstered, huh?"

Her wink made his cheeks burn. He'd never been so happy to have her teasing him.

"Call your mom. I'll give you some privacy."

He pulled her into his lap. "Stay." He dialed, using speaker so Marisa could hear the conversation.

His mom answered on the first ring. "Mijo. Are you coming?"

"I'll be there. You said noon?"

"Yes. Your father is grilling steaks."

"Do you need me to bring me anything?" He toyed with his mother, knowing what question she liked to ask.

"You can bring someone with you, you know, if you'd like us to meet her."

Ben winked at Marisa. "I think I will."

Clapping echoed from the other end of the line. "You are bringing a date?"

"Yes, Mom. I'll see you on Sunday." He thought he heard sniffling. "Love you."

Marisa rested her head on his shoulder. "You made her cry."

"Imagine when she meets you."

When they got to Marisa's apartment, he motioned for her to stay right behind him. Gun drawn, he cleared each room, then bolted the front door. "With all this fingerprint powder everywhere, I'm thinking you won't get your deposit back. My blood drips won't help either."

She shrugged. "I'll just be a few minutes." On her way to the bedroom, she called out instructions. "Grab the tamales out of the freezer. We can have them for lunch."

"Where'd you get them?"

A thud sounded from the bedroom. "Oh, ow."

Ben rushed down the hall. "You okay?" He glanced around the room. "Marisa?"

A hand waved from inside the closet. "Help. My hair is caught on the suitcase, and it's falling off the shelf." Her shoulder bore the weight of a hard-sided suitcase.

Ben breathed a sigh of relief as he lifted it, letting her untangle from the handle. "No more scares. Please. My heart can't take it."

"You gotta at least hold out until tomorrow. Then I'll give your ticker a run for its money." She kissed his cheek, then hurriedly threw her clothes in the suitcase. "Grab the boxes, will you?"

~*~

That evening, Marisa snuggled on top of him again for another viewing of her favorite movie.

But before he hit play, she sat up. "Ben, about tomorrow."

He laid the remote on the table and pulled her close. "I told you that whatever you want, I'll support."

"Please don't make any reference to what happened. I promise to let you know what I need, want, or don't want." She dropped kisses on his neck. "I want you thinking about me, us—not about what happened."

Ben slid his hands down her sides, letting them rest on her hips. "I can hardly wait until tomorrow." He kissed her head. "Do you want me to stay in my room all day, so I don't see the bride before the wedding?"

"I want to go out to breakfast—the same place where you proposed. Then I want to go buy you a ring and whatever else we need to make this into our honeymoon suite."

"Satin sheets and a mirror?"

"Start the movie, Casanova."

# CHAPTER 50

*Friday, July 1*

Marissa ran her hands down the sides of her dress and smiled as Ben whistled a tune in the next room. *He'll be so surprised.* Again, she tried unsuccessfully to zip the back of her dress. A quick tap on her phone, and his rang somewhere else in the apartment.

"Yes?"

"I can't get the back of my dress zipped."

"Okay?"

"But you need to close your eyes."

"You want me to zip your dress with my eyes closed?"

"Surely that won't be a problem for my talented detective."

He tapped on her bedroom door. "I'm here. Lids shut."

She opened the door, stepping back into his outstretched hands. After a moment of fumbling, he slid the zipper up.

Marisa turned. "You can open your eyes now."

Ben held her gaze. Dashing and handsome in his suit, he'd forever be etched in her memory looking just like that. The look in his eyes would forever be etched on her heart.

"Miss Ramirez, shall we go get married?" He held out his arm.

She looped her arm through his and nodded. "I'd love to."

Fluorescent lights hummed above as Ben promised Marisa forever, and they exchanged vows. She held a cluster of blooms they'd picked up from the florist that morning.

"You may kiss the bride," the judge said.

Marisa, dressed in a fitted pale pink dress, wore her happiness like pearls. Ben slipped his arms around her waist and tasted her lips, sweeter and softer than he'd even dreamed. And he had dreamed of that moment many times.

Music played, and office staff tossed silk petals as Marisa looped her arm through his. Mr. and Mrs. Torres were presented to the world, or rather a sparsely filled room.

After exiting between the rows of chairs and out of the courtroom, he pulled her into the nearest corner. "One more kiss, then we'll go home."

After multiple stops for quick and not-quick kisses, Marisa and Ben made it to his car. She leaned across the console before he backed out of the parking space. She wanted another kiss before he drove home.

"I love you, Detective." She cradled his face, and he pressed his mouth to hers. She nibbled on his bottom lip, tugging gently, and rubbed her hand along his chest. "And I want …" She sat back in her seat but kept her hand on his chest. "This. You."

He smiled, his brown eyes twinkling with desire. "I want to get you home."

"I gave notice to my complex this morning."

"We don't need two apartments."

"Really? What if I want to keep a separate apartment?"

"Then I definitely need to buy a robe. And slippers."

She pictured him shuffling down the sidewalk and laughed. "I want you close. Those coeds gawk at you way too much."

"What coeds?" He winked. "Do we need to stop for anything on the way back?"

"I don't anticipate needing anything other than what God gave me for the next several hours."

Ben downshifted and shoved the accelerator closer to the floor.

"Do not get pulled over!"

After racing back to his complex, Ben pushed open his apartment door and swept her into his arms. "Welcome home, Mrs. Torres."

She cradled his face in her hands, kissing him while he blindly made his way inside. After kicking the door closed, he turned, and she flipped the locks. He carried her down the hall and into the bedroom.

He stood her next to the bed and shed his jacket. His lips never more than a breath away from hers, he teased open the zipper on her dress. Her olive skin aflame with the heat building inside her, she loosened his tie, pulling it off when they paused for air. While he slowly separated the metal teeth at her back, she unbuttoned his shirt. His clothing littered the floor. Stripped of all but his pants, he danced his fingertips on the fabric of her dress, whispering plans for what he wanted to do to her, for her, with her.

When he reached the hem, she lifted his head. "Please." Green pools of desire pleaded for the tease to stop.

Locked in her gaze, he lifted the hem, anticipating the brush of silk or lace that never came. Once over her head, the dress dropped to the floor. She stood before him only in heels that nearly matched the color of her skin.

"Marisa." He gasped her name, words barely escaping the constriction in his throat. He lifted her onto the bed and made the whispers come true.

# CHAPTER 51

## *Saturday, July 2*

Ben awoke to kitten teeth gnawing on his big toe. Warm breath tickled the skin above his heart. Hair blanketed his chest. Marisa lay snuggled on him, the scent of pomegranates awakening his memory.

Tito pounced on Ben's hand.

"I'll feed you. Just hang on." Ben kissed the top of her head and slid out from underneath her.

She rolled onto her side. Pulling on boxers, he smiled at her naked back. He'd married a twenty-five-year old goddess with fewer imperfections than a piece of fine art.

Tito meowed again, pulling Ben out of his daydreams and fantasies.

"Shhh. Let her sleep. Come on." He padded down the hall, Tito batting at Ben's ankles. "Keep this up, and you'll be locked out of the bedroom at night."

After flipping the switch on the Keurig, letting it heat, Ben picked up the kibble canister. The kitten meowed with excitement and twirled circles around Ben's ankles.

Ben dropped a scoop of food into the cat bowl. "Eat up."

While Tito enjoyed breakfast, Ben brewed two mugs of coffee. Staring into the dark liquid, he chuckled. He didn't know how she liked her coffee. The last few days he'd served her tea, but never coffee. He added sugar and a splash of cream to one and left the other unadulterated.

Two mugs of coffee in hand, he stopped half-way down the hall when a knock sounded at the door and called out, "Just a minute."

He set the mugs on the table next to Marisa.

She stretched, the sheets falling away. "Who's here?"

He brushed hairs out of her face. "Don't know yet. I have to get dressed first." He pulled on a shirt and sweats before returning to the door.

When Ben opened it, Alex stepped in, Kate right behind him. "Marisa canceled her lease? Apparently, my number is also listed with the office." He dropped onto the couch. "I've tried to be patient, but my sister still hasn't contacted me."

Kate sat next to him, rubbing his back.

"Hold on. Wait." Ben tucked his left hand in his pocket.

Alex ignored Ben and continued. "She lost her job but didn't say anything. Lucia saw a letter at the apartment and only called me about it yesterday. Marisa still isn't answering her phone, and now I find out she's moving out of her apartment." Alex jumped up and paced. "I stopped by her apartment this morning. No one answered. When I looked in the window, I didn't even see the kitten."

"We talked about this." Ben understood the frustration of feeling in the dark.

Alex forked his fingers through his hair and continued, "You asked me to trust you, but I'm worried about Marisa. It's like she's disappeared."

Tito jingled his way across the room, and Ben winced when the kitten jumped up on the coffee table.

Confusion registered on Alex's face, but it morphed into something else entirely when Marisa spoke.

"Alejo, what are you doing here?" Her voice full of tease, she stood at the end of the hall wrapped in the bedsheet. Red spaghetti straps hinted at what lay underneath.

*Wow.* Ben stared, forgetting there were others in the room.

He snapped back to reality when Tito meowed, and Ben tore his gaze away from his wife.

Anger flashed in Alex's eyes. "Trust you? *This* is what you meant? You lied to my face."

Ben readied himself to duck. "Please listen to me."

Marisa waved. "I'm not missing. I'm married." She held up her left hand and wiggled her fingers.

Kate dashed across the room and tangled Marisa in a hug. "Y'all are perfect together."

Alex focused on Ben. "I'm not sure whether to hug you or hit you. When?"

"Yesterday afternoon."

"Why didn't you say anything?"

"She wanted it to be a surprise." Ben picked up the kitten. "We haven't told anyone. Only Tito." He scratched the blue-eyed ball of fuzz behind the ears.

Alex pulled his shoulders back and drew up to his full height. "You give her everything she wants?"

Ben set the cat on the sofa and stepped up, getting toe to toe with Alex. "If I can, *always.*"

"Welcome to the family. I hope you know what you've gotten yourself into." Alex wrapped his arms around Ben. "I kinda thought you'd ask her out before getting married."

"I did ask her out."

"When? Tuesday? Y'all spent the entire evening dancing and chummy."

"Long before that." Ben slipped his arm around Marisa's waist as she eased up beside him. "I'm her plus one for the wedding, by the way. Now, if you don't mind, the missus and I haven't even had our coffee yet."

Alex gripped Kate's hand as he beelined for the door. "Call me later. I want us all to go to dinner. To celebrate. For now, I'll leave you alone, so you can *have your coffee.*"

~*~

Marisa laughed as her brother frantically left the apartment, Kate chuckling behind him. "Serves him right. I almost came out wearing this." She let the sheet fall to the floor, revealing a red nightie.

Ben pulled Marisa against him. "Why do you tease your brother like that?"

"He worries about me too much."

"He loves you, Marisa, but I'm guessing he'll ease up on the worry part at least a little bit now."

"Why?"

"Because you have someone to take care of you."

She winked. "My detective."

He released the clip from her hair, letting wavy strands tickle her shoulders. "I don't know how you like your coffee."

She slipped the straps of her nightie off her shoulders. "Let go of me a second."

Ben lifted his hands, and red satin pooled near her feet.

"This is how I like to *have my coffee.*"

He tugged her to the couch. "We definitely surprised them. Why was that so important to you?"

"You want to talk? Now?" She pushed him back onto the cushions and climbed on top of him, yanking off his shirt.

"Only for a minute." He nibbled on the curve of her neck.

Her reasons had been selfish. "You want complete honesty?"

"You aren't exactly dressed for concealment."

Resting on her heels, she trailed her fingers along his chest. "Because I didn't want anyone talking you out of it. Marrying me isn't the most well-thought out idea you've ever had."

"Less than twenty-four hours into our marriage, and you're already questioning my judgment?" He danced his fingers along her curves. "No one could have changed my mind."

"I hope your parents won't be upset."

"Like I already told you, they'll just be happy I finally settled down." He pulled her down for a kiss. "I do need to tell Gram."

"Gram? I'm confused."

"She pulled me aside at Kate's party."

Marisa pictured his blush. "What did she say that colored your cheeks?"

"Oh, you saw that? Gram isn't like a normal grandmother. She's very studied in the art of people."

"You are trying to talk your way around what she said. That's not fair."

"She said if I kept looking at you, I might catch fire." The blush returned.

"You liked me."

Ben pulled her closer, desire overwhelming any thought of conversation. "A lot."

"After that first day, I kept thinking about you. Little things. I just didn't think a guy like you would want a girl like me. You knew too much."

He teased his lips along her collarbone. "A guy like me?"

"You were different." Her body reacted to his touch. "You turned around."

He lifted his head, remembering her standing between him and the rack of chips.

She kissed his smirk. "Both times."

He leaned her back, her stomach his new playground. "What if you didn't like my kisses?"

"I'd have pretended I did."

He stopped. "Ouch. Seriously?"

"Oh, Detective, a keen eye like yours would quickly spot the difference." She reversed their angle, leaning into him. "That morning, when you told me I was gorgeous, which sounded to me like *I love you*, from that moment, I was putty." She teased her fingers along the edge of his waistband.

He groaned.

She sat up again ogling him, her hands where he could see them but not where he wanted them. "You were so insistent. You kept up the chase." She slipped off his lap and popped his waistband as she stepped away. At the end of the hall she fluttered her fingers and winked.

Ben tripped in his race down the hall, wanting that putty in his hands.

Hours later, Marisa kissed his shoulder as he reached for his phone.

Dropping kisses on his chest she pulled the phone out of his hand and tossed it on the floor. "Whoever texted can wait."

He rolled her onto her back. "Let me make us something to eat."

"In a bit."

"Ay, Marisa." He groaned as she traced his collarbone with her tongue.

She let her breath tickle his ear. "I don't want you to starve. Come on. I'll make you breakfast."

"At two?" He stood up and pulled on the nearest clothes.

"Lunch, then." Marisa slipped on her robe.

Tito pouted and flicked his tail when they opened the bedroom door.

"Sorry, bud. Will a few treats make it all better?"

"You're going to make him fat giving him treats all the time." Marisa never tired of seeing Ben interact with the kitten.

After they'd eaten, Ben dropped onto the couch. "Come here, sugar."

"Sugar? That's new." She picked up her phone as she sat in his lap.

"Who texted?" He untied her robe.

Marisa forgot about the phone as he let his hands roam. "Hmm?"

"Am I distracting you?" He pulled her down to his lips.

"Kate—Detective!—she wanted to know if tomorrow night was better for dinner."

He slid the satin off her shoulders. "Whatever you want, dear, sweetie, love."

Conversation was lost in the tangle of limbs and kisses.

Ben sighed as she collapsed on top of him. "So what do you think?"

"I'd give you a nine and a half." She yawned, choking out a giggle.

"I meant about nicknames, you know, the pet names." He moved her hair off her shoulder and dotted kisses on her olive skin. "But I'll try to do better."

"Dear sounds like you want something. I'm definitely not a sweet-ie." She shifted, curling into her napping position.

He picked up his phone.

"You're googling pet names?" Humor glinted in her eyes.

He snickered. Her phone lit up with a message: *No, sweet girl. Just texting my honey.*

She picked up her phone off the table. "No and no." After tossing it aside, she nestled back into him.

He traced her curves. "How about Princess?"

"Call me that, and I'll run the other way. Do I need to think of one for you?"

"You already call me Detective. And the way you purr that name. Mmm."

"Purr? Really, Detective?" Her breathing slowed, the escaping air tickling his chest.

Ben coiled a curl around his finger. "I know what I'll call you."

"What?" Her voice sounded far away and dream-like.

"I'll tell you later. Go to sleep." He yanked the blanket off the back of the sofa and covered her.

He picked up his phone and, one-handed, texted Kate and Alex: *Tomorrow night is great. Will send contacts to invite. Thanks for helping me surprise her.* He forwarded the numbers to Alex, then dropped his phone onto the coffee table.

With his arms wrapped around Marisa, he closed his eyes. When she slept on his chest, almost like a drug, it summoned dreams, sweet and vivid.

# Chapter 52

*Sunday, July 3*

Ben rolled over when Marisa whimpered. She hadn't yet begun fighting the sheets and grunting as if her mouth was taped.

He spooned behind her, his cheek on her shoulder, his arm around her. "Shhh."

She lifted his hand and moved it off her stomach. "Not tonight, Paul." Rolling onto her stomach, she mumbled something else, but he couldn't make out what she said.

The pain, jealousy, and guilt that stampeded through his chest caught Ben off-guard. Being rebuffed using another man's name tore his heart to shreds. Images of another man touching her were hard enough, images of him hurting her made Ben sick. He hadn't been there to help. He slipped out of bed and pulled on his running shorts.

Restless, he paced the hall, wanting to go for a run but unwilling to leave her alone. He hung the pullup bar on the guest room door and over and over, let his muscles burn away the frustration pumping through him. His anger wasn't directed at her. He hadn't married her under any guise of ignorance. But in spite of all his head knew, his heart wasn't prepared to hear her say the name, not in bed. Jealousy pulsed with each up and down motion. Guilt pounded in his chest.

He closed his eyes, continuing without counting, hoping exhaustion would clear his head.

"What happened, Ben?"

Startled, he opened his eyes and dropped from the bar.

She stood facing him, wearing only her wedding ring. "Don't stop on account of me. It's most pleasant to watch. Although, I'm guessing it isn't good for your stitches."

"I'm fine."

"You lie like a two-year-old with cookie crumbs on your mouth. It's the middle of the night, and you're doing pullups. While that may make for very sweet dreams for me, for you, it means something's wrong."

"I don't want to talk about it."

"Ben, please." She sank to the floor. "Somewhere in my head, I know the voice. While I sleep, it's as if my mind searches my brain. I think that's why the nightmares are so frequent. If I said someone's name, it might be important."

"When I tried to calm you, you said 'Not tonight, Paul.' Okay?" He turned away and walked down the hall. The pang of jealousy was hard enough. Admitting it to Marisa reduced him to a child.

Her lips touched his back before her arms circled his waist. "Ben, I'm sorry."

"You never even asked about the apron or anything about my past. I don't want to be jealous." He pulled her in front of him. "I know I shouldn't be."

"It's easy not to ask when whoever brought the apron here is clearly no longer part of your life. But seeing Officer Andrews—why do you think I haven't called her back? The apron wasn't hers, was it?"

"No. Marisa, I never—you shouldn't—" He slid his hands down to her hips.

"I love you." She wrapped her legs around him as he lifted her into his arms. "Can I watch when you exercise all the time? Because wow. You are delicious, Detective."

"You don't fight fair."

"My mom always said to fight naked when you're married. She always added the married part."

"That's quite a tidbit of motherly advice."

"You should hear my grandmother's advice. I think you'd like that even better."

Ben carried her to the bed. "I find that incredibly hard to imagine."

"Her recipe for a good marriage ... Be both wife and mistress."

"I think family recipes are important."

"I bet you do, Detective."

When the sun crested the horizon, Marisa slipped out of bed and pulled on her robe. Tito followed as she padded into the kitchen. "What should I make him for breakfast? For you, I have kibble and a couple treats."

Blue eyes tracked her as she picked up the food container, and the fur ball meowed his excitement.

"Think he'll like a Dutch Baby?" She flipped the switch on the coffee maker before digging through the fridge. She set eggs, bacon, butter, lemon juice, and milk on the counter. After shuffling through cabinets, she added powdered sugar and flour to the pile.

She turned on the oven, slid in a pan of bacon, and brewed herself a cup of coffee. Scrolling through her phone, she resisted the urge to update her relationship status on Facebook. Very few would believe it anyway.

She set the pan of crispy bacon on the stove and tiptoed down the hall. Ben still lay face down, snoring. It was the soundest she'd seen him sleep since Wednesday, and she didn't want to disturb him. Breakfast could wait a while. She put away the groceries and covered the bacon—mostly to keep Tito honest—then wandered back to take a shower.

Suds dripping down her body, she smiled when she heard the bathroom door open and close.

"Can I join you, baby doll?"

She winced at the name. "Yes, but please don't call me that, not baby, not doll, and especially not together."

"I'm sorry. I was only trying to be funny. I mean, you are Barbie-like in shape, but calling you baby seems hazardous to my health."

She grinned at his well-directed poke. Her reaction to his childish comment hadn't been forgotten.

Ben didn't ask about who'd called her doll. He knew who called her baby and silently kicked himself for forgetting. If she wanted to talk about it, she would. He squeezed her pomegranate scented shampoo into his hand. "May I?"

She nodded, then turned, giving him her back.

Trying to be gentle, he fumbled at first when he caught a tangle. "Sorry." Slowly, rubbing small circles on her scalp, he worked his fingers through her hair, lather building as he massaged the pearlescent liquid into her dark strands. Working down the length of her hair, he made sure the shampoo covered every inch. "Turn around."

She tilted her head back, the spray from the shower washing the suds away. Tears cut paths through the lather sliding down her face.

"Why the tears? Did I get soap in your eyes?"

She shook her head, and the last remnants of soap disappeared. "You. This. Us." The smile that said he'd done something very right lit up her features. "The way you love me."

Wrapping his arms around her, he kissed the tears from her cheeks. "Thank you for letting me." More words weren't needed to convey what he meant.

Understanding seeped from her eyes. "Forever?"

"'Til death do us part." No matter what pangs of emotions berated him, loving her was worth it.

Over breakfast, they discussed how and when to tell friends and family.

"Are you just going to let your parents be surprised when we show up on Monday wearing wedding rings, or tell them beforehand?"

"As tempting as it is to surprise them, Mom will want to do something special, and I'm not sure I want to rob her of that." He imagined his mom scolding him for not letting her welcome Marisa properly.

"I need to call Lucia, Nico, and Sam. Alex texted that he'd wait and let me tell them."

"Go call." Ben dusted the powdered sugar off her lips. "I'll tell my parents."

"Think the guys at work will be shocked?"

"Maybe just a little." Ben chuckled, wondering what bets had been made on his love life.

"You going to just show up married on Wednesday?"

"I'll tell a few before then. Probably the ones you met at dinner that night."

That evening on the way to the restaurant, Marisa admired Ben's profile. "My parents would have loved you." An overwhelming sense of pride expanded in her chest at the thought of being introduced as his wife. "They'd say I chose well."

He flashed her a smile.

She spotted Becca's car. "Is it only Kate and Alex?"

Hand in hand, they walked toward the front of the restaurant.

"You were the one texting Kate."

Marisa paused, drawing his gaze. "You aren't upset with Becca for trying to set me up with the neighbor?"

"You mean Phillip? Nah. She didn't know."

"You had nothing to worry about. I wouldn't want to live in that little town."

"And that's the only reason?" Ben bumped her with his shoulder.

"He's a bit odd, secretive, and arrogant."

"Well, that little town will become a possibility if the craziness continues."

She appreciated his careful choice of words but didn't like that thought of moving there. "Because that's helped keep Kate so safe."

"Touché."

As they entered the courtyard of the restaurant, he pulled her off to the side, next to the large metal sculptures of a mariachi band. "I hope it goes without saying, but every secret you've asked me to keep, I have. And I will."

She cradled his face. "I know. Please don't make me cry twice in one day."

"Can't promise anything."

She walked toward the glass doors where the hostess sat just inside.

"This way." Ben nodded toward doors opposite the courtyard.

Through the glass doors, Marisa recognized more than a few familiar faces. "What—?"

He chuckled softly and moved behind her as he pulled open the door. Friends and family clapped and cheered.

Alex shushed the crowd. "We asked y'all here to surprise Ben and Marisa. What you don't know is that they have a surprise for you."

Ben cleared his throat and clutched Marisa's hand tighter as he lifted his left hand. "I said 'I do.' Say hello to Mrs. Torres."

The entire room gave a collective gasp.

Marisa cradled Ben's face and kissed him, drawing shouts and whistles. "My happily ever after started Friday."

Kate handed Ben and Marisa each of a flute of champagne, and Alex raised his glass.

"To my baby sister and a man I'm proud to call a brother—to Marisa and Ben, happiness always."

"Here, here." Everyone lifted their glasses.

Marisa let her lips tickle Ben's ear when she asked, "You did this?"

"Mostly Kate and Alex." Ben didn't give himself enough credit.

Marisa squeezed his hand. "I love it. Thank you."

She and Ben moved through the room, talking with everyone who'd shown up on such short notice. She'd expected Kate and Alex and maybe Becca and DJ, but the room was full of her friends, his friends, and their friends.

Ben hugged his partner's wife. "Marisa, you remember Dana, Miller's wife."

"Congratulations. I've been asking about you ever since you showed up to dinner that night." Dana wiped her eyes. "We were hoping Ben would find a good one. He sure has."

Ben beamed as they greeted the Daniels and the Robbins, who Marisa remembered from that night at dinner. Names and faces became a blur as people swarmed her, excited about the nuptials.

Becca threw her arms around Marisa. "You didn't say a word! But we wondered about you two that night we went dancing. He seemed pretty starry-eyed."

"By that night, I was completely smitten." Marisa grinned and hugged DJ. "Did you bring your Rubik's cube? In case the party gets slow?"

"Forgot it at home." He chuckled and shook hands with Ben.

Bethany retreated toward the back wall, her body language almost apologetic for coming. Marisa let go of Ben's hand and headed to the corner.

"Thank you for coming." She smiled, thinking of Ben's likely horror at her comments earlier, knowing Bethany would be attending.

She fiddled with her loose blonde locks, almost as if she wasn't used to wearing it down. "Congratulations."

"Thanks." Marisa glanced around to make sure no one was within earshot. "I'm sorry I haven't returned your calls."

"Marisa, I almost didn't come because I didn't want to be a reminder. But your brother texted, and Miller called me."

"The night Ben bumped into me near the food trucks…" Marisa glanced at him across the room.

Bethany's eyes widened. "You don't have to explain anything to me."

Without viewing all Bethany's actions through a green lens of jealousy, Marisa could appreciate the help and concern. "He really didn't know my name. And though we had met once, he was trying to protect me by not admitting it. I don't want you to think badly of him."

"His thoughts were written all over his face, but Ben's a good guy. I think you'll be good for him. It's obvious he's crazy about you."

"Bethany, I'm sorry for—"

"Excuse me." Phillip tugged at the collar of his dress shirt.

Marisa flashed her warmest smile. "It's Phillip, right?"

"You remembered. We met at Kate's. Congratulations. I don't know Ben well, but he seems pretty awesome."

"He is." Marisa had no trouble agreeing to that statement. "Have you met Bethany? She works with Ben."

"We aren't in the same unit. He's a detective, and I'm in uniform." Bethany held out her hand. "Sorry. I'm rambling. Nice to meet you, Phillip."

He dropped into a chair, focused on her.

Marisa gave Bethany a quick hug before walking away. "I'll call you."

～＊～

Ben worked his way down the buffet. Lexi popped up beside him as he stacked street tacos on his plate.

"Hey, Detective. Congratulations."

"Thanks."

"Glad Marisa found you. She deserves someone better than the guy sending stuffed cats and roses."

Lexi and Marisa were closer friends than he'd realized.

Alex motioned toward his table. "Hey, Ben, over here."

"Yeah." Ben returned Alex's wave, thankful for the excuse to step away. "I'm lucky to have her." He joined the other men at a table.

After taking a seat, he scanned the room for a glimpse of Marisa. Seated at a table with several of the other women, she talked and laughed, her radiant smile lifting the apples of her cheeks.

Miller stood near the entrance, talking with Maddox, and raised his glass when Ben looked his way. *He's guarding the door.*

DJ poked Ben in the shoulder. "You realize there is no prize for the shortest engagement."

"I'm not sure they were even engaged." Alex elbowed Ben.

He snagged a few bites while the guys laughed. "We were. Almost a week."

Travis tapped Ben on the shoulder and motioned him away from the table. "I need to head out soon. I'm catching a red-eye in the morning."

"Thanks so much for coming."

"Ben, you're part of the reason I have my daughter back. You've helped Kate and Alex whenever they've needed it. He is like a son to me, and you just married into the family. If you ever need anything, please don't hesitate to call." Travis handed Ben an envelope and shook his hand before walking over to Marisa.

Ben winked at her as she hugged Travis, and she smiled.

DJ stirred his drink. "Hey, I don't mean to bring up unhappy stuff, but can I ask a question about that business with Paul? I'm assuming you know about all that."

Ben reminded himself that DJ didn't know about the attack. "I know about it."

"Alex mentioned she lost her job over it."

Ben's glance shot to Alex. *Who else did he tell?*

"He told me because I asked about her. It was my house that got broken into."

Ben nodded.

DJ kept his voice low. "No one found anything that tied her to the break-ins. I guess I'm really confused about their findings."

"Honestly, I don't know. It doesn't really make sense."

"Well, from where I sit, she did everything right." DJ picked up his plate. "I think your partner wants to talk to you."

"Thanks, DJ."

Ben handed Miller a fresh drink. "Thanks for coming and guarding the door."

"You didn't invite your partner to the wedding?"

"We didn't invite her brother or my family either."

"Well, you did good. Amazingly, I think she really loves you. Has that look."

"You're just full of compliments tonight."

"Ben, she's a lucky girl." He shook his glass and downed most of the iced tea. "We need to be headed home. You okay if I leave my spot?"

"Of course. Thanks again. I'll see you Wednesday."

"I'll believe it when I see it." Miller laughed as Dana stepped up beside him.

Marisa dropped into a chair next to Kate, resting sore feet while Alex and Ben carried presents out to the car.

She had tears in her eyes. "You look really happy."

"I am. Ben is…" Searching for the right words, Marisa eyed him across the room as he loaded his arms with pretty packages.

"Home?" Kate choked on the word.

"Yes. Home." Marisa pulled Kate close. "Alex chose well. I'm so excited about your wedding and having you as a sister."

Kate fanned her eyes, then waggled her fingers. "Stop. You'll make me cry."

Marisa turned when a hand touched her back. Her brother wrapped her in a bear hug. "Mom and Dad would be so proud of you. I am, too. He clearly loves you and will take good care of you."

"Thank you. You have no idea what that means."

"Love you." He tweaked her chin. "I wish Lucia, Nico, and Sam could've been here. They are happy for you, too."

When they were finally alone in the car, Ben leaned across and kissed Marisa before starting the engine. "You look beautiful."

"What happened to no secrets?"

"This was a surprise. That's different." He winked. "Lexi seemed happy for us."

"Lexi's liked you from the first time she saw you, but you were there to hear that."

"Yeah." Ben grinned, remembering the evening at the food truck park.

"I can't believe all the presents. They didn't have to do that. Your family didn't come?"

"We already had plans with them on Monday, so I didn't put them on the list. I hope you don't mind." Ben handed Marisa an envelope. "Travis gave that to us."

"Want me to wait until we get home?"

"Go ahead and open it."

She tore open the flap and slid out the card. "Ben, oh wow!"

"What is it?"

"It says—Ben and Marisa, congratulations. I couldn't be happier for you. In many ways, you feel like family. Consider this my contribution to your happily-ever-after. Use it toward a honeymoon getaway or anything else you need to start your life together. Wishing you years of love and happiness. Travis." Marisa sniffled her way through the end of the note. "He enclosed a check."

"Dare I ask how much?"

"A lot."

"A thousand?"

"Multiply that by ten."

"Seriously? It's too much."

"You going to tell him that?"

"No. I guess not. What are we going to do with it?"

"I don't know. While a honeymoon sounds nice, I feel like we've had a private cabana this weekend." Marisa trailed a finger down his arm.

"Adding that to what I have saved, we could buy a house."

"Let's sleep on it."

"Sleep?" Ben chuckled. "Your cabana boy had other things in mind."

# Chapter 53

*Monday, July 4*

Ben woke with a start when the bed jolted. The sun hadn't yet crested the horizon. The thrashing preceded the tears in her nightmare. He pulled her to him and whispered in her ear. "Marisa, I'm here. Open your eyes. Put your arms around my neck." He repeated similar versions of the same until her lids flickered open.

"Sorry." She buried her face in the pillow.

He rubbed her back. "Want me to make you tea? We can—"

"Just hold me." She wiped her tears with the sheet and used his shoulder as a pillow.

He hugged her close and kissed the top of her head, swallowing back fury toward a faceless voice. Only these moments in the dead of night interrupted their honeymoon bliss with reminders of what happened. How would Ben leave her to go to work on Wednesday? Pushing worrisome thoughts aside, he gazed down at her, glad to have her in his arms and bed where he could comfort her. "I love you."

She smiled into his chest.

Ben stroked her hair, expecting her to fall asleep.

She gazed up at him. "Make love to me."

"Are you sure?" He wished he hadn't asked when sadness creased in her face for a moment.

She rolled to her back, pulling him to her. "It was only a nightmare. It's over."

He lay on top of her, holding himself up with his elbows. With his fingers in her hair, he dropped kisses on her neck.

"That day, when you showed up—" She interrupted herself kissing him. "I feel it all over again when you hug me close during my nightmares, like you're saving me all over again. With you, like this, the rest of the world disappears. Nothing bad can happen to me."

Ben pressed against her. "I'd give my life to protect you, Marisa."

She caught his lips in hers and mumbled, "No more talking."

~*~

Marisa opened her eyes, the nightmare waking her before she cried out. She snuggled close to Ben. He had a job. And soon he'd be gone all day, leaving her alone. Just thinking about it sent chills down her spine.

He mumbled her name, sounding like he did the night he'd called her. She kissed his back, regretting all the times she'd pushed him away, not telling him about the notes and roses.

Married three days, and she couldn't remember not loving Ben. She had little doubt that he loved her before she allowed herself to love him, but none of it mattered now. The doubts that she had about him leaving when he learned more about her vanished that night in the hallway. No matter what she'd done, he loved her. It only made her love him more.

Since it was still early, she ignored the paw poking under the door and closed her eyes, letting Ben's breathing lull her back to sleep.

~*~

Mid-morning, Ben closed himself in the guest room and called Miller. "Any updates? Leads?"

"Sorry. I would've called. Only a smudged partial on the bolt. Not enough."

Ben dropped back on the bed. "He'll come after her again. What will I do on Wednesday?"

"Take off a few more days."

"I'm out of leave. A full paycheck is more important now than before."

"Maybe her brother will come stay with her."

"He doesn't know, and she doesn't want him involved."

"I wish I had more to offer." Miller mumbled something Ben couldn't hear. "Sorry, Dana was talking to me."

"I'm sorry, Jack. Get back to your barbeque. I'll see you later."

"Maybe you can talk her into staying home for a few days?"

"We'll figure it out." Ben ended the call as he opened the door.

Marisa stood with an eyebrow raised. "Miller?"

"No update."

"Ben, if you're worried about going to work, don't be. At least for a few days, or until I go crazy, I'll stay behind a bolted door while you're away from the apartment."

"We can go out every night if you want."

"I'm stubborn, not stupid." She rubbed his back. "You don't have to respond to that. What time are we supposed to be at your parents'?"

"In an hour."

"I better get ready."

"Dress casual. Dad's grilling. At least that was the plan." He tucked a strand of hair behind her ear. "Whatever you wear, you'll be stunning. As always."

"Come teach me everyone's names while I change."

Ben sighed. "Torture." Watching her undress and making it to his parents on time weren't both possible, at least not in his mind.

Marisa took a deep breath, dismissing the butterflies that danced in her stomach. Meeting his parents was no different than meeting prospective clients, except she was sleeping with their son and convinced him not to mention the wedding beforehand. How much had he told them about that?

"Ben, what did you tell your parents about not saying anything about the wedding?"

"I didn't. I just told them I got married."

"They didn't ask?"

"Mom was too excited about the married part."

"If it comes up, what should we say? I mean, I don't want them to think…"

"I'll tell them I was in a hurry."

"Ben Torres, if you say that, they'll think—"

"They'll think I was in a hurry. Any other assumptions would be wrong." He laughed as he parked along the curb. "Don't worry about it."

Marisa squeezed his hand as they walked up to the door. It flung open before they even made it to the porch.

"Mijo!" His mother handed her apron to her husband as she ran down the steps. "Marisa. We are so excited to meet you." She hugged Marisa, then Ben, then Marisa again.

Mr. Torres patted Ben on the back. "Congratulations, Son. You, too, Marisa."

The apron got passed to him, and his dad pulled Marisa in for a hug.

A curvy blonde with an infant in her arms motioned toward the door. "At least let her come inside. Hi, Marisa."

Ben rubbed Marisa's back as they walked in. "Marisa, this is Gracie, Frank's wife. And Lola in her arms."

"So nice to meet all of you." Silently, Marisa ran through all the names Ben had taught her.

A little girl, brown curls bouncing as she ran, dashed across the room squealing. "Uncle Ben." Her brown eyes dazzled with admiration.

He scooped her up and smoothed the ruffles on her sundress. "Well, hello."

She kissed his cheek, arms wrapped tightly around his neck. He nuzzled her shoulder, grinning as she giggled.

Marisa fell in love all over again watching her husband. It was about the sexiest she'd ever seen him. After glancing at her, the girl pressed a small hand to each of his cheeks and whispered in his ear.

"She is pretty, isn't she?" Ben shifted her to his hip and stepped closer to Marisa. "Gabby, this is your Aunt Marisa."

"Hello. Did you marry Uncle Ben?"

"I did." Marisa smiled.

The little girl wriggled out of his arms. "I'm glad." She disappeared into the other room. A minute later, she reappeared with other kids in tow.

Marisa glanced at Ben as their nieces and nephews gathered around. Gabby slipped her fingers into Marisa's hand. Marrying Ben had been an easy choice. Gaining more family—especially these nephews and nieces—was an added delight Marisa hadn't even considered.

After a few minutes, she'd met all three of Ben's brothers, their wives, and the seven grandchildren. With the exception of two names, she'd been able to remember what Ben taught her.

"Mind holding her for a minute." Gracie passed a bright-eyed infant to Marisa.

"Sure." Meeting strangers and making a good impression she could do, taking care of babies was a whole different story. She hadn't held an infant in years. "How old is she?"

"Two and a half months."

Marisa counted back in her head and remembered the night in Alex's office. "She's very alert."

~*~

Ben half-listened as mom gave family updates, his focus on Marisa cradling Lola.

When his mom noticed he wasn't listening, she turned, and a knowing grin lit up her face. "Never enough grandbabies. You two will have beautiful *niños. Preciosos.*"

"Slow down, Mom. We haven't even been married a week."

"Ay, but *mijo,* you aren't getting any younger."

"Thanks so much. I'm going to see if Dad needs any help." He pulled his gaze away from Marisa and wandered into the backyard. "What can I do to help?"

"Keep me company. Your brothers are all chasing kids." His dad opened the grill and flipped the steaks. "Married, huh?"

"Yeah. Mom's not too upset that we didn't say anything beforehand?"

"Nah, she's okay. There a reason you were in such a rush?"

"How long did you wait to marry Mom?"

"That was forty years ago."

"Love hasn't changed that much, Dad. We didn't have to get married. We wanted to."

"I hope you are both very happy." He piled steaks on a platter and called everyone to the table. "Steaks are done. Come and eat."

At dinner, Ben fell more in love with his wife. The way she interacted with his mom, her delight with the kids—she fit in as if she'd been around for years, and he loved it.

While Ben helped with the kitchen after dinner, Marisa sat on the sofa, holding Lola, surrounded by his nieces and nephews. With the baby asleep on one arm, she turned the pages of a book one-handed, reading aloud.

Gracie poked him in the ribs. "I'm pretty sure that platter in your hand has had time to air dry."

"Sorry. A little distracted I guess." He tucked it away in the cabinet.

She laughed. "I've known you, what, ten years? This is totally out of character for you."

"How so?" Ben chuckled, knowing full well what she meant but still putting her on the spot to explain it.

"Showing up married. This is the one, the not-Rachel, isn't it?"

"Yeah, turns out, she liked me. From day one, there was something about her. I'm friends with her brother so that made things interesting."

"I like her."

Ben glanced into the den, and Marisa smiled at him. "Me too."

"Yeah, I can tell." Gracie nudged him. "Your mom asked about kids yet?"

"As soon as you handed Lola to Marisa."

She bubbled with laughter.

Marisa waved as Ben pulled away from the house. "I love your family."

"That's a good thing."

"I worried that I'd feel like an outsider. Anything but." The commotion of the evening brought back memories of her own family be-fore the accident. "Lola was born on Kate's birthday?"

"You remembered."

"Vividly." Marisa touched Ben's arm. "That night when you turned around and opened your arms … I wanted things to end this way."

Ben cracked a smile. "I didn't do so well at the taking it slow part."

# CHAPTER 54

### *Wednesday, July 6*

Marisa grabbed Ben's tie and pulled him closer. "Bye, Detective. I'll miss you." After so many days together, she wasn't ready for him to leave, even for work.

"You'll stay inside?" He lifted her onto the table.

She straightened his tie and patted his chest. "Yes, sir." Adding a small salute earned her an eye roll.

"If I don't leave soon, I'll be late." He untied her robe and snaked his arms around her waist.

"Keep that up, and I promise you'll be late."

"I'll have a surprise for you after work."

"Oh?"

"You have to wait."

"No fair."

He kissed her again before untangling himself. "I really have to go. When is your car supposed to be ready?"

She slid off the table and tied her robe. "Tomorrow, at the earliest."

"Love you." He kissed her one last time before running out.

She blew him a kiss and closed the door behind him. Her first order of business was getting dressed. Then she'd rearrange closets. Surely, Ben wouldn't mind if she moved his stuff to the guest room.

Ben called Alex on speaker phone as he drove to the office. "Hey, you found it?"

"Yep. And made a copy for you."

"Any chance you can meet me for lunch? I want to surprise her with it after work."

"Text me when and where. I'm sure glad I thought to give you her number."

"Save the ribbing. I'll text you when I get to the office."

Ben made it to his desk seconds before Miller dropped a file in front of him. "Morning."

"She agree to stay home?"

"She offered, thankfully." Ben sipped his coffee and opened the file. "What's the latest on this case?"

"The case can wait a moment." Miller climbed into a chair. "Can I get everyone's attention, please?"

The room quieted, and all eyes turned toward Miller.

"Please take a minute to congratulate my partner. He got himself hitched on Friday."

Ben shook his head, and the officers and detectives around him cheered and made their way toward him. "You didn't have to do that."

"It was no bother." Miller slapped Ben on the back. "I'm happy for you."

Marisa dialed Bethany's number. It rolled to voicemail. "Hey, it's Marisa. Give me a call whenever you are free. No hurry." She hung up and went back to moving Ben's clothes to the guest room closet, tucking love notes in the pocket of each pair of pants.

When her phone rang a little while later she was surprised to see a different name on the screen. "Lexi, hi."

"You free for lunch? I want to hear the whole story!"

"You were there Sunday night. There isn't much else to tell."

"Please, my treat. Where do you want to go?"

Marisa hesitated. She didn't intend to break her promise to Ben, and giving Lexi Ben's address gave Marisa pause. What if someone followed Lexi? "Can we do it a different day? I'm knee deep in a project right now, so I don't want to leave, but I can talk for a few minutes."

"Everyone at the office was so shocked. I didn't think you'd fall in love so quickly. Should've guessed though when you threw away those flowers."

Marisa winced at the memory. "Ben didn't live far from me, and we bumped into each other a lot, like that night at the food trucks. Both times actually. He's also friends with my brother."

"I'm so happy for you, Marisa. And super glad you ditched that Paul guy. Detective Torres is so much better."

"Lexi, you always talk about how much you didn't like Paul. You met him like twice."

"I had to call him for Mr. Jenner all the time and occasionally made deliveries to his office. He'd hit on me all the time. I should have told you, but that's not easy, you know. Hey, your boyfriend is hitting on me. I decided keeping quiet was better."

"Lexi, I'm sorry. I had no idea."

"Thankfully, I don't have to do it as much anymore."

Marisa grew antsy talking about Paul. "Listen, can I call you later? Ben just texted."

"Go talk to your husband. I'll catch you later."

Marisa grinned as she read Ben's text: *I keep picturing you in that red dress you wore the day we met. It's making the minutes crawl by.*

She ran to the closet, trying to remember if she'd brought the dress to his apartment. Deep red silk peeked out from behind other dresses. She responded: *Maybe you'll get to see me in it later.*

An emoji with hearts for eyes popped up as a response, and she laughed.

She went back to resorting closets. After finishing her project, cleaning up the apartment, and prepping dinner, Marisa dropped onto the sofa. If staying home was what the near future held, she needed a hobby. She opened the house hunting app and scrolled through houses for sale in the area. Knowing what was available would help when she and Ben discussed what to do with the money from Travis. She jotted down a few houses, then her phone rang.

"Bethany, hi. Thanks for calling me back."

"Hey. Sunday night was fun. I'm really happy for you two."

"I'm glad you went. I think Ben enjoyed shocking a room full of people."

"Seemed like it. How are you doing?"

Marisa poured herself a glass of tea and curled up at the end of the couch. She'd shut down all questions from Bethany the last few days, but everything wasn't perfect. Marisa reminded herself that there was no reason to be jealous.

She had no doubt about Ben's feelings. "I've only been back to my apartment once. And nightmares still wake me, but each day is better than the last. Ben is wonderful, very caring and supportive."

"I'm glad you're not going through it alone." Bethany sighed. "Hopefully, when we catch this guy, the nightmares will disappear completely."

"Oh, I hope so. Any news on that front?"

"I'm working with Detective Fuller. They didn't get any viable prints out of the apartment. We aren't giving up, though."

"Thank you. And if I need to unload, I'll call you."

"And I'll keep you updated about progress on the case."

Marisa checked the time as she wandered into the bedroom. *4:30 pm.* Ben would hopefully be getting off soon.

Ben nearly ran Miller over, trying to get to the elevator.

"Slow down, lover boy. You're going to hurt someone." He dodged to the side as Ben slipped in.

"See ya tomorrow." The doors slid closed, and he watched the numbers flash as the elevator sank toward the ground floor. When the doors opened, he raced out to the parking garage and texted Marisa: *Leaving now. Be home soon.*

As he approached his car, the phone chirped Marisa's text tone. She'd replied: *And my surprise?*

Grinning, he tapped out: *Not yet.*

A sharp jab stung his leg. He whipped around.

A man holding a gun and an empty syringe smirked and opened the passenger door of the car parked next to Ben. "Hello. You should sit down. What I just gave you will take effect pretty quickly."

Tingles raced through Ben's arms, and the ability to run evaporated as whatever he'd been injected with seeped throughout his body. His legs useless, he dropped into the passenger seat after a small shove from the man.

Recognizing the voice, Ben tried to tap out a text, but his fingers didn't want to cooperate.

The familiar voice moved closer. "I'll take that phone. Thank you." The man picked it up and tucked it in his pocket, then put a baseball cap on Ben's head and pulled it down low.

Ben's arms grew heavy, and then Ben didn't feel them at all. He could see his legs and feet, but his brain no longer controlled them, or even seemed aware of their attachment to his body. Buckled in, he watched as the man left the garage and drove. He exited the highway, taking the roads that led to Ben's apartment.

*Not Marisa. Leave her alone.*

"No." Ben's tongue refused to obey. All Ben could muster was the one word.

A haughty, pompous laugh echoed next to him.

Not far from the apartment, in the nearby hills, the car pulled into a long driveway. Hidden behind a wall of trees and shrubs, they parked in front of a large brick home. The man jumped out and fiddled with a lockbox. A key dropped out, and he unlocked the door.

Ben stared at the house. He glanced from the man to the open door. Marisa stood just inside, arms crossed, tears streaming down her face. Ben blinked, and the doorway was empty.

"Seeing things?" The man lifted Ben from the seat. "I've heard that's a side effect. Never tried it myself. Special K, I think they call it."

*Do whatever you want to me but leave my wife alone.* "What." What was wrong with his tongue?

"What am I going to do? I told you. I'm not done with her. I intend to finish what I started. You've earned a front row seat." The man dragged Ben down a long hallway. "I didn't expect her to run off and get married."

Propped up against a wall, Ben watched Marisa run into the

room, headed for him, wearing nothing more than a smile. Just as she touched him, the stalker grabbed her and threw her to the rug.

*No. No. No!*

Ben struggled against the drug. A slap to the face startled him. The man was the only other one in the room. Ben tried to focus. The hallucinations made it nearly impossible to sort the clouded images in his head from reality.

His phone danced in front of his face. Laughter bellowed from the man. "How convenient. You've already set her up to be surprised. She'll be so excited to learn that you want to buy her this house." His fingers jumped up and down on the phone.

*Don't listen to him, Marisa. It isn't me. Run away.* "Princess." Ben managed to utter that one word.

"Is that what you call her? How sweet." Tapping away, the man sneered. "When Paul introduced me to Marisa, I expected that all her talents had been credited to the beauty department. Boy, was I wrong about that. She's got brains to go with that body. And that was why I had to have her canned. Too smart for her own good."

Marisa buttoned the last button on her dress and grabbed her phone as soon as Ben's text popped up: *Ready for your surprise? I'm sending you a map link. Meet me there.*

She grabbed her red heels and slipped them on as the next text flashed on the screen: *And hurry, Princess. I want to buy my doll this house.*

"Oh, Ben." Marisa backed over her fat fingered reply and sent: *Give me a few minutes to change, and I'll be on my way.*

After replying to the text, she called Lexi. "Hey, I need your car."

"Sure, when?"

"Right now. I need to meet Ben."

"Are you serious?"

"Please, Lexi, hurry."

"I'm on my way."

Ben opened his eyes. Had he been asleep? He scanned the room as best he could, moving only his eyes. How late was it? The dark man with horns floated on the other side of the room.

*He doesn't have horns.*

Ben focused on his service weapon sitting on a table near the door.

*It might as well be on the other side of the Grand Canyon.*

Too much time had passed. Marisa wasn't coming. She'd read his mind. *She listened.* But the drugs weren't wearing off. That was worrisome.

Blinds rattled. That howling laugh started again. "She's here. Isn't it wonderful to have a piece like that who comes at your beck and call?" The man with the voice Ben had nightmares about squatted next to him. "Can't have the drug wearing off during the show." He jabbed Ben in the leg with a needle again.

Marisa stilled her shaking hands before getting out of the car. She glanced down the driveway as she walked up to the door, listening for other cars and smoothing the silk of her dress. She had a surprise of her own. Hopefully, it would arrive soon.

She jumped when Ben texted: *Come on inside.*

She pushed open the door and clicked through the opulent entry. Pictures of the property flashed in her head. The house had been listed for weeks, but in a price range few could afford, it saw very little traffic. She wandered to the back door, then into the utility room.

She texted back: *Where are you? This place is amazing.*

The reply popped up as soon as she clicked send: *In the bedroom, doll.*

She took a deep breath and made her way down the long hall.

"Princess." Ben didn't sound right.

She broke into a run, shedding her heels as she went. "Ben?" She cleared the doorway and scanned the room. He lay slumped against the wall. Tripping over the rug, nearly falling on her face, she raced toward him. "What have you done to him, Ted?"

Ted's smug smirk nauseated her. "Surprise."

Marisa drop to her knees next to Ben. "Say something to me. Please be okay."

Ted tapped her with the gun. "Get up. You aren't here for him. He just gets to watch."

Marisa squeezed Ben's hand before standing up.

*Ted?* Ben tried to claw through the invisible restraints on his arms. He had to save her. She landed on top of him as he grabbed her arms, then he rolled on top of her. He'd be her shield. He blinked, trying to battle the hallucinations. Marisa stood in front of the dead man. Ben hoped that would be true soon.

Ted waved the gun. "Stand over there."

Marisa stepped around Ben and onto the rug in the center of the room.

"Take off your dress." Ted crossed his arms on top of his head, a hideous gnarl of a sneer curling his lips.

"No." Marisa folded her arms in front of her.

Ben looked into the end of the gun.

"He doesn't *have to watch.*"

"Leave him alone." Moving around the room, she reached for the lowest button.

Reality sailed further away. Ben undid her buttons, slowly, listening to her heart race. *Focus. She needs your help.*

The bottom of her dress hanging open, her fingers moved to the top. Deep red lace, the same color as the dress, peeked around the edges.

Ben willed his arms to move. Clawing at tile, he dragged himself to the rug, toward her feet. The gun—he had to reach the gun. Almost to the rug, he glanced back over his shoulder. He still sat slumped by the wall. Marisa needed him, but he couldn't save her.

Forcing his eyes into focus, he stared at her. Calm, she glided across the rug, the Ted guy turning to keep his eyes on her. Another button opened. The tick of the clock on the wall slowed. Marisa straddled Ben, her buttons all undone. He struggled against the ecstasy of the dream as her hips moved in an enchanting rhythm. *It's not real. She's in trouble.*

His vision blurred, Ben could no longer control his eye movements. Staring at the rug, only Ted's feet and Marisa red toenails stayed in view.

No ski mask blocked the leering smile of Ted when he leaned down in front of Ben. "Stunning, isn't she?"

Marisa stepped between Ben and the man. "What are you going to do? Give me the same drug?"

*No, don't give her this stuff.* Ben gave all his attention to a single finger, willing it move. Nothing. He couldn't help her. She would suffer. He was there but couldn't even lift a finger to help.

"Oh no. I'm not giving it to you. I want to feel you writhing underneath me. I want him to hear you screaming my name. You don't have to pretend anymore. I know you want me." Ted's feet moved closer to Marisa's toes. "Want me to undo the rest of those buttons?"

Marisa moved back off the rug. "I want you to go to hell."

"Drop it!" A new voice yelled.

Ben's eyes shifted from one wall to the other, the room a blur of color. Focusing on the rug again, he flinched at a burst of loud sounds. Blood red silk pooled on the rug, crawling toward the edges of the room. Without her dress, she was in trouble. Ted could see her, touch her. Ben's eyes burned. Pushing through the fog, he focused on Ted. He lay on the rug, the red underneath him.

His eyes closed, Ben surrendered to the black hole that tugged at him. *It's too late. But you can't leave her.* He stared at the rug, at the silk. It continued to creep toward the walls. Not fabric, blood. The burnt red liquid moved across the tile. He struggled to comprehend what happened.

*Ted killed Marisa.*

Ben fought for air. His heart rate accelerated, his heart racing to escape his chest. Every beat thundered in his head. Panting, his breath struggled to keep up. His chin fell to his chest. His heart on a trampoline, darkness pulled at him. His body stiffened, then his arms and legs danced a rhythm he hadn't choreographed.

The floor opened up, and he relived his life in the span of a moment. Losing her was his greatest regret. He closed his eyes, his limbs still detached from his brain. *I'm sorry. I love you.* "Marisa."

Marisa skirted the sticky pool of blood, leaving Miller to deal with Ted. "Call an ambulance. He's having a seizure."

Miller radioed as he knelt over the lifeless body.

Bethany ran into the room, several officers right behind her. "I got here as quick as I could. Glad you were close, Jack."

"Ambulance is on the way. Hope they hurry." Miller somehow sounded calm, through his expression showed that he was anything but.

Marisa knelt beside Ben and clutched his hand. "I'm here, Ben."

The seizure ended, and he stopped shaking.

She dropped into his lap, facing him. "Sweetheart, stay with me. It hasn't been forever yet. You promised." Blinking away tears, she ripped off his tie. She fumbled with his buttons, trying to unfasten them. As the last button slipped free of its snag, she pulled open his shirt. She slid her hand inside his t-shirt and pressed her hand over his heart. "His heart is pounding too fast."

Pressing her lips to his, she prayed the physical contact would penetrate his drugged haze. "You can't leave me. I need you." She grabbed his limp hands and held them against her cheeks. "Look, I'm here. It's me, sweetheart."

She moved his hands down her body. "I'm not hurt. He never touched me." Leaving his hands on her thighs, she cradled his face. "Look at me, Ben. Please. Open your eyes."

His lids fluttered open, revealing brown pools. Confusion and pain swirled in his wide pupils. "Princess."

"He's talking." Her relieved laugh drowned out her cry. "You told him to say that, didn't you?"

Ben gazed at her, but she wasn't sure if he could make sense of what he saw. "You didn't listen."

Overjoyed by the full sentence, she choked back emotion. "I couldn't run away when you were in trouble." She wiped drool off his chin. "You needed me."

Sirens drew closer.

"No hospital." He glanced over her shoulder.

"Oh, yes. You are." She pointed to her ring. "See this. You're incapacitated. This means they'll let me decide where you go. You *are* going to get checked out." She leaned in, brushing her lips on his ear. "I need you all in one piece. Okay?"

"Torture."

The thought hadn't occurred to her. A chill scurried down her spine. "What did he do to you?"

"You, *kitten*." Ben tickled the inside of her thigh.

Relief washed out the last of her floodgates. "Oh, Detective."

He shifted his head, focusing on her unbuttoned dress. "How did you…?"

"She'll tell you all about that later. You going to live, Torres?" Miller wiped his forehead.

"Go away." Ben's lip curled slightly, and he danced his fingertips on her leg. "We're busy."

"Andrews, I think they want to be alone." Miller jingled the keys in his pocket and laughed.

Marisa climbed off of Ben as paramedics swarmed in and circled him. "They need to make sure you're okay."

"What did he give him?" The medic glanced from Marisa to Miller.

"We don't know." Marisa knelt next to Ben and rattled off the effects that she'd observed.

"Special K." Ben tightened his hold on her hand, catching her dress in his grip.

"Ketamine. We don't need the Narcan." The medic checked Ben's vitals.

Ben clutched at Marisa's silk dress as she got up, but it slipped through his fingers.

"I'm right here, sweetheart." She stepped back, giving the medic room to work.

Miller patted her on the shoulder. "He'll be okay."

"He has to be." Marisa crossed her arms, the swell of emotion spilling out of her eyes.

She wouldn't let herself melt into a puddle of sobs. Ben needed her. For him, she had to be strong. She wiped her tears.

Miller waggled a finger at her. "We'll talk about your crazy stunt later."

"Not before I know he's going to be okay." She stared at Ben. "I don't care what you tell him *after* this is all over."

Ben wiggled his fingers searching for Marisa. Cold settled where she sat moments before. His eyes darted from side to side, searching, as medics stuck a needle in his arm and attached a tube. "Marisa."

"Heart rate is increasing." The young medic called out numbers.

The chariots raced through Ben's chest again, trampling the clear thoughts in his head. "Marisa."

"Ma'am, could you stand over here, where he can see you, please?" The tech motioned to her partner. "Let's hook up the EKG."

Marisa came into view, her dress all buttoned up. "Ben, I'm here. Let them help you. May I hold his hand?"

"Earlier, he calmed down when she touched him." Miller hovered close by.

"Try it." The medics shifted, letting her kneel near Ben.

Her soft lips grazed his fingers. "I'm still here." Her touch cleared a path through the fog.

"Kitten."

"Yes, Detective." She kissed his hand between words. "Please stay calm."

Ben closed his eyes, the commotion in the room making him dizzy. With great effort, he pulled her fingers to his lips. "Love you, Mrs. Torres."

She kissed his head. "I love you too, Ben."

He battled against heavy lids. "I'm so tired. The surprise will have to wait."

Marisa let go of his hand as medics lifted him onto the gurney. "I'll stay close. You have to stay calm."

Ben puckered his lips, blowing her a kiss.

The sun had long set, and nurses cleared visitors from the hospital halls. Marisa sat next to Ben's bed, dozing, his hand clutched in hers.

"How is he?" Miller held out a cup of coffee.

"Still asleep." She sipped the hot liquid. "Doctor said he may not wake for hours. His vitals are better."

"Anybody you need me to call?" Miller lingered near a chair without sitting down.

"No." Ben squeezed her fingers. "No visitors."

Marisa jumped out of her chair. "You're awake." She smiled as he opened his eyes and kissed him.

He tapped the blanket. "Come here."

"I'm going to let you rest." Miller rubbed his eyes. "Call if you need me."

Ben motioned Miller to the bed. "Thanks for keeping her safe, Jack."

"Of course. We're partners." His voice cracked. "I'll be back in the morning."

Marisa touched his arm as he stepped away from the bed. "I'll keep you posted."

He nodded and left the room.

Ben lifted the covers. "Please, Kitten."

Marisa laid down beside him, her head on his chest. "The nurses might not like this."

"Where's your dress?"

"Bethany brought me clothes. Since they were trying to keep your heart rate down, I figured wearing sweats was a better option." She closed her eyes, listening to a chuckle rumble in his chest.

~*~

Ben kissed her hair and breathed in the scent of pomegranates. "You understood my warning but ignored it."

"There were so many things wrong with the text Ted sent. Asking me to meet you was my first clue it wasn't you texting. Princess warned me to run away. The doll jogged my memory. That's what Ted called me, and I hated it. I knew you were in trouble."

"So you called Miller?"

"What? No more Jack?"

"Moment's passed. He's Miller again."

"I didn't have his number. That's been remedied, by the way. I called Bethany."

"What took them so long to come into the room?"

"Please don't be mad at me. I borrowed Lexi's car, and drove to the house by myself. I knew that Jack and Bethany were on their way. I unlocked every entrance, then kept Ted talking until Miller arrived."

Ben raised his eyebrows and stared at her. "Never. Promise me, Kitten. Don't ever do that again. You should have let Miller handle it."

"No. Ted might've killed you, and I wasn't going to let that happen."

"Good thing Miller showed up when he did. It was such a blur. I remember you telling Ted to go to hell and loud noises."

"Ted didn't drop the gun. He fired. Hit a mirror. It brought him bad luck courtesy of Jack."

"Who is Ted?"

"Paul's friend. He's the realtor that got me the job."

"He said he got you canned because you were too smart for your own good."

"That doesn't make any sense. Too smart about what?"

"Don't know." Ben rested his head on hers. "The surprise is in my car. We'll have to wait until I get out of here, I guess."

"Jack brought it up here." She pointed to the gift laying on the side table. "He parked your car in the garage."

Ben handed her the package. "Open it."

She sat up long enough to tear away the paper. "Oh, sweetheart." She ran her fingers over the old photo in the double frame, her parents' wedding picture. Then patted the picture in the other frame, taken less than a week before by the clerk at the courthouse.

He smiled at the endearment that made them sound like an old married couple. "Alex said it was a tradition in your family."

Marisa hugged the gift to her chest and laid down again, nodding against his shoulder.

Ben moved the picture back to the side table. "I'm falling asleep again. Stay where you are. Tell the nurses police orders."

"Whatever you say, Detective."

# Chapter 55

*Thursday, July 7*

The bed jostled, and Marisa opened her eyes. She smiled when the nurse waved. "Do you need me to move?"

"I think I can get what I need with you there. His numbers haven't looked this good all night, so you must be what the doctor ordered."

"Thank you for taking such good care of him." Marisa glanced at the time. *4 am.* She must've slept through the other nurse visits.

"Happy to do it. I'm all finished. You go back to sleep. Need another blanket?"

Marisa shook her head. "I'm okay."

The nurse hurried out, and Marisa snuggled back against Ben.

Ben jolted awake, but the warmth cuddled next to him calmed him. He brushed her hair out of her face. *Maybe a honeymoon getaway is a good idea.* He shifted so that they lay nose to nose.

Her eyes peeked open. "You're staring, Detective."

"And if I keep it up, I'm going to set off my heart monitor."

"Please don't. They might keep you longer. I want to take you home." She kissed him on the cheek. "I'll get out of bed, so you can sleep."

"I can't sleep if you move. Nightmares." Ben told her the truth, but flippantly, hoping not to worry her.

"All right, but not like this." She rolled him onto his back. "I'll only stay if you close your eyes."

He picked up his phone and texted her: *Yes, Kitten.*

"Go to sleep."

He sent the text again and chuckled, his eyes squeezed shut.

They lay snuggled in the dark, neither asleep.

Ben kissed the top of her head. "Thank you for coming to my rescue."

"That's what partners do."

The door swung open. Ben watched as a man in a white coat closed the door and made his way toward the bed. Ben recognized the face.

He closed his eyes and pressed his lips to Marisa's ear. "Paul's here."

~*~

Marisa sat up and whipped around. "Paul?"

"Hello, baby." Paul approached the bed, his features sinister-looking in the light of the monitors. "I gave Ted enough of that K stuff to take down a band of horses; your *husband* probably hasn't even woken up yet."

Marisa gasped but recovered quickly. "He hasn't. Movement hasn't completely returned." She slipped off the bed, pulled the covers up over Ben as if that added any protection, but kept hold of his hand. "You helped Ted?" She tried to figure a way to get to the call button.

"You turned me in, *and* you left me without even a goodbye. That wasn't right, Marisa. Just not right. I couldn't let you get away with that." Paul stood at the foot of the bed.

"You planned it?" Her head swam, trying to remember each note and gift. Had Ted left them? Had Paul sent them? She inched toward the bed, ready to jump up and grab the button from the other side of Ben.

"Ted had no scruples and even fewer morals. I told him that you whispered his name in your sleep and that you called out his name in moments of passion." Paul paused, staring at her face, wanting a reaction.

She gave none. Ben stroked her palm with his pinky, then slipped his hand from hers. *What is he planning?* She needed to alert the nurses. Moving as quickly as she could, she climbed on the bed and reached to the table on the other side.

Paul beat her to it. "No need to invite anyone else to our party." He set the button out of reach.

Ben's best hope of getting the upper hand against Paul lay in the element of surprise. He peered out from barely open lids while putting the first step of his plan into place. Acting asleep when Marisa crawled over him hadn't been easy, but Paul didn't seem suspicious.

Marisa jumped down and ran toward Paul. "Get out! Just leave us alone." Yelling, she likely hoped the nurses would hear.

He grabbed her and slapped a hand over her mouth. "I'm not here to hurt *you.*" He pulled a syringe out of his coat pocket and stepped near the IV stand.

Marisa struggled to get free.

Ben forced himself to be still, waiting for the right moment.

"After Ted heard that about you, he was a man on a mission. I knew you'd get punished for what you'd done to me. Sadly—poor Mr. Jenner—things didn't quite work out like I'd hoped. Is he dead or in jail?" Paul pointed at Ben. "He wasn't supposed to live. There are consequences for the choices you made."

Marisa eyed the needle, whatever she was trying to yell blocked by Paul's hand.

Paul sneered. "I had more of that K stuff. After what he's been through, injecting this directly into the IV should send him over the edge."

Ben kept still as Paul poked the needle into the IV. Marisa beat on Paul, but he acted unfazed. He pushed the drug into the line, while Marisa grappled with him.

"That was easy." Paul let her go and tossed the syringe into the trashcan.

"You, monster." She bent over the trashcan and threw up.

Paul patted her on the head. "Bye, baby. Have a nice life. Maybe next time you'll think twice about turning me in."

Ben threw back the covers and launched out of bed, the IV formerly in his arm dripping saline onto the sheets. Paul turned around just as Ben tackled him.

"Ben!" Marisa hugged the wall, trying to stay clear of the punches being thrown.

"Stay back." He grunted as Paul's fist landed a blow. The beep of the heart monitor grew more and more shrill. "Nurses will be in any minute. You aren't getting away."

Paul untangled himself and jumped to his feet, fishing in the pockets of his coat. "Lucky for me, I brought back up." He uncapped a syringe and lunged at Ben. "I'm sure you remember what happens when you get stabbed with this."

Dodging the needle, Ben moved out of Paul's reach. He couldn't bear the thought of that drug in his system again, but Marisa's ex didn't give up easily.

Poised to pounce, Paul rocked from side to side. "I've heard it causes nightmares. Is it true?" Just as he shifted his weight to the balls of his feet, Marisa brought the frame down on top of his head. Paul dropped to his knees, stunned.

Ben wiped at the blood dripping from his arm and yanked the remaining wires off his chest, giving him more freedom to move. He shoved Paul backward, who landed hard on his back, somehow still clinging to the needle. Ben sat up, pinning Paul to the floor, and clutched the arm holding the threat.

Marisa ran out of the room. Shouts and screams echoed behind Ben as nurses flooded into the room. Ignoring the distraction, he held Paul's wrist, while feeling around the floor. A sharp pain on his index finger brought a smile to his face. He gripped the shard of glass and jabbed. The syringe flew out of Paul's hand.

Paul scrambled backward, not as brave without the syringe full of drugs as a weapon. As he stood up, Ben grabbed Paul's head and arm, then swung around behind him, restraining Paul in a choke hold.

Marisa pushed past the nurses and picked up the syringe. She rushed at Paul. "Is this what Ted gave him?" She stopped in front of him, rage flaring in her eyes.

"Marisa, don't. He's going away for a long time, and I want him to remember every minute." Ben locked eyes with her. "There are consequences for the choices he made."

"I'll give you something to remember. I should've done this months ago." She raised her knee, striking Paul in the groin.

He yelped and doubled over. Ben wrestled him upright. After a minute of moaning, Paul struggled against the headlock, shifting and turning. Ben held on. Behind him, security ran in, and Ben released his attacker to them.

A second later, Marisa pressed against Ben's backside. "Bravo, Detective." She tied the strings on the back of his gown. "Now, let's stop distracting the nurses, okay?"

Ben leaned back into her. "Next time I fight, I'll wear pants."

"We'll see about that." She kissed his neck. "The ties aren't worth anything. You need to get back in bed."

He climbed back under the sheets but grabbed her hand.

Two hours later, after the police had taken their statements, collected evidence, and hospital staff had returned the room to order, Marisa snuggled next to Ben on the bed.

"I'll get you another frame." He brushed a knuckle along her cheek.

"It was the first thing I saw to grab. I'm sorry."

"Knowing Paul was behind what happened, does anything Ted said make more sense?"

Her smile fell away. "Ben, I don't want to talk about them anymore. They'll never bother us again."

"We have to talk about it, Marisa. It's important. What did he mean by you being too smart for your own good?"

"I don't know. I thought I was dismissed because Paul only broke into houses I had listed. They thought I somehow gave him info or codes, I guess. But I didn't."

"He broke into all of them?"

"All but five. Four were vacant. I'm not sure why he didn't break into the other. It had lots of expensive art, actually."

"What was different about that house?"

"Ben, is this really necessary?" She sat up and pulled a strand of hair into the corner of her mouth.

He rubbed her back. "Marisa, I know it's hard to relive right now, but I think it is necessary. Something had to be different."

"It was one of the houses I listed on my own."

"On your own?"

"Ted didn't paw at me as I snapped photos." She rubbed her forehead. "That's it, Ben. That's how Paul got the information."

"Slow down. Start from the beginning."

"When I started at the office, as part of my *training*, Ted accompanied me when listing houses. I hated it. Couldn't stand the way he looked at me, touched me, but I never suspected he was capable of—anyway, he was in every one of those houses."

"Wouldn't the police have looked into that?"

"I'm not sure I thought to mention it. It didn't seem important. And he wouldn't have sent info to Paul in an email or text, he had to have another means of sending the info. I guess he could have just told him. I need to call that robbery detective again and tell him what I remembered."

Ben rolled her on top of him. "Maybe this will help get you your job back, if you want it. I mean, that's up to you."

"Are you trying to say that I don't have to work?"

"We'll be okay if you don't. I'm not saying that you have to stay home, either."

"You're just giving me the option."

"Right." Ben tangled his fingers in her hair and let his lips dance a tango with hers, wishing they were at home in bed. "You choose."

Miller strode through the door, a brown paper bag in hand. "Whoa. You realize that when people say, 'get a room.' they aren't talking about a hospital room."

Marisa jumped off the bed. "Jack, you're here early."

"I got a phone call. Something about a fight. I figured you'd both need a real breakfast." Miller held up the bag and a large Styrofoam cup. "Chorizo and egg tacos and a Big Red."

"You have the best partner, Ben." She accepted the offered goodies and climbed back on the bed, then pointed to a chair. "Have a seat."

While they ate, they recounted yet again what happened.

"Paul and Ted both deserved what they got, or are going to get, as the case may be. You said they were working the burglaries together, too?" Miller leaned forward, waiting on more information.

Marisa shook Ben's arm. "Lexi. She didn't like Paul, said she had to run him messages for Ted. Maybe she has evidence that shows they were in cahoots." She grabbed her phone and dialed. "Lexi, hey."

"I'm not letting you borrow my car again. You were gone for hours, and a police officer dropped it off. She only said you were on your way to the hospital and would call me later. That was yesterday!"

"Sorry about that. Listen, you said you had to take Paul messages. Do you still have any of the notes Ted sent to Paul? Did you ever read any of them?"

"Why?" Lexi's voice lost all emotion.

Suddenly all the bits and pieces that hadn't made sense before, made sense in a horrible and twisted way. "I'm grasping at straws. What am I going to do without a job?"

Marisa muted her phone. "She was in on it. She knew. That's how Paul knew where to find us."

"You never told her about the stalking?" As Ben asked the question, he reached for his phone.

"Never." Marisa took a deep breath and unmuted the phone. "I'm sorry about your car. Ben got hurt and had to spend the night in the hospital. I should have called."

He jumped out of bed and handed her his phone opened to a note. *Address?* was typed at the top.

Marisa tapped out both her work and Lexi's home address and pointed at the word *work*. "Lexi, you there?"

"Yeah, sorry. One of the agents needed something. What happened to Ben?"

He snatched up his phone and huddled in the corner, his back to the wall, whispering to Miller. Ben motioned for Marisa to keep Lexi talking as Miller rushed out of the room.

Marisa twisted the sheet in her hand. "Ben got into a fight. He's okay, though. You should see the other guy." She tried to maintain a light-hearted tone. "Thanks for letting me vent. This whole job thing has me stressed. Has anyone said anything about me being gone?"

"Not really. Whispers I guess, but I try to stay out of the gossip." Lexi stayed out of the gossip like squirrels stayed out of bird feeders. "Maybe I can talk to Ted and see if he'll put in a good word for you."

"That'd be great, Lexi. Thanks." Marisa tried to think of what else to say. "You wanted me to tell you all about how Ben and I got together. Have time now?"

"I'm at work, but go ahead." Lexi's lack of interest didn't deter Marisa.

Dragging out the story as much as possible, she recounted how she'd bumped into Ben multiple times, how he'd chased her until she let herself be caught. Describing the day at the zoo took up several minutes, but Marisa was running out of content. "So, when are we going to lunch? Sorry I couldn't go yesterday."

"We could go today. About one. That work?" Papers shuffled on Lexi's end of the line.

Marisa waved her husband back to the bed. "Should I bring Ben?"

He winked at her.

Lexi sighed. "Really, Marisa? Can't you be away from him at all?"

"I *can*. I just don't like to be. He's all that *and* a scoop of ice cream." Marisa strained to hear as Lexi spoke to someone in the office.

"The police, really? Paul was right about you." Lexi gave a humorless chuckle. "I really thought you'd be too stupid to figure it out."

"Please hang up the phone, ma'am." The voice was unmistakable. "We're going to need you to come with us."

Marisa ended the call.

"They got her?" Ben slid back under the covers.

"I heard Fuller say she needed to go with them."

"What was all that about lunch?"

"She wanted to meet for lunch yesterday. Insisted. But I didn't want her to come to the apartment in case anyone followed her."

"And she was the one to be worried about." Ben shifted, thumping his pillows, trying to make himself comfortable. "Any word on when that doctor is supposed to let me out of here?" Exhaustion showed in the lines in his face, only made worse by the need to stay in bed to avoid flashing people.

Marisa poked her head out of the room, and the nurse hurried over. "When is the doctor coming by? My husband needs to rest, and that's not going to happen here."

"I'll see what I can do to get him here. We'll see if we can't get your detective released to go home."

"Thank you so much."

The nurse had the doctor in the room within a half-hour. After hearing the account of all that happened, he had no qualms about releasing Ben.

Marisa laid Ben's clothes on the bed. "I didn't have Bethany bring you fresh clothes, sorry. I wasn't thinking."

"Not a big deal. You got out of your sweats."

"I only have my heels, so I changed back into my dress."

He grinned.

Ben grumbled about riding down in a wheelchair. He hated the role of patient. When Marisa pulled up to the curb, he slid into the passenger seat. "I can't wait to be home."

She drove home, glancing at him at every stop. Worry still evident in the tightness of her smile. As soon as she parked, she ran around to open his door.

"I'm okay, Kitten." Ben pulled her close. "Really."

Her eyes misted. "Please can we not talk out here?"

When they stepped into the apartment, as he closed the door behind him, she buried her face in his chest. "I thought I'd lost you. Twice."

He smoothed her hair and tugged her to the couch. "I'm sorry."

She nestled into his lap. "Don't apologize. You didn't do anything wrong. I just…" Her words dissolved in tears.

Tito jumped onto the couch, purring loudly, lonely after a night alone. He curled up on Ben's shoulder but jumped away when Ben shifted.

"Shhh." He kissed her head and undid the top button of her dress. "You need to rest."

"I've spent the better part of the last eighteen hours dreaming of you in this dress." Ben continued, letting his fingers graze her skin as he worked his way to the last button.

"In the dress or taking me out of it?" She'd read his mind.

He traced his fingers over red lace. "Yes. So unless you intend to make me chase you …"

Marisa danced her lips on his. "Oh, you caught me, Detective."

# Acknowledgments

Special thanks go to Sheri, Jessica, Glenda, Jennifer, Laura and all the members of the Schatzenburg, TX group on Facebook for reading, listening, and giving feedback when it was needed. And huge thanks goes to Kevin for answering my many questions.

And as always, I have to send a big thank you to my husband and boys for allowing me to do what I love.

# About the Author

Pamela Humphrey is the author of Finding Claire, Finding Kate, Finding Treasure, The Chase, Researching Ramirez: On the Trail of the Jesus Ramirez Family, and The Blue Rebozo. She started writing fiction in 2015 after discovering a christening record that revealed a surprising secret. It opened her eyes to the stories around her, real and imagined.

Using the beautiful Texas Hill Country as the setting for most of her books, she looks to the places and people of the region for inspiration. If you've never visited, pick up one her stories and get a glimpse of the landscape and residents. She lives in San Antonio, Texas, with her husband, sons, black cats, and a leopard gecko.

Find out more at www.phreypress.com.

# Connect Online

Website: www.phreypress.com
Facebook: http://www.facebook.com/phreypress
Twitter: @phreypress


If you want to read more about the town of Schatzenburg, TX, or the characters who frequent that little town, check out the website for extras and short stories.

http://www.phreypress.com


Interested in reading more about Travis, Kate's father? *Just You*, a romance novel, tells his story. Look for it in Fall 2018.

www.ingramcontent.com/pod-product-compliance
Lightning Source LLC
Chambersburg PA
CBHW030541190726
48283CB00006B/1961